TED TAYLER

A MORNING MURDER

VINCI BOOKS

By Ted Tayler

The Freeman Files

Fatal Decision

Last Orders

Pressure Point

Deadly Formula

Final Deal

Barking Mad

Creature Discomforts

Silent Terror

Night Train

All Things Bright

Buried Secrets

A Genuine Mistake

Strange Beginnings

Dead Reckoning

A Normal November

Into the Sunlight

Tame the Storm

One True Friend

Whispered Truths

A Morning Murder

Quick to Anger

Red Herring Season
Gathering Clouds
Still Standing

Vinci Books

vinci-books.com

Published by Vinci Books Ltd in 2025

1

A CIP catalogue record for this book is available from the British Library.
Paperback ISBN: 9781036705060

Chapter One

BURNHAM-ON-SEA

Saturday, 6 October 2018

GUS REACHED HOME EARLY on Saturday afternoon. He'd had a busy morning.

Amazing Grace had arrested Becky Hood for the murder of three illegal immigrants. But, despite never having set foot in Burnham-on-Sea, he and the team somehow solved the original case Kenneth Truelove had handed them.

Suzie had returned from the big shop and made a detour to the horses fifteen minutes before Gus wandered through the front door.

"I read your note," said Suzie, popping her head around the kitchen door before continuing to prepare a late lunch. "I hope you won't make a habit of dashing off with Amazing Grace on Saturday mornings. After all the things you've said about her, it's disconcerting. Don't worry. I've put everything I bought away safely."

1

"I would rather have braved the supermarket with you than have to deliver such dreadful news to Becky Hood."

"Oh dear," said Suzie. "What happened after I left here?"

Gus explained how drugs had been the dominant passion for the three Chippenham men in their late teens. They never used the evil stuff themselves but were happy to satisfy the demand among their peers if they could earn extra money. But, in the beginning, they weren't as security conscious as they later became, and Ian Hood got caught.

As Gus's team had thought, Ian had agreed to take the fall for his friends. When he returned to Chippenham, Ian found Sam and Mark were married to Mary and Mandy. Sam Webber was doing okay with his burgeoning car dealership, while Mark had an excellent job with a major local employer.

Ian married, too, once he found the right girl, Becky Roker, but he didn't fancy a career where he started at the bottom and worked his way up. So he imported goods from China that he hoped to sell at a handsome profit. However, most of the early items Ian purchased were cheap for a reason. The quality was shoddy, and Ian got his fingers burned. But, as always, he had the answer.

The cheap products he bought would need to make a brief stopover on their way to the UK. Drugs were hidden inside the items in the Middle East. The quantities involved weren't huge, and the system worked undetected for years.

"So, they smuggled small amounts destined for a select clientele," said Suzie. "A little and often. These products arrived in containers docking at Portbury or Avonmouth."

"Ian Hood arranged collection and transported the goods containing the raw material to a middleman," said Gus. "It was still profitable but risky. The middle man then cut and bagged the end product. Ian's transport system collected and delivered the finished article to their contacts in the Chippenham area."

"When Mark met Sylvie Tilson, he realised they could simplify the process," said Suzie.

"Shane Prosser's gang could get the finished product across the Bristol Channel to Burnham-on-Sea, stash it in Mark's caravan, and the three friends could transfer it to the end-user," said Gus. "The percentage profit rose steeply."

"Will you still need to go to the seaside next week?" asked Suzie.

"It would be rude not to," said Gus. "I'd like to delay meeting with Kenneth Truelove for as long as possible. We close the office on Friday, and I don't want him to have too long to bend my ear about uncovering more problems than I solved."

"Jim Francis?" asked Suzie.

"For one," said Gus. "Then there's Jessie North. Don't start me on Annie Drew and who she's working for these days."

"Plus, if this London gang bumped off Gavin and Sylvie Tilson, someone needs to start the search for their bodies."

"It looks like another two murders solved for which we can name a killer but never put them in front of a judge and jury."

"Never mind, Gus," said Suzie. "It's not as if you do it deliberately. Kenneth will understand."

"I hope you're right," sighed Gus. "How long before lunch is ready?"

"You've got time to change into your gardening clothes. I thought we'd make the most of this sunny spell and eat it on the patio."

Gus couldn't think of a better option, so he headed for the bedroom. When he joined Suzie in the back garden, he was surprised to see she'd poured him a glass of wine.

"A refreshing change," he said as he tucked into his BLT.

"My mother collared me while I was grooming my horse in the stable," said Suzie. "She reminded me it's been a while since we had Sunday lunch with them."

"That explains the wine," said Gus. "When are we dining in Worton?"

"Tomorrow," said Suzie. "Do you mind?"

"Not at all," said Gus. "I'll get as much done at the allotment this afternoon as I can. Whatever's left outstanding can wait until next weekend. If Bert Penman thinks otherwise, I'll give him cash to supplement his cider money."

"You shouldn't encourage Bert to overdo things," said Suzie.

"Gardening or drinking?" asked Gus.

After finishing their lunch, Suzie encouraged Gus to get out from under her feet and visit the allotment.

"The sooner you start, the sooner you'll finish," she said. "I'll wash these few things by hand, put them away, and then hoover around. We're booked in for a meal at the Fox & Hounds tonight, and we won't want anything to eat after Mum's finished with us tomorrow, so the dishwasher can rest until Monday. You can take your turn at the sink after breakfast in the morning."

"Will everything be so organised next April, do you think?" asked Gus, kissing Suzie before leaving the bungalow.

"We'll cope," said Suzie. "It's a case of having to."

Gus looked to the heavens as he strode along the lane

towards the church. The sun was still warm enough to allow him and Suzie to enjoy a pleasant lunch on their sheltered patio. With mature trees screening the rear of the property, it was a bit of a sun trap.

Once exposed to the elements, it was a different matter. He would have to keep working this afternoon. If he stopped to chat to Bert or the Reverend for any length of time, the cool breeze would play havoc with his back. That was the last thing he needed with two weeks' holiday around the corner.

He needn't have worried. Bert must have made an early start. Perhaps, when Irene returned from her sister's, she'd wanted him out of the house to get it shipshape. Gus doubted whether Bert was as keen on hoovering and dusting, especially after a session in The Lamb following his morning's labour.

Gus opened his shed door and consulted the oracle. The notebook he'd compiled from every lecture Bert had given him about what needed doing and when throughout the seasons. The oracle was a well-thumbed yet vital document.

"Things may be winding down in October, Mr Freeman," Bert had told Gus. "But there's still plenty to do, including harvesting late crops, planting for next year, and improving the soil."

Gus worked his way down the list; with runner beans, courgettes, and his main crop of potatoes to harvest, there was plenty to keep him occupied. As he gathered his produce by the shed door, he spotted someone waving a walking stick in the distance. Bert was leaving The Lamb after his liquid lunch and looked a little unsteady on his feet as he made his way up the lane towards home.

Gus redoubled his efforts. Suzie might be right. So, he sowed his broad beans, divided his rhubarb crowns, and then rooted around in the shed for his stock of canes. Bert reckoned they prevented the heavily-laden Brussels sprout plants from blowing over in the autumn winds.

"Why go to the effort of growing the darn things only to stand by and watch them rot on the ground?" Bert would say.

Gus made sure nothing was getting blown over anytime soon. He smiled at an item in the notebook he'd crossed through a couple of years ago. No way was he bothering with planting a variety of peas.

As the church clock prepared to strike the hour, Gus realised five o'clock had crept up on him already. Enough was enough. He hadn't managed to start improving the soil on his patch of land today, but manuring would have to wait until next weekend.

Gus was locking the shed when Suzie arrived in her Golf.

"Were you wondering where I'd got to?" he asked.

"No, but I did wonder whether you'd be able to carry everything home with you. So, just as well that I popped along based on what I can see."

They loaded the vegetables into the boot and drove home.

"You had the place to yourself by the looks of it," said Suzie.

"Bert worked this morning," said Gus. "No sign of Clemency today. I expect she's writing her sermon and getting ready for tonight."

"Are we giving them a lift to the pub?" asked Suzie.

"I didn't arrange anything with Brett on Wednesday night," said Gus. "Perhaps they'll cycle? It's only four miles."

"I can't tell if you're joking or not," said Suzie. "I'll

drive your car, and then you and Brett can have a drink. The Reverend rarely indulges these days. I think she has a soft drink to keep me company."

"We can blame Irene North and her homemade wine for Clemency not drinking," said Gus. "I'll call Brett and tell him we'll collect them from the vicarage just after half-past seven."

"Leave that to me," said Suzie. "You can shower and change while I make arrangements with the Reverend. We don't want her parishioners getting in a tizz if someone sees us dropping the couple at the Rectory close to midnight."

"Whatever you say, darling," said Gus.

"You're learning," said Suzie.

Gus was ready to leave within fifteen minutes but knew he had time on his hands. Suzie had spent several minutes rummaging through her clothes, lamenting the lack of something different to wear, before disappearing into the bathroom.

Gus went into the lounge and thumbed through a magazine Suzie had picked up while shopping that morning. The content was uninspiring, with news of offers any sensible shopper could identify on the shelves if they took their nose out of their phone while inside the store.

The colourful menu suggestions looked great, but why did every dish include so many exotic ingredients when we should encourage people to grow their own? First, the ingredients needed to be imported, and second the amount required for each dish was tiny. As a result, the customer would need to eat the dish five times a week to finish the packet, tube, or bottle before it went out of date.

Gus heard the bedroom door closing, which signified progress. He waited with bated breath. If Tess was anything to go by, he was in for a fashion parade. The decision on what to wear had been his responsibility. The trick was to pick the dress Tess had already chosen. Woe betide him if he got it wrong.

The bedroom door opened, and Suzie emerged barefoot in a floaty floral wrap dress.

"What do you think?" she asked.

"Give me a twirl," said Gus.

Suzie obliged.

"I like it, and I'm certain I've never seen it before," Gus said.

"More to the point, nor has Clemency," said Suzie.

She returned to the bedroom. Had he said the right thing? Gus was none the wiser.

When Suzie re-emerged, the only change was she now had flat shoes on her feet.

Gus found he could breathe more easily.

"Right, I'm ready," said Suzie. "Let's go."

Gus joined her in the hallway, dropped the magazine in the waste bin by the kitchen door, and handed over his car keys.

"Be gentle with her," he said.

"We need to have an urgent conversation about our transport needs," said Suzie. "I struggled to get the vegetables you harvested in the boot of my Golf earlier. Imagine trying to accommodate everything we'll need with the little one. As for your Focus, it's been on borrowed time for several years. What if it lets us down when I need to get to the hospital?"

"I'll make a mental note," said Gus. "We'll add it to the list of things that need sorting out while I'm on my so-called holiday."

Gus was impressed with how Suzie coaxed the Focus through the gateway without spraying tonnes of gravel toward the climbing roses. They arrived outside the Rectory at seven-thirty-five, where Brett and the Reverend were waiting on the pavement holding hands.

Once the couple was inside the car, Suzie drove just over the speed limit to the Fox & Hounds. The car park was almost full, but Suzie parked the Focus without adding to its war wounds.

"We've not been here before," said Clemency. "It's busy, which is always a good sign."

"You must book, especially on a Saturday night," Gus said. "We like its ambience and seasonal yet affordable menu."

"We like the Waggon & Horses for the same reason," said Suzie. "It's good to have somewhere that's not on your doorstep and gives you a chance to be alone. If you approve, perhaps you two can add it to your list of places to visit for a special occasion."

"Like tonight, do you mean?" asked the Reverend, brushing a loose lock of hair behind her ear.

Gus led the way into the pub, and they were shown to their table. The four friends ordered drinks and studied the starter menu.

"I'll be back in a minute," said Brett, heading towards the bar.

"What have you two been up to today?" asked Clemency.

"I was working this morning," said Gus. "Not a pleasant experience, but a positive outcome. Then, this afternoon I worked on my allotment. I saw Bert leaving the pub. I could tell he'd worked on his patch this morning."

" I know what you're going to say. I'm afraid I couldn't get there today," said Clemency.

"With Gus working on a case in Chippenham, I battled

the crowds alone doing the weekly shop," said Suzie. "Then, I drove to Worton before lunchtime to groom my horse, and I caught up with chores at the bungalow this afternoon. I imagine you had parish duties to perform, home visits, and a sermon to write?"

"All of the above," said the Reverend. "Although, I tackled the lion's share last night. Brett convinced me we must take a trip into Devizes this morning."

Brett returned to the table, followed by two staff members. One carried a tray with their drink order, and the other waiter delivered four flutes of champagne.

"Bubbly?" asked Gus. "What did I miss?"

"Call yourself a detective, darling?" said Suzie. "When I mentioned a special occasion in the car park, Clemency gave a big hint something was going on."

"Brett proposed last night," said Clemency, stretching her left hand across the table for Suzie to see the engagement ring more clearly.

"We were to blame for Bert having one or two more drinks than usual at lunchtime," said Brett. "We dropped in on him and Irene after returning from the jewellers in Maryport Street. Irene joined us in The Lamb for an hour, and then we took her home. She wanted to ring her sister to check she was okay."

"Congratulations, you two," said Gus. "I can't recall the last time anyone I know got engaged, let alone married."

"We don't plan on a long engagement," said Brett. "So you won't have long to wait."

Suzie and Gus raised a glass and wished the smiling couple every happiness.

"It's time we ordered food," said Suzie. "My bacon, lettuce, and tomato sandwich seems a lifetime ago."

When they finally made their way outside to the car

park when the pub closed, everyone agreed it had been a splendid evening. The food didn't disappoint, and on some occasions, alcohol wasn't required to get everyone in high spirits.

Suzie drove back towards Urchfont and slowed as they approached Brett's house.

"You can drop us at the Rectory, Suzie," said the Reverend.

"Gosh," said Suzie. "What will the Bishop say?"

Clemency giggled.

"Brett cycled to my place earlier," she said.

"I'll cycle home later," said Brett. "Honest."

When they reached the Rectory, Brett and Clemency got out of the Focus and waved as Suzie pulled away.

"I bet he won't leave until *much* later," said Gus.

"I'm happy for them," said Suzie.

"So am I," said Gus. "It was plain from the start they were meant for each other."

"I'm still happy with things the way they are if you were getting ideas."

"Me too. If it ain't broke, don't fix it," said Gus.

Suzie parked the Focus under the rambling roses, and they went indoors.

"Do you want a nightcap, darling?" asked Suzie.

"It's not the same when we can't enjoy it together," said Gus.

"We can't eat breakfast too late in the morning, or we'll never finish our roast dinner."

"I've just remembered something we *can* enjoy together," said Gus.

"Now you're talking," said Suzie heading for the bedroom.

Sunday, 7 October 2018

WHEN GUS OPENED HIS EYES, he could hear Suzie already working in the kitchen. He rolled out of bed and strolled through to join her.

"Morning, sleepyhead," she said. "After last night's meal, I thought you deserved blueberries and Greek yoghurt for breakfast."

"Deserved is a stretch," said Gus. "Roll on when we can have bacon and eggs again. Oh well, a mug of coffee will ease the pain."

Suzie handed him a mug of black coffee.

"You were snoring well last night," she said, "so that's not why you're like a bear with a sore head this morning. What's the matter?"

"I had a weird dream," said Gus. "Brett had developed a refinement to those microchip cat flaps he was talking about the other night. So if anything other than the authorised moggie tried to enter the house, it got Tasered."

"That's dreadful," said Suzie.

"I couldn't agree more," said Gus. "Just before I woke up, Brett told me he'd sold a million units in the first year."

"You've never mentioned any of your dreams before."

"That's the first one I've been able to mention," said Gus as he poured himself another coffee.

"I'm off for a shower," said Suzie. "From the sound of things, you had better have a cold shower this morning."

"I can wash the breakfast things later," said Gus. "I'm coming with you."

"Incorrigible," said Suzie.

They left the bungalow ten minutes before noon, and

Suzie delivered them to the Ferris farm in her Golf just as Jackie's kitchen clock struck the hour.

"They're here," she called.

Blessing Umeh came downstairs and hugged Jackie.

"Jamie will be here soon," she said. "We'll get out of your hair, and you can spend quality time with your family."

"John's somewhere on the other side of the farm," said Jackie. "I told him when to return, but the land and the animals control his time, not me."

"Good morning, guv," said Blessing as Gus entered the kitchen.

"Gus, when we're off-duty, Blessing," said Gus. "Have you got five minutes?"

"Jamie's picking me up," said Blessing. "So it will have to be quick."

"He followed us along the lane from the main road. Suzie's chatting to him outside. I wanted to update you on what happened yesterday morning."

"That's okay, Gus," said Blessing. "Grace phoned yesterday afternoon. She was too excited to wait until Monday."

"Oh, okay. Well, I'll tell the others when we get together in the morning."

Suzie came indoors and hugged her mother.

"Your young man can't wait to see you, Blessing," she said. "Enjoy your afternoon."

"We will," laughed Blessing as she dashed outside.

She bumped into John Ferris in the doorway.

"Sorry, Mr Ferris," she said.

"Don't worry, Blessing. It was a soft landing."

Gus could still hear Blessing laughing until Jamie's car roared out of the farmyard.

"That was a mad five minutes," said Jackie. "Now, let's

eat, and you can tell us what you've been up to since we last got together."

"It's not been that long, mother," said Suzie.

"Humour her, Suzie," said John. "She's a grandmother-in-waiting. I tell her not to fret, but I might as well talk to that wall."

The delicious aroma of Jackie's cooking filled the kitchen as Suzie and Gus filled in the blanks on their daily lives over the past couple of weeks. Of course, Suzie's parents didn't expect to hear details of any cases Gus and the team worked on, but they were keen to learn what Gus might do during his vacation.

"Nothing has been decided yet," said Gus. "Although, at the weekends when Suzie is available, we've got a list of items that need both of us to thrash out."

"I won't ask whether you're planning any major projects at the farm," said Suzie. "Nothing ever changes."

"Everything will continue in the same pattern as it has for decades, Suzie," said her father. "Change is inevitable, but it happens slowly. If you think back to when you were leaving school, we didn't have the equipment we have in the barns now. There were more farmhands, and the materials we used were efficient but not good for the long-term future of the land."

"My brothers were still living here then, too," said Suzie. "You're right, there have been changes in the past fifteen years, but they were subtle."

"It's high time that roast beef was carved, John," said Jackie, busying herself on the other side of the kitchen. "Food first, and then we can put the world to rights later."

John Ferris winked at his daughter.

"Perhaps you were right. Nothing changes."

Sunday lunch was always a leisurely affair with Jackie in

charge. After polishing off his second bowl of rhubarb and custard, Gus leaned back from the table and realised it was approaching four o'clock.

"That was fantastic, Jackie," he said, "I'm stuffed."

"Coffee?" she asked.

"Just the ticket," said Gus.

Suzie noticed her father didn't seem in a rush to get away. That was odd. He usually headed out to a remote corner of the farm to tend to something urgent.

"I'll just get these plates and dishes into the dishwasher," said Jackie. "The rest can wait."

"Okay," said Suzie. "What's going on? I should have known there was an ulterior motive for the sudden lunch invitation."

"We don't need a reason, sweetheart," said John. "Go on, Jackie, you'd better tell them."

"Blessing put the idea in my head," said Jackie. "Before she arrived, the two of us rattled around in this old farmhouse. You had moved in with Gus, and I suddenly realised how quiet the place was without young folk. The way things are going with Jamie, I can see we'll be losing Blessing too in time, so I thought we could rent out another bedroom."

"That makes sense," said Gus.

"On Thursday evening, Blessing brought a young lady home with her. She lives in Easterton, in one of Monty Jennings's properties."

"Amazing Grace," said Gus.

"The very same," said Jackie. "A polite girl, the same age as Suzie. I had prepared a meal for Blessing, and the three of us chatted while they shared the food between them."

"Grace is a vegan," said Gus. "That can't have been easy."

15

"Different rather than difficult," said Jackie. "After Grace drove home, Blessing told me how lonely Grace was in Easterton. She doesn't know anyone in the village and finds it tough to make new friends. So I thought as she works with Blessing, it would make sense for her to move here. They can take turns driving to the office. I'm sure they will appreciate the extra cash in their purse. As for me, I would welcome the company and the challenge of adapting my menus to suit their different requirements. I'm not too old to learn."

"Grace will only be with us until Christmas," said Gus. "Unless Kenneth and Geoff can't find a suitable replacement for Luke Sherman."

"Grace still needs to be close to London Road," said John. "Her and Blessing might not be able to car share for more than a couple of months, but every little helps. I'm happy to have Grace living here. Jackie reckons she and Blessing get on well."

"Grace did mention her visit here when we were in Chippenham on Saturday," said Gus. "Although, she spoke about a regular Thursday evening invite for an evening meal. I didn't realise things had moved so quickly."

"We haven't asked Grace yet whether she wants to move here," said Jackie. "I wanted to check you were happy with the arrangement first."

"What are you thinking, Gus?" asked Suzie.

"Any chance of a brandy to go with this coffee?"

"I'll join you, Gus," laughed John. "You two haven't always seen eye-to-eye, am I right? Blessing was explaining it to us yesterday evening."

"We sit in very different camps," said Gus. "I represent the old regime who those preaching the modern policing mantra want to disappear. While Grace was carrying out a special project at London Road for Geoff Mercer, we crossed swords on several occasions. I sensed trouble was just around the corner. When Luke left us, it would have been better if Geoff had conjured up a transfer for a bright, young detective sergeant. Someone I could educate properly before they were beyond help and brainwashed. Geoff insisted good candidates were thin on the ground, and DI Packenham was a rising star."

"How's it been so far, with her working in the CRT office?" asked Jackie.

"Grace is making progress," said Gus. "Teamwork wasn't in her vocabulary before she joined us. It worries me that she seems to be doing far better than I feared."

"Perhaps you misjudged her, darling," said Suzie.

"Time will tell," said Gus.

Chapter Two

Monday, 8 October 2018

"I'LL EXPECT you when I see you," said Suzie as they stood outside the bungalow beside their respective cars.

"There's no telling how long we'll be in Burnham-on-Sea," said Gus. "What will be, will be. But, either way, we need to wrap things up by Friday."

One slice of toast and honey was all either of them could manage this morning after yesterday's visit to Worton. They had left John and Jackie to return to Urchfont at eight o'clock, meeting Jamie's sports car on the long driveway. Blessing Umeh gave them a wave as they drove past.

Time would tell whether Grace and Blessing would soon be sleeping under the same roof.

"Think positive thoughts, Gus," said Suzie. "Grace could have rented a cottage in the village, like Brett."

Gus grunted and slipped into the driving seat of his Focus. He followed Suzie through the gateway, and they turned left. The start of another week and the now-familiar detour. Gus tapped the steering wheel to the lyrics of a song that entered his head. *I'll tip my hat to the new constitution, take a bow for the new revolution, smile and grin at the change all around*…. He was sure that was The Who. Why did 'Won't Get Fooled Again' come out of the ether like that? Then the penny dropped. The Detours was the band's first name. It preceded The High Numbers, and the final name change gave the group the golden ticket to chart success. Somehow Gus felt The Detours would never have been as popular.

Gus arrived before nine despite the circuitous route to the Old Police Station office. The others were already there.

"Morning, guv," said Neil.

"Did you have a good weekend?" asked Lydia.

"Wonderful," said Gus. "What have you heard about Saturday morning?"

"Grace told us the gory details, guv," said Neil.

"Becky Hood torched the caravan," said Alex. "She didn't realise it wasn't merely somewhere for her husband and his mates to stash their drugs."

"We also know Gavin and Sylvie Tilson are missing, presumed dead, guv," said Lydia.

"There's not a lot to keep us here then, is there?" said Gus.

"We'll see you outside the Burnham nick, guv," said Lydia.

"We'll try not to keep you waiting too long," said Gus.

Alex and Lydia were soon inside her Mini, leaving the Church Street car park.

"Shall I go with Neil, guv?" asked Blessing.

"It looks like it's you and me, Gus," said Grace.

"Indeed," said Grace.

Gus returned to his car and waited while Grace fitted a

steering wheel lock to her Smart car. Why anyone would want to steal it, he couldn't imagine.

"Do you have a plan for today, Gus?" asked Grace when she joined him.

"We'll play it by ear," he replied. "Jill Crooks knows the terrain better than we do, even if she hasn't lived in the town for years. I know you were based in the area more recently, but most of your time in the county was either at the Avon & Somerset HQ or driving to and from Portishead."

"Fair comment," said Grace. "By the way, I had a phone call yesterday evening."

"From Jackie Ferris. Yes, I was aware she was calling you. Suzie and I had lunch with John and Jackie yesterday. They asked whether I thought you were house-trained."

"I have to give notice to my landlord, Mr Jennings," said Grace, ignoring Gus's remark. "So, I can't move in for at least twenty-eight days."

"You didn't accept the offer immediately?"

"I didn't want to appear too eager. But I'd be a fool not to make the switch. The rent is way lower than I'm paying for my current property, and Blessing and I can car share."

"The rental situation is straightforward enough," said Gus. "At the farm, you'll get bed and board. You will have seen how valuable that could be when you went to the farm with Blessing the other evening. Jackie's cooking is sensational. I suppose you need to weigh the reduced outgoings against the loss of independence."

"I've rented ever since I left university, Gus," said Grace. "I've no idea when I'll get my foot on the property ladder."

"What about the bank of Mum and Dad?" asked Gus. "Is there no possibility of help from that direction?"

"None whatsoever," said Grace. "No, I hope moving to Worton will give me more than a financial benefit."

"You've spoken to Blessing, I can tell," laughed Gus. "She calls the farm her home from home."

Grace didn't reply. She thought Blessing was lucky to have somewhere to call home in the first place.

Gus joined the M4 on the other side of Chippenham and headed for the Almondsbury interchange. Once they were on the M5 and heading west, he kept watching for Junction 22. They would be just two miles from the resort if he didn't miss it.

"We should reach the Burnham Police Station by a quarter to eleven," said Gus.

Grace was staring out of the window, watching the world go by.

"This must be the B3140," said Gus. "It's more like a country lane after travelling forty miles on the motorway. The first signs of life are up ahead. A holiday park on the outskirts of town."

"Don't you find it odd?" asked Grace. "Every coastal town I've visited has this style and mix of housing. They have bungalows and villas on the outskirts and rows of terraced housing near the town centre. Most have a Grand Hotel on the seafront. Yet, the weather in the UK is rubbish compared to the Spanish Costas, which have three hundred days of sunshine yearly. No resort on this coast can claim visitors are holidaying at the seaside. That's the Bristol Channel in the distance, not the Mediterranean. It's dirty and notoriously tidal. I don't see the attraction."

"Did your parents never take you to the seaside, Grace?" asked Gus.

"We visited Great Yarmouth for two weeks every summer. That's no better. The North Sea will have reclaimed most properties built on the cliffs in the next two decades. We were ecstatic if we had three sunny days during our fortnight's holiday. My mother prepared for four seasons daily, taking every scrap of clothing we possessed with us in our old Countryman."

"The Rolls Royce?" asked Gus.

"My father was a High Court judge. He wouldn't be seen dead in an Austin Seven."

"The Radford Countryman is as rare as hen's teeth. They sell for anything up to half a million depending on condition. Does he still own it?"

"No idea," said Grace. "Is that the police station on our right?"

"Not hard to spot, was it?" said Gus. "Lashings of red brick and zero character. Abandon hope all ye who enter here. That's for the staff's benefit, not the criminal's. We're the last to arrive. I don't recognise the lady speaking to Alex, but she fits the persona of the DI Jill Crooks I spoke with on Saturday."

Gus parked the Focus next to Lydia's Mini, and he and Grace joined the others.

"You made it then, guv," said Neil. "We were about to send out a search party."

"Good morning, Gus," said Jill Crooks. "I've met the team and your resident joker."

"I'm here all week," said Neil.

"The Berrow Road caravan site is a mile and a half north from here," said Jill, ignoring Neil. "It might be better if your team stays here while I show you around. Henry Gibbs suggested I bring DS Kurt Burgess with me from Bridgwater. He knows the Burnham and Highbridge crime map in all its grubby detail and can bring the team up to speed. We don't want to advertise that we have half a dozen

Wiltshire detectives on our patch. Kurt's inside, waiting for your people to join him."

"Fair enough," said Gus. "Grace, can you do the honours, make the introductions, update DS Burgess on our progress, and then listen to what he has to say about the main players operating in the area."

Grace nodded, and Gus and Jill were soon alone in the car park.

"My BMW's behind you," said Jill. "It has far too much power under the bonnet for my driving these days, but it looks the part."

Gus sat in the passenger seat, expecting a sarcastic comment about his vehicle.

"Did they offer you a car when you came out of retirement, Gus?" asked Jill as she drove out of the police station car park.

"The budget didn't stretch that far," scoffed Gus. "My partner and I are looking to buy a replacement in the next couple of months."

"I hope the Focus lasts that long," said Jill.

"I can't see the point of Suzie getting rid of her Golf," said Gus. "She'll return to work after she's had the baby, and if I'm still working with the Crime Review Team, we both need a car. So I expect I'll settle for a small family saloon."

"Don't sound so downhearted," laughed Jill. "You'll be a father. That's something to celebrate, even at your age."

"Do you have kids?" asked Gus.

"Never found the time," said Jill. "Didn't marry until my early thirties. That lasted three years before he left me for an Australian barmaid. I met my second husband at the Bridgwater carnival five years later. Pete Crooks was a lorry driver, and we had a great marriage, probably because our jobs often kept us apart. Sadly, Pete died of a heart attack at the wheel of his truck three years ago. The only godsend was he careered off the M5 and didn't take anyone else with him in the crash."

"What rotten luck," said Gus. "How do you keep going, Jill?"

"My faith and work get me through life one day at a time," she replied.

Gus spotted the sign for the caravan site up ahead. He thought once you'd seen one site layout, you'd seen the lot, but this did differ from the norm, as Jessie North had explained. Only a handful of caravans were visible on the top level. The main car park, clubhouse, and office building occupied the rest.

Jill Crooks parked her Beemer by the office building, and they went inside.

Adam and Tina Watson, the current site managers, sat at desks on either side of the office. Gus described them as being in their late thirties and early forties, overweight, and not welcoming any interruption to their well-ordered day.

The building reminded Gus of a 1930s flat-roofed cricket pavilion, the lower half brick-built and the upper half containing wooden-framed windows on three sides. Every inch of the office's solid back wall was covered in town maps, site diagrams, notices, brochures, bus timetables, and an array of helpful phone numbers for doctors, dentists, taxis, and takeaways. All were designed to give a visitor the answer to their question without the need to bother the management.

"I'm afraid I don't have any news for you about the caravan," Jill told the couple. "Forensics should finish with it today. Then we can arrange to remove the debris, and you can source a replacement."

"It's costing us money," moaned Adam Watson. "Even in October, we could expect to have a customer eager to find a residential pitch."

"I wish I had better news, but three people died," said Jill. "Your income is way down the list as far as priorities go. I have a colleague from Wiltshire Police with me today. He's arrested the person responsible for the fire, but his superiors have unanswered questions regarding Gavin and Sylvie Tilson."

"Josie Clift should be in the clubhouse getting ready for the lunchtime trade," said Tina Watson. "We weren't here when Sylvie worked in the bar, but Josie was, so perhaps you should speak to her?"

"We'll pop next door," said Jill. "I'll update you about the caravan as soon as I get the all-clear. We'll try not to delay Josie for too long."

Adam Watson wasn't listening.

Jill and Gus went outside and walked to the main door of the clubhouse.

"The far corner of the upper level is a good place to have the clubhouse," said Gus. "The bar windows look out over the caravans on the hillside below and out to the Bristol Channel. I spotted the opening and closing times on a notice on the back wall of the office. Midday to midnight in the summer season, but the residents prefer a quieter time after the August Bank Holiday. The clubhouse shuts at ten-thirty every night between September and the end of March."

"The fire officer thought the fire was set after midnight," said Jill.

"The M4 camera clocked Becky Hood's car heading this way at midnight, so that fits. But unfortunately, it also means the clubhouse was in darkness before she arrived. Zero chance of eyewitnesses."

Jill and Gus climbed the three steps into the building. They couldn't see anyone, but the chink of glass bottles suggested Josie Clift was somewhere to their left.

"The equivalent to a pub cellar must be over there," said Gus.

"Josie Clift?" shouted Jill. "Police. Can we have a word?"

A rosy-cheeked woman in her early thirties appeared in the doorway of the room at the far end of the building. She was carrying a crate of bottles.

"I'm Josie," she said, lifting the crate easily onto the bar counter. "I need to get on with bottling-up. Will this take long?"

"I saw you on Saturday morning when I attended the aftermath of the fire," said Jill. "You drove away before I had a chance to speak with you. Mr Freeman is with Wiltshire Police and has some questions for you."

"Were you working on Friday night, Josie?" asked Gus.

"Not me; I cover lunchtimes only, five hours a day, seven days a week. Adam told me not to bother on Saturday. That's why I went home early."

"Who serves behind the bar in the evenings?"

"Adam and Tina," said Josie. "Then, casual staff from an agency cover the peak periods. The clubhouse doesn't warrant any extra permanent staff. Visitors to the holiday parks in town want entertainment after spending a day in the resort and are more likely to spend their evenings in a clubhouse. Here, the demand isn't as great. Many retired residents drink at home if they drink at all. Several owners rent their caravans out to friends and family, which means Adam never knows from one week to the next whether we'll be busy or quiet with a different crowd on site. It's easier to watch for unfamiliar car registrations in the car park and then make a phone call to the agency if there's likely to be an upturn in trade."

"What can you tell me about Sylvie Tilson?" asked Gus.

"Sylvie did this job before me," said Josie, "but the manager in those days wasn't married. So, Sylvie also worked behind the bar in the evenings every other day. Lennie, the manager, did the bottling-up before she arrived in the mornings to cope with the lunchtime bar trade."

"How did you come to get the job? It sounds as if Lennie had everything covered."

"Sylvie's husband wasn't keen on her working here. She didn't drive, so he had to make four trips a day in his BMW, and this place is open until midnight in the summer. He didn't appear to have a regular job, but somehow he always had plenty of money. If you ask me, Gavin Tilson was a nasty piece of work; I don't know why Sylvie stayed with him. I never trusted him. Lennie wanted a regular female face behind the bar because he reckoned the residents preferred it. So he advertised for someone to cover the lunchtime shifts, which suited me down to the ground. Sylvie showed me the ropes, and that was it. I rarely saw her after that."

"Did she ever mention anything about leaving Burnham?" asked Gus.

"Sylvie was too frightened of Gavin to go off on her own," said Josie. "Then, one morning, Lennie asked if I could work here that evening. Sylvie hadn't arrived at six the night before as planned. Lennie had rung her mobile but got no answer. Nobody knew where Sylvia and Gavin went; they just vanished. Lennie assumed whatever business Gavin was involved in must have failed, and they'd left town, leaving their creditors to whistle for their money. If that was the case, I never heard anyone mention it. Sylvie wasn't around to work here in the evenings. Life just moved on. We had agency staff help out when required."

"What happened then?" asked Gus.

"I agreed to work with Lennie for a week or two in the evenings. It was cheaper for him than employing someone from the agency. But it got too much for me. Lennie decided he'd had enough too, and it wasn't long before Adam and Tina took over. They leave me alone, saving them from having to do anything before six in the evening. That suits my home situation.

"What happened to Lennie?" asked Gus.

"He was getting on, a lot older than Adam. Lennie moved to a retirement village on the other side of Weston-super-Mare. I heard he died last year."

"You told us you rarely saw Sylvie after taking over this lunchtime job," said Jill. "Where did you bump into her?"

"We used to shop at the same supermarket in town on a Friday afternoon," said Josie. "Gavin didn't go with her, of course. That wasn't his style. So instead, we had a coffee and chatted while she waited for a bus to their place in Highbridge. The buses run every thirty minutes, so Sylvie took advantage of time away from him."

"Did Sylvie ever give you the impression she was afraid of anyone?" asked Gus.

"Apart from Gavin? There have been a few new faces in the area since I left school. People you would do best to steer clear of, you know?"

"People with a London accent?" asked Gus.

Josie nodded.

"Did they ever visit this clubhouse?" asked Jill.

"I wouldn't know whether they came here in the

evening," said Josie. "As I said earlier, it's quiet at lunchtime. So, no, I've never been bothered by them."

"Lennie would have been next door in the office," said Gus. "I don't suppose you would know whether he had visitors?"

"I'd have to leave the bar unattended and go outside to see," said Josie.

"On the other hand, when it's quiet, you could relax in the seating area on our right," said Jill. "Perhaps chat to the handful of customers in the bar. Lennie wouldn't mind. He told you the customers preferred someone friendly."

Gus walked to the large picture window at the end of the bar.

"From here, it's possible to keep an eye on the door and have an unrestricted view across the bay and most of the caravans. Anything to pass the time when you're not busy."

"Did you ever see any of those newcomers wandering through the caravans?" asked Jill.

"Hard to tell from that distance," said Josie.

"So, hypothetically," asked Gus. "If you had seen someone in the distance, would they have been close to the pitch where the fire broke out last Friday night?"

"I suppose so," said Josie.

"We believe Gavin Tilson was a regular visitor to that caravan," said Gus. "Sylvie sold it to a man called Mark Fennell. Before the London newcomers arrived on the scene, it suited Gavin for Sylvie to work here throughout the day. Nobody batted an eyelid when he dropped her off in the car park or sat outside in his BMW waiting for her to lock up late at night. He could visit the caravan, let himself in with a spare key, leave certain items for Mark Fennell, then lock the caravan behind him as he left."

"This is all news to me," said Josie. "Lennie never

mentioned that Sylvie used to own one of the vans. She didn't speak to me about it. What sort of items, anyway?"

"Drugs," said Gus. "That's how Gavin Tilson earned a living."

"I'm not surprised," said Josie. "Did Sylvie know?"

"We're positive she did," said Jill.

"Let me ask you again, Josie," said Jill. "Did you ever see any of those newcomers wandering through the site? Or another person that you know was associated with them?"

"I saw Ben Mulligan hanging around more than once. He was about twenty back then, a few years younger than me. The first time Ben was in trouble with the law, he would have been about ten."

"Kurt Burgess told me Ben Mulligan was a runner from the age of twelve, Gus," said Jill. "Ben moved drugs from one trap house to another and made deals on the streets. So it makes sense that Gavin Tilson had nurtured him. Perhaps Newbold and Atkinson persuaded him to work for them."

"When was the last time you saw Sylvie?" asked Gus.

"August Bank Holiday Monday, in 2006," said Josie.

"How can you be so certain?" asked Jill.

"My birthday is on the twenty-eighth of August. I finished work here, went into town, and met friends in a bar. Later that evening, as we moved to another pub, I saw Gavin arguing with someone on the other side of the road. The guy had his back to me, so I couldn't see who it was. Sylvie was standing five yards away. She looked across the road, and I'm sure she saw me waving, but she didn't respond."

"You couldn't hear what was being said?" asked Gus.

"We'd all had a few drinks, my mates were noisy, and the streets were full of holidaymakers. All I could see was two blokes shouting and pointing at one another. I spotted

Sylvie, waved, and then my friends dragged me through the door into the pub. I never saw either after that day, but people come and go, don't they? They don't have to ask anyone's permission if they fancy moving to a different town or city looking for a better life."

"Where might we find Ben Mulligan these days?" asked Gus.

"He was strung out on coke the last time I saw him," said Josie. "I can't remember when he was a regular in this part of town."

"We can ask Kurt when we get back to the station, Gus," said Jill.

"Will that be all?" asked Josie.

"For now," said Gus. "Thanks for your time."

Jill and Gus walked outside and made their way down the hillside to the remains of what had once been Mark Fennell's caravan. They stood in silence, studying the wreckage.

"Did the fire officer comment on how the fire spread?" asked Gus.

"He wasn't very forthcoming," said Jill. "Why?"

"Becky Hood is a mild-mannered suburban housewife. I can understand her losing her rag with her husband and Sam Webber. I can even imagine her attempting to damage the structure of the van to make it unusable. But, somehow, I couldn't see her capable of obliterating the van before the emergency services arrived. Would you know where best to start a fire and which accelerant to use?"

"I take your point, Gus," said Jill, "but Becky Hood admitted she drove here to do just that, and you've charged her."

"Becky didn't know there were three illegal immigrants locked inside," said Gus. "Someone else did, though."

"Newbold and Atkinson," said Jill.

"You told Adam Watson the forensic people hadn't finished with this pitch yet. Where is everyone? Perhaps we should get back to the station and follow up on that. The fire officer might have more he can offer us."

Gus and Jill walked up the steps to the top level and returned to her car. She drove them back to the police station, and once inside the building, they joined Kurt Burgess and the others in what had been the detective squad room.

Grace spotted the newcomers and came over to speak to Gus.

"DS Burgess has just ended his presentation, Gus. So we now have a complete picture of how things were in the Burnham and Highbridge district from the turn of the century until August 2006."

"Monday, the twenty-eighth," said Gus. "Bank Holiday Monday."

"Your trip to the caravan site was informative then?" said Grace. Gus thought she almost smiled.

"Josie Clift, the barmaid who took over from Sylvie Tilson, gave us that snippet of information," said Gus. "While Kurt, Jill, and the others grab a coffee, why don't you take me through the highlights of Kurt's presentation? Then, we can get a drink later."

"I'll see you in fifteen minutes, Gus," said Jill.

Within ten seconds, Grace and Gus had the room to themselves.

"You can see the wallboards," said Grace. "Kurt came in yesterday morning to prepare everything. The board in the centre shows Shane Prosser, the leader of the gang based in Cardiff. We know he died of cancer in 2006. Prosser was a career criminal who had been active for over three decades. South Wales Police had made dents in his organisation without ever reaching those at the top of the tree. All the other faces on that wallboard were based in Cardiff, Swansea, and various towns in the Rhondda Valley and the Brecon Beacons."

"We can ignore everyone on that board except the man on the extreme right, Gavin Tilson," said Gus.

"True," said Grace, "but DS Burgess had good news to pass on. I'll return to that. On the board to the left is the structure this side of the Bristol Channel around the time Mark Fennell holidayed in Burnham-on-Sea. The arrows on the main board indicate that Gavin Tilson reported directly to Shane Prosser. Tilson had met Sylvie after Prosser urged him to move from Cardiff to grow their business on the North Somerset coast. The names and faces on Tilson's board were locals he conscripted into his operation. Jack Carr, James Devine, and Gary Ellis were responsible for the distribution system. We already knew the drugs arrived by boat from Cardiff. Sylvie's details didn't appear on the wallboard because she was never deemed significant in the Prosser gang.

"A young tearaway named Ben Mulligan had the job of moving a small quantity of those drugs to the Berrow Road caravan site," said Gus. "Josie Clift saw him there, even after Gavin and Sylvie disappeared."

"Mulligan doesn't appear on the wallboard either," said Grace. "He was one of several youths the gang used that were expendable. Tilson could always find another feral teen to take their place. The picture changed dramatically after Paulie Atkinson and Jonny Newbold arrived. Kurt Burgess wasn't certain which London borough spewed them out, but in his words, they were different gravy from anything the local criminals had ever met. Within weeks of them moving to Highbridge, they targeted James Devine. Devine was from a fishing family. Although he had no intention of earning his living from fishing for mullet like his ancestors, he did have access to small craft that could put to sea and meet larger vessels further out in the deeper stretches of the Bristol Channel. That's where the transfer of illegal immigrants occurred at the dead of night. Devine brought them ashore and thus became the first link in the Tilson chain to break. Atkinson and Newbold convinced Devine that smuggling people into the country was a better prospect than handling a few kilos of cocaine."

"How did Tilson respond to that?" asked Gus.

"He recruited Adam Wilson from Bridgwater. Ellis and Carr continued to handle the drug imports from Cardiff. With Prosser's cancer making it tough to keep control of his operation, Tilson saw an opportunity to expand his empire by venturing further afield. Wilson had contacts in Taunton. Gavin Tilson wasn't prepared to take on the gangs in Easton or St Paul's in Bristol. However, he realised there was scope in the west of the county, avoiding the intergang warfare that undoubtedly would have been sparked if he'd ventured north-east."

"Jill Crooks told me on Saturday morning that Avon & Somerset weren't idle during this period. Of course, they had their successes, but it was mostly identifying illegals in whichever enterprise they'd been set to work and trying to repatriate them."

"The same old story, Gus," said Grace. "Low-hanging fruit, similar to the story from the Cardiff side of the water. The good news I hinted at earlier was down to a DI Williams."

"I know it's a long shot in Wales with that surname," said Gus, "but if it was Dai Williams, then I've met him."

"Dai Williams, that was the name Kurt mentioned. A bit of a character. Shane Prosser had died a few months before Tilson disappeared. South Wales Police had an undercover officer inside the Prosser gang who tipped off Dai Williams when a meeting was scheduled to arrange the break-up of the various parts of the organisation. Other gangs from Wales wanted a piece of the action. Williams led a raid of a meeting held in a Hells Angels' chapter clubhouse in Pembrokeshire. That raid resulted in a series of arrests."

"I remember things didn't go as smoothly as they would have wished," said Gus.

"Does it ever?" said Grace. "However, the Prosser organisation was destabilised to such an extent that Dai Williams and his colleagues could dismantle it over the next four years. As usual, other gangs moved in to fill the void."

Conversation in the corridor indicated that Jill Crooks and the others had returned from their coffee break.

"Just as we were getting to the interesting part," said Gus.

"What did you learn at the caravan site, guv?" asked Alex.

"We'll pick this up again in a minute, Grace," said Gus. "Well done. Right, what did we learn? Well, the barmaid who replaced Sylvie Tilson last saw her on the evening of Monday, the twenty-eighth of August 2006. Her husband, Gavin, was arguing with another man several yards away on the other side of the road. It appears to be the last occasion when anyone saw the couple."

"Did the barmaid describe the man talking to Gavin Tilson, guv?" asked Neil.

"He had his back to her, Neil. I thought it had to be either Atkinson or Newbold, but based on what Grace heard from DS Burgess, it could easily have been James Devine."

"Was this sighting in Burnham, sir?" asked Kurt Burgess.

"Yes," said Gus. "Josie Clift was celebrating her birthday with friends in various bars near the seafront."

"In that case, it couldn't have been Devine. He was in Highbridge that day. Traffic police stopped him for running a red light, and once he'd opened the car door, they smelled the cannabis. He was done for possession and driving under the influence. Devine was nowhere near Burnham that evening."

"I believe Gavin and Sylvie Tilson died within twenty-four hours of that last sighting," said Gus. "Atkinson and Newbold weren't strangers to using violence to achieve their ends. So where would they ditch the bodies, Kurt?"

"There's an awful lot of open ground within ten miles of the town in either direction," said Kurt. "Brent Knoll to Lympsham to the north and Sedgemoor to the south. When a criminal disappears from our patch, we tend to breathe a sigh of relief. It's rare for a friend or relative to report them missing, so we don't send out a search party."

"You rely on an elderly lady walking her dog in the countryside to find a bone," said Lydia.

"Pretty much," said Kurt. "Nobody has ever found anything in the past twelve years."

"There could be a good reason for that," said Jill. "If Atkinson and Newbold had two bodies to get rid of on Tuesday morning, they had other options."

"Devine would have returned from a night in the cells," said Neil. "He could have buried the bodies at sea."

"We'll never find them if that's the case," said Blessing.

"There could be a way to determine a possible location," said Kurt. "This station was operating twenty-four-seven in those days. My predecessors monitored activity between here and the Welsh coast. It was nigh on impossible to learn when and how the drugs reached these shores, but we did find instances where a small craft was in areas not generally used by the fishing fleets. GPS for a journey like the one you're describing might show an outward trace to an odd destination and a subsequent inward trace to Burnham marina."

"That could give us a general idea of where to look," said Alex.

"Better than that," said Kurt. "If we have the details on record, we can pinpoint the location of the bodies within five to ten yards. At seventy miles long and between five and forty-three miles wide, the Bristol Channel is the UK's largest natural inlet, with a depth of thirty to two hundred and forty feet. To avoid detection, they would have chosen deeper waters."

"Even if we found where the bodies were buried could we prove Atkinson or Newbold was responsible?" asked Grace.

"How does it help our case, guv?" asked Neil. "We're positive Gavin Tilson killed Mark Fennell and Helen Roker."

"True, but the conversation Jessie North overheard suggested that after Devine switched allegiance, Tilson soon realised he needed to do Atkinson and Newbold's bidding. He told Sylvie to relax. The switch to illegal immigrants becoming a major part of their business was just around the corner."

"You're suggesting that by August, with Prosser out of the picture, Tilson was working for Atkinson and Newbold."

"Although he liked to see himself as a leader, Tilson was

a follower," said Gus. "I don't reckon he had much choice if those two villains are as tough as Kurt makes out. The London crew were already in Highbridge by 2005. Devine jumped ship later that year. The newcomers started making noises about getting out of drugs and into people trafficking. Tilson drove to Kington Langley to dispose of Fennell. We can't know what happened over the previous weekend when Mark and Helen visited their caravan for the last time. It might have prompted Tilson to act alone. Prosser was a spent force, and Tilson was some way from throwing in his lot with Atkinson and Newbold. Helen Roker was a loose end. We may never know who decided she had to die. Perhaps, the London crew ordered the hit to incentivise Tilson's gang to follow their boss's lead and work for them. Whichever way it played out, Helen died in January, and although Sam Webber managed to maintain access to the caravan on Berrow Road, the balance of power had changed. Within six months, Atkinson and Newbold had removed Tilson and his wife and controlled everything in the region."

"What about between then and today?" asked Blessing.

"We've arrested dozens of people whose faces appear at the bottom of the other wallboard over there," said Kurt. "The senior members have the best defence lawyers in the country on speed-dial. We can never get evidence to connect them to any offences. They're untouchable."

"Find where they buried the bodies," said Lydia. "That will wipe the grin off their faces."

Chapter Three

"I'LL DRIVE to Marine Drive for a chat with the senior fire officer," said Jill Crooks. "Do you want to come with me, Gus?"

"I can leave that in your hands, Jill," Gus said. "You know the right questions to ask."

"I'll take DS Hardy with me to Bridgwater, sir," said Kurt Burgess. "We can chase those GPS records. I'm confident we'll still have them, but it could take an hour or two."

"No problem," said Gus. "We're committed to staying here until at least three-thirty."

"I could accompany Alex, guv," said Lydia. "Then we could drive straight home if we finish after three-thirty. We'll be outside the Old Police Station office tomorrow, awaiting your instructions."

"Another pair of hands won't hurt, Mr Freeman," said Kurt.

"Off you go then," said Gus.

Jill Crooks was the first to leave. Kurt collected his

things together, and Alex and Lydia followed him to the car park.

"Just the four of us, guv," said Neil. "What's next for Blessing and me?"

"I'd like to start looking for Ben Mulligan," said Gus. "Where are these characters, Devine, Carr, Ellis, and Wilson?"

"I can help with some of that, Gus," said Grace. "I hadn't finished telling you what Kurt told us happened between 2006 and the present day."

"We're ahead of you for a change, guv," said Blessing.

"Right," said Gus. "Grace and I were about to take a break. I'd like to see more of the resort than the four walls of this office. Neil, take Blessing with you and drive into Highbridge."

"Are we looking for anything in particular, guv?" asked Blessing.

"We know Atkinson and Newbold settled in that neck of the woods, but I guess they live a mile or two out of town. The higher-priced detached properties guys like them favour won't be on the small housing estates and terraced streets you'll visit. So, it's unlikely you'll stumble across them. No, it's the local riff-raff I want you to observe."

"We'll find somewhere inconspicuous to sit and watch, guv," said Neil.

"The longer we can stay here without anyone associated with Atkinson and Newbold knowing we're on their patch, the better," said Grace.

"I wouldn't be surprised if they already know," said Gus.

"Do you suspect the new site managers at Berrow Road are dodgy, guv?" asked Neil.

"I don't think they see half of what goes on," said Gus.

"I'd be surprised if the gang didn't control more than one caravan on that site. Adam and Tina Watson don't care who stays there as long as the money gets paid on time. If I'm right, someone will have reported back to Atkinson and Newbold that the DI who was there on Saturday morning had returned with a colleague this morning, and they were nosing around."

"Come on, Blessing," said Neil. "Let's do a spot of covert surveillance."

"Where are we off to, Gus?" asked Grace after Neil and Blessing left the old squad room.

"It won't take long, Grace," said Gus. "The Esplanade is a mere three-minute walk from this office. We can stroll along the seafront searching for a cafe."

"Do you want me to continue Kurt Burgess's story as we walk?"

"I don't imagine it will take long," said Gus.

"The wheels of justice move extremely slowly," said Grace. "The main players are still thriving, as Kurt indicated. They believe they're untouchable. As for the human trafficking routes they established, Avon & Somerset Police and other agencies from the UK and Europe managed to close two routes for good. However, the threat of new routes always remains."

"James Devine?" asked Gus.

"He's still responsible for getting the immigrants ashore," said Grace. "As a more senior member of the organisation these days, Devine doesn't make the trips himself. The problem for the authorities is knowing when these exchanges occur and where. They can't afford to have boats patrolling the Bristol Channel every night, nor can they cover every possible beach or cove where the boats can land their human cargo. Devine understands the tides and the coastline. He wouldn't risk a boat carrying immigrants running aground on the mudflats. Even if they had the resources, Kurt reckoned it would still be a stroke of luck to come across a boat coming ashore."

"What about Jack Carr and Gary Ellis?"

"They originally handled the distribution of the drugs arriving from Cardiff. Since Tilson's disappearance, Kurt believes they are more involved in moving the illegals from the landing point to a place of safety. However, they've never been spotted at the caravan site on Berrow Road."

"I presume the gang has other properties available in the area?" said Gus.

"Kurt and his colleagues believe those properties are close to the coastline. The shorter the distance from the beach to a locked room, the better."

"Was there a future in the new business model for Adam Wilson?" asked Gus. "The Bridgwater contact who Tilson hoped would help expand his business?"

"Police found his body in a ditch on the other side of Combwich in February 2008," said Grace. "That's a village between here and Bridgwater. Wilson had been shot in the back of the head. He was just thirty, with a wife and one child."

"Wilson chose the wrong people to mess with," said Gus. "Nothing to add?"

"That was it, as far as Kurt's presentation was concerned."

Gus nodded towards a café up ahead.

"We could try there unless you wanted to walk further and visit the Pier."

"This café will be fine," said Grace.

"They're an internationally-known brand," said Gus,

"We've got more chance of finding your choice of drink on the menu than in one of the local places."

Gus was right. Ten minutes later, Gus had his black coffee, and Grace could sip her green tea concoction.

"I've read about it but never been to this corner of the country," said Gus looking along The Esplanade. "It has a certain charm."

"The Pier you mentioned is reputed to be the shortest in Britain," said Grace. "That's its only claim to fame as far as I could gather when I lived nearby. Unfortunately, these resorts dotted along the coast are stuck in a Victorian or Edwardian time-warp. Some have progressed to the 1950s, but they're the exception rather than the norm."

"So much cynicism for one so young," said Gus. "I bit my tongue earlier when you spoke about the similarities in housing development in seaside towns such as Burnham. Isambard Kingdom Brunel started the beachball running with the rapid development of the railways in the middle of the nineteenth century. After centuries where people lived their whole lives in towns and villages where they were born, it was suddenly possible to travel by train to the coast."

"I did study history at school, Gus," said Grace.

"We received a broader version many years earlier," said Gus. "Life wasn't like today, where people get weekends and as much as five weeks' holiday to spend how they please. Only the wealthiest people went abroad. Some rich people came here and stayed in the Royal Clarence Hotel, a five-minute walk from here. The terraced housing was home to the families associated with the new businesses on this promenade. As the resort's popularity grew, the more successful business owners had bungalows and villas built further inland. More and more families in the terraced

43

properties helped develop the burgeoning bed and breakfast model. They rented rooms to holidaymakers between April and October, hoping to earn enough money to tide them over until the following year. Burnham was a sleepy fishing village before buckets, spades, ice creams, and fish and chips came here. The railway changed it forever."

Grace had finished her drink and was scrolling through items on her mobile phone.

"Sorry I was boring you," said Gus. "It's this case. I can't help feeling we're too late to achieve anything worthwhile. Even if those bodies were wrapped in tarpaulin, weighted down, and buried in waters with freezing temperatures, we'd never retrieve enough of the remains to make a case."

"I'm afraid you're right, Gus," said Grace. "I was checking the history of the railway. Highbridge still has a station, but Burnham's Pier Station, fifty yards from where we're sitting, closed for good in 1962. They ran summer excursions for a decade before that to bring the holiday-makers the extra mile closer to the action."

"Where do we go next, I wonder?" said Gus.

"To find Ben Mulligan?" asked Grace. "What do we know about him?"

"Josie Clift told us the last time she saw Mulligan; he was barely functioning. If he's an addict, his handlers can't rely on him for anything but basic tasks. They'd be more likely to cast him adrift and let his chosen life take its course."

Grace was interrogating her mobile phone again.

"There's a rehabilitation centre for drug addiction on Berrow Road," she said.

"That's as good a starting point as any," said Gus.

They left the café, walked back along The Esplanade

and within five minutes, Gus was driving them to Berrow Road.

IN HIGHBRIDGE, Neil and Blessing had cruised through the parts of the town Gus thought worth a look. They stopped, here and there, watched and waited but saw nothing untoward.

"It's so normal, Neil," said Blessing.

"Gus didn't have anything better for us to do," sighed Neil. "What's the point of coming back here tomorrow?"

"Is there anywhere we haven't tried?" asked Blessing.

"Gus thought Atkinson and Newbold would live further afield. So why don't we find their addresses?"

Blessing searched her phone for an online directory based on 2011 census details.

"Atkinson lives near Edithmead, Neil. It's only two miles away, but it's off the beaten track. No way could we get close without drawing attention to ourselves."

"What about Newbold?"

"He lives in Brent Knoll, a village one mile further on."

"Right, let's give that place a whirl," said Neil. "Keep your phone handy to take a few holiday snaps to show the rest of the team. Perhaps today might not be a total waste after all."

"Be careful, Neil," said Blessing.

Neil followed the A38 Bristol Road out of Highbridge and soon reached the junction leading to Brent Knoll.

"Newbold's five-bedroomed property is two hundred yards ahead on your left," said Blessing.

A Royal Mail van was parked on the right-hand side of the road, and Neil slowed to allow a tractor and trailer to come through before moving off again. The driver gave Neil a friendly wave.

"That's odd," said Blessing. "Did you see that car parked in the lane back there?"

"I wasn't looking," said Neil.

"The hedges on either side were overgrown, but I caught sight of a dark saloon car tucked away, out of sight."

"A pity," said Neil. "We could do with a vantage point like that."

"We need to go back, Neil," said Blessing, grabbing his arm.

"Okay, keep your hair on, Blessing."

"Now, Neil," she yelled. "I parked near that car often enough to know it was Luke's."

Neil swore under his breath. They were one hundred and fifty yards from Jonny Newbold's home. Could they find a safe place to turn around?

"Where did that tractor and trailer come from?" asked Blessing.

"The farm could be further on," said Neil. "Can we get back to Burnham this way?"

"Drive through the village and take a left onto Station Road," said Blessing, checking the map on her phone. "That lane will take us to the coast road. We'll get back to the police station in twelve minutes."

"We need to speak to Gus," said Neil.

What on earth was Luke Sherman doing in Brent Knoll?

MEANWHILE, Gus and Grace were already returning to the police station.

"That was a waste of time," said Gus.

"Patient confidentiality," said Grace. "We would need the warrant to get anything out of them, and we don't have enough to secure one. We should get hold of Jill Crooks or Kurt Burgess. If Mulligan is still hanging around Burnham, they will know if he's sleeping on the streets or squatting in an abandoned building. He might not have tried to turn his life around."

"I wonder how Alex and Lydia are getting on in Bridgwater?" asked Gus.

"Jill Crooks is back," said Grace as Gus steered the Focus into the car park.

"Let's hope she has something for us," said Gus.

They found Jill in the old detective squad room.

"I wondered where everyone had got to," she said.

"DS Davis and DC Umeh are carrying out covert surveillance in Highbridge," said Gus. "At least, I hope it's covert. Grace and I visited a café on the promenade and then made an abortive attempt to find Ben Mulligan. Can you point us in the right direction?"

"I checked on people I thought you might be interested in before I called you on Saturday. Unfortunately, Mulligan wasn't among them. Josie Clift's recollection suggests that my first port-of-call would be Newtown Road."

"Does Ben Mulligan have a permanent address?" asked Grace.

"I left town long ago, Grace," said Jill. "Somewhere at the back of my mind, I seem to recall that was where his family used to live. Like father, like son, the old man was well-known to the custody sergeant in this station. Someone in Newtown Road might know what happened to Ben. You said you made an abortive attempt to find him. Where was that?"

"We visited the rehab place on Berrow Road," said Gus.

"What can you tell us about that? Could Mulligan be tucked away inside? They wouldn't admit a thing."

"Residents in Berrow Road were furious over plans to convert a B&B into a residential care home for a dozen patients," said Jill. "They collected a petition of several hundred names. As a result, the county planners received many letters objecting to the scheme. Residents feared it was in the wrong place, might bring more crime to the area, and devalue property prices. Town councillors weren't in favour either. They didn't want the town's tourist industry to lose a very important B&B and thought the care home would cause traffic and parking problems."

"What did the local police think?" asked Grace.

"They gave a cautious thumbs-up to the scheme and suggested a security system, including access control, was an important consideration. Rehabilitating known misusers positively affects local crime figures, as you well know. Well-managed centres serve to reduce actual crime and the fear of crime. Despite the objections, the scheme went ahead, and from what I've heard, the place is well-managed and successful."

"Perhaps a visit to Newtown Road would help," said Gus. "Maybe that's a job for Neil and Blessing. Come on, Jill. I'm sure you're itching to tell us what you learned from the fire officer."

"You must get fed up with Gus always being right, Grace," said Jill.

"This is only the second case we've worked on together," said Grace. "I agree. It can be annoying when he's clutching at straws one minute and has the solution to the mystery the next."

"Ed Gunstone, the Forensic Fire Investigator in charge of the Berrow Road caravan case, has concluded that a small fire started at the rear of the caravan," said Jill. "I don't know if you're aware, but arsonists have started using packets of crisps to help them start fires. The fat and calories in a packet of crisps can prove a potent accelerant."

"How did Becky Hood get inside if the door was padlocked?" asked Gus. "Surely, the crisp packets method wouldn't work on outside surfaces?"

"Ed suggested the rear window could have been poorly secured, or Becky could have dropped a number of burning packets through the skylight," said Jill. "Fabric seating and curtains would have been ablaze in under a minute. Bags of crisps have an advantage to criminals in being far more innocuous than a can of petrol and burn in a way that leaves little evidence behind. Police wouldn't have suspected a thing if they had stopped Becky Hood on her way to Burnham."

"No one's going to look twice at someone with a few bags of crisps," said Gus. "I get that. I wonder where Becky Hood learned this method to make a deliberate fire look accidental?"

"Ed Gunstone told me the first he heard about it was from a colleague in the prison service," said Jill. "Criminals had tested the method inside, found it worked and passed on the information to all and sundry."

"Ian Hood must have heard on the grapevine from people he met in prison," said Grace. "I can imagine him telling Sam Webber and Mark Webber in front of Becky, thinking she was too dim to understand."

"Why did Ed Gunstone believe Becky used packets of crisps anyway?" asked Gus.

"He called Geoff Mercer at London Road first thing this morning and asked Geoff to check with Becky Hood," said Jill. "Geoff called back while I was in Ed's office. Becky

Hood explained how she'd started the fire using packets of crisps. When she left, the seating area was well-alight, but she didn't intend the caravan to be destroyed. Becky only wanted it to be damaged enough to be a write-off. She thought someone would call the fire brigade within minutes of leaving the car park."

"What else did Ed discover?" asked Gus.

"A connected gas cylinder was stored outside on a level, concrete surface, together with a backup cylinder," said Jill. "The parts of the caravan away from the fire were doused in petrol and set alight. The two cylinders exploded, and destruction was swift and inevitable, regardless of how quickly the emergency services had arrived. Ed showed me proof that the major fire had emanated from the opposite end to the minor fire set by Becky Hood."

"The gang had someone on-site," said Grace. "They couldn't have been alerted to an attack by Becky Hood, so why were they there?"

"After Jill left us earlier, Neil asked if I thought the site managers were dodgy. I don't believe so, but I reckon the gang had other safe houses at their disposal. We'll never know whether there were illegal immigrants elsewhere on Friday night, but we have the names of a couple of gang members we can bring in for questioning."

"Jack Carr and Gary Ellis," said Grace. "They'll have their high-priced lawyers with them."

"It would be nothing more than a fishing expedition, Gus," said Jill. "We would need to place one, or both, of them on the caravan site at the right time. The town's CCTV system has been problematic and suffers from faulty hardware. It still has analogue cameras installed. As a result, only half of the cameras work at any time. They did get a new one installed in the Pier Street car park six months ago to help tackle a boy racer problem. There's nothing useful close to the caravan site."

The squad room door opened, and Neil and Blessing entered.

"Finished already?" asked Gus.

"We've got a problem, guv," said Neil.

"I spotted Luke's car in Brent Knoll, guv," said Blessing. "He had to be on a stakeout. His car was tucked away in a lane, masked by a hedge, less than two hundred yards from Jonny Newbold's house. It was just a glimpse. I couldn't see whether Luke was in the driver's seat."

"What were you doing that far afield?" asked Gus. "I thought I asked you to keep an eye on the lowlife in Highbridge."

"We did," said Neil. "Well, we visited the hot spots you selected, but if there's any criminal activity, it doesn't happen that early in the day. It was like watching paint dry."

"Neil thought you just wanted to give us something to do, guv," said Blessing. "I found the addresses for the main men. We agreed to leave Paulie Atkinson alone because his house was in the middle of nowhere. Someone would spot a strange car before it got within half a mile."

"Newbold's house is in a cul-de-sac off the main road in the village," said Neil. "With more through traffic, it seemed a drive-by was less risky. Blessing was primed to take photos of any people or cars outside the property when she spotted Luke's car. We carried on driving through the village and made our way back here. I guarantee we weren't followed, guv."

"Did you know anything about this stakeout, Jill?" asked Gus.

"News to me, Gus," she replied. "Portishead keep us in

the loop with ongoing surveillance to avoid uniformed officers tapping on car windows and accusing undercover cops of being kerb-crawlers. Although, certain investigations must be carried out in strict secrecy. Even if we don't hear a whisper about what they involve, we usually get a heads-up that we should steer clear of a particular area."

"Luke Sherman worked with this team until recently," said Gus. "He transferred to Gablecross, Swindon, last month."

"You weren't expecting him to be assigned to a case in Somerset," said Jill.

Gus wondered whether something else was behind Luke's appearance in Brent Knoll.

He called Luke's phone.

"Hello."

"It's Gus Freeman here. I wanted to speak with Luke Sherman. Who is this?"

"DS Tom Spencer. We met at the Waggon & Horses a couple of weeks ago."

"Why do you have Luke's mobile phone?" asked Gus.

"He's on special assignment with Avon & Somerset Police, guv. Luke had to leave his personal belongings behind. He's carrying a burner phone. The SIM card only carried the numbers of the other team members. I can't call Luke, and he shouldn't call me under any circumstance. I'm afraid I've no idea how long he'll be away."

"You two are close," said Gus. "Did Luke indicate the nature of the assignment he was on?"

"Luke couldn't tell me much at all. When I asked whether it involved organised crime, he said it did, but not in the way I thought. I've tried to fathom what that meant ever since he left."

"The red-haired man," said Gus.

"Sorry. You've lost me," said Tom. "Why did you need to speak to him? Was it anything one of us here can help with?"

"We investigated a double murder last week that we all-but finalised at the weekend. One victim and his associates had strong links with Burnham-on-Sea. So we arrived here this morning to tie up a few loose ends. I asked two of my team to carry out surveillance near Highbridge. Luke should have spotted their car as it passed the junction if he was good at his job. He was parked just up the road from the home of a criminal called Jonny Newbold, whose gang are responsible for ferrying illegal immigrants into the UK via the Irish Republic."

"Do you want me to pass that up the chain of command?" asked Tom.

"I've got a DI from Taunton working with me, Tom. She's unaware of any operation in the neighbourhood. So I guess we'll do more harm than good by getting more people involved."

"Do you think the gang could have someone on the inside, guv?"

"One can never rule it out, Tom. I trust Blessing. If she says it was Luke's car, then I believe her. However, with such a brief sighting, Blessing couldn't tell whether Luke was lying low in the driver's seat. So I'm going to call the Chief Constable for guidance. His counterpart at Portishead will let us know whether to withdraw or carry on hunting for clues relating to our case."

"Where does the red-haired man come in, guv?" asked Tom.

"I don't mean to confuse you further, Tom," said Gus. "From what I've learned, pretty much wherever he chooses."

"I hope to hear good news from Luke soon," said Tom. "I miss him. Good luck with your case. Sorry I couldn't be of more help."

"Thanks, Tom," said Gus, and he ended the call.

"I could make that call to our Chief Constable, Gus," said Jill Crooks. "It might be better coming from one of his officers. If you call your boss, we can compare notes and take whatever action they decide."

"Fingers crossed, they both want to go in the same direction," said Gus.

"That's why they get paid the big bucks, Gus," said Jill.

She walked to the far corner of the room to make her call.

Gus called London Road, and Vera Butler answered.

"Vera, it's Gus here. Is Kenneth available to talk?"

"I'll put you through," said Vera.

"Truelove speaking. What have you done now, Freeman?"

"I'm sure I don't know what you mean, sir," said Gus. "What have you heard?"

"Nothing, as usual," moaned the Chief Constable. "Nobody tells me anything."

Gus explained in brief what they'd done since arriving in Burnham. He wanted to build up to the revelation that Neil and Blessing might have scuppered surveillance on the Atkinson-Newbold gang.

"So, you've proved the woman you charged on Saturday morning didn't murder the three people trapped inside the caravan. This story has a familiar theme, Freeman."

"It didn't sit right with me, sir," said Gus. "The more I thought about it over the weekend, the more I thought Becky Hood was a mischief-maker, not a killer. She had no idea there was anyone inside the caravan. The Forensic Fire

Investigator confirmed my suspicions. What DI Crooks needs to do now is find the person responsible."

"When do you expect to hear back from DS Burgess?" asked Kenneth.

"He could return from Bridgwater at any time, sir," said Gus, crossing his fingers. "DS Hardy and Ms Logan Barre will encourage him to produce a result for us later today."

"You mentioned surveillance on certain areas in High-bridge and district. How did you select those areas?"

"Frequent appearances on the crime map, sir," said Gus. "I'm a firm believer in studying statistics and utilising them to our best advantage."

"Mmm," said Kenneth. "You've changed your tune since you returned to duty, Freeman. Either that or you're extracting the Michael."

"It's possible our surveillance team visited a no-go area, sir," said Gus. "Would you like to venture a guess where that might have been?"

"Don't talk in riddles, man," said Kenneth. "Spit it out."

"Blessing thought she caught sight of Luke Sherman's car in Brent Knoll, sir."

"Ah," said Kenneth. "Is everyone inside Burnham Police Station, apart from DS Hardy and Ms Barre?"

"That's correct, sir," said Gus.

"Stay put," said Kenneth. "Ask DI Crooks to contact Burgess. As soon as those three return from Bridgwater, I need you to drive straight home. Then, at nine in the morn-ing, I'll get Mercer to brief you in the Old Police Station office."

"We had no idea something was going on, sir," said Gus. "A warning would have been welcome."

"I'm as much in the dark as you are, Freeman," said

Kenneth. "Rest assured. I'll know what's what by the time I leave this office."

Gus looked up to see Jill Crooks shrug her shoulders.

"Was it news to your guy, too?" asked Gus.

"He revealed as much as the people running the operation would allow, Gus," said Jill. "Which was very little."

"Please don't tell me the name Curran was mentioned during your conversation."

"He's with the National Crime Agency, isn't he? So, no, he isn't involved."

"Can you call Kurt Burgess, please? They need to wrap up what they're doing and return here at once. We've been ordered back to base."

"I don't have Kurt's number," said Jill.

She called Bridgwater Police Centre.

"Kurt signed out of the building ten minutes ago, Gus, " said Jill. "He should be halfway back by now."

"I was looking forward to hearing what they'd discovered," said Neil.

"I want to know that Luke is safe and well," said Blessing.

"Someone knows what Luke was doing there this morning," said Gus.

"Whatever it is must be way above our pay grade," said Jill.

They didn't have long to wait. Lydia was first through the door. Gus could tell she was excited. He dreaded having to burst her bubble.

"We found the spot!" she cried.

Kurt and Alex soon joined her, both grinning from ear to ear.

"We have to leave immediately," said Gus. "Don't

discuss today with anyone. DS Mercer will explain everything in the office tomorrow morning."

Jill Crooks took Kurt Burgess to one side and told him to return to Bridgwater. She would be in touch in the morning.

Lydia turned to Neil and Blessing for an explanation.

"What's going on?" she asked.

"Beats me," said Neil.

"Make sure we don't leave anything behind," said Gus. "Grace and I will be right behind you."

Gus watched as the disconsolate team members left the squad room.

"Well, this is a first," said Jill. "If we don't work together again, I hope everything goes well with the baby, Gus. Nice to meet you, Grace. Goodbye."

Gus and Grace walked outside to the car park.

"Some days, the gap between the end of one working day and the start of another seems so brief," said Grace.

"It won't come any quicker if you fret over it, Grace," said Gus. "On nights like this, I used to turn to a good single malt for help."

"You drank to forget. Did it work?" asked Grace.

"There was one positive to come out of it," said Gus. "No matter how bad a situation I was in the next morning, it was nothing compared to how rough I felt."

Chapter Four

GUS HAD ARRIVED home well before Suzie last evening. He drove Grace back to the Old Police Station car park, watched her remove her steering-wheel lock, and trundle away in her Smart car. The others were long gone.

Suzie had asked how their day went. Gus told her what they'd learned about the caravan fire and how much a black coffee was in a café on The Esplanade.

"Why did you leave Burnham so early?" she asked.

"Kenneth's orders," said Gus. "Don't ask. I won't know until Geoff gives us the lowdown tomorrow morning."

Gus knew that wouldn't stop Suzie from trying to fathom what was behind those orders. She was a detective, after all, and a mystery needed to be solved.

"Let's eat," said Gus. "Then we can spend a quiet evening watching TV."

"How can you not want to work out what's going on?" asked Suzie.

"It will all come out in the wash," he shrugged.

After a long evening and an even longer night, they were in the kitchen before eight.

"You need a hearty breakfast," said Suzie. "Sausage, egg, and bacon."

"I thought that was the condemned man?" said Gus. "Things aren't that bad. But look, we didn't alert the criminals we're after, and if Lydia's excited face was anything to go by, we're closer to tying up another loose end. Suppose we get an explanation for this other business; we can return to Burnham and pick up from where we left off."

"You can't tell me what this other business is, though, can you?" asked Suzie.

"No, and that's because I don't know what it is myself yet," said Gus.

Suzie placed the plate of fried food in front of him.

"I'll interrogate you further tonight," she said.

"I would expect nothing less," said Gus.

They left the bungalow at eight twenty-five.

Suzie led the way through the gateway in her Golf and turned left. Gus followed and soon descended into the valley en route to the office. He thought he spotted Geoff Mercer's car in the line of traffic ahead. Parking could be an issue for someone this morning.

Gus was the last to reach the Church Street car park. The others were upstairs in the office, no doubt discussing yesterday's events despite being off-limits.

Gus saw Geoff Mercer waiting by the lift as he parked in the last remaining CRT space. Geoff had risked the wrath of the locals by parking his large car in one of the small public bays.

"Good morning, Geoff," said Gus. "Or am I being a trifle optimistic?"

"Let's get upstairs and get this over with," said Geoff.

They rode in the lift to the first floor. As the doors opened, the conversation died.

Neil Davis stood up.

"I decided to go further than the Highbridge streets you specified, sir. DC Umeh just did as I asked. I take full responsibility."

"Sit down, DS Davis," said Geoff Mercer. "This has nothing to do with what you did yesterday. I'll provide what background I can, but DS Sherman has more to answer for than either of you."

Gus sat next to Grace Packenham while Geoff stood behind Gus's desk and reminded them not to breathe a word about what he had to say. Then, happy he had their full attention, Geoff began.

"Organised crime has been the biggest thorn in our sides for decades. We have had to withstand significant threats, both internal and external. The move from a police force to a politically-correct police service has damaged our relationship with the public we serve. Successive governments have reduced our numbers, and the courts are less likely to convict the guilty than at any time in our history."

"We can struggle to find sufficient evidence to break these gangs and put them in jail," said Grace. "It's not *all* down to the number of officers on the streets or the legal system."

"I agree it's a complex problem, DI Packenham," said Geoff. "Bear with me. At the beginning of 2015, it's understood a meeting took place in the office of the then Chief Constable for West Midlands Police. He spoke with representatives of a group using methods outside the law to get results. Of course, he couldn't condone their actions, but evidence gathered over the previous five years highlighted instances in various parts of the country where criminals had disappeared without explanation."

"They were getting help from vigilantes," said Neil.

"Shades of the sniper at Cheney Manor Industrial Estate," said Alex.

"That shooting took place in May, eight months before that secret meeting," said Gus.

"Why haven't we heard about this meeting and its ramifications?" asked Lydia.

"Not everyone wearing a uniform is singing from the same hymn sheet, Lydia," said Gus. "When we visited Larcombe Manor earlier this year, we met Callum Wood, a former Detective Sergeant who once worked downstairs in this building. Callum believed he could help more people by working outside the police than he could while stationed at Manvers Street in Bath. I'm struggling to see how this connects with Luke's assignment."

"Each of you spoke with Luke before he left the Crime Review Team," said Geoff. "Did he elaborate on the preliminary meetings he had at Portishead? What about the abortive raid on Larcombe Manor that Rick Chalmers went on?"

"I spoke to Luke here in the office," said Neil. "At first, it was to check he was still coming to our night out at the Waggon & Horses. He'd spent the past couple of days at Portishead. Luke was staggered at the number of incidents where Larcombe Manor played a significant role. He said he found it hard to accept the view the people involved were criminals. I told Luke we can't have vigilantes running riot around the country sorting problems we don't have the resources to tackle."

"That's what I would expect you to say, DS Davis," said Geoff.

"Luke said the Assistant Chief Constable he'd worked with at Portishead held the same view, sir," said Neil. "But Luke had studied the names of people who were no longer a danger to the public. He argued things would be much worse if they were still alive and kicking."

"That was what I was afraid of, DS Davis," said Geoff.

"I chatted with Luke at the pub, Geoff," said Gus. "He told me he was playing catch-up with his colleagues on the team at Portishead. At that time, they were no closer to finding the red-haired sniper, David Scott; but their surveillance was ongoing. Senior charity officers had resurfaced at Larcombe Manor since the raid Rick Chalmers took part in, and people were working normally again. I jokingly suggested if they could disappear into thin air at a minute's notice, perhaps they had an under-ground bunker on the estate. When I heard Luke's car was in Brent Knoll yesterday, I wondered whether he was carrying out surveillance on Scott, or one of his Larcombe Manor colleagues, with others from the Portishead team."

"If he was," said Alex, "it suggests Scott was targeting Jonny Newbold."

"DI Crooks didn't know of any surveillance on Newbold, did she, guv?" asked Lydia.

"She was as much in the dark as we were, Lydia," said Gus. "And unless her Chief Constable was being economical with the truth, neither did he."

"What I'm hearing this morning lines up with how London Road sees the problem," said Geoff. "Before that meeting in 2015, certain regional forces had turned a blind eye to incidents where known criminals suddenly disappeared. They had more than enough criminal activity to handle without hunting for missing persons. Those regions reaped the benefit of a gang leader no longer being in control."

"When someone removes a snake's head, death is not immediate," said Gus.

"True, but the body is fatally weakened," said Geoff. "The removal of its leader helped reduce a gang's hold in a particular town or city, but failings within a neighbouring region often offset the gains. For example, grooming gangs have operated unchecked for decades in the North. Moreover, organised crime gangs have identified serving officers in the Metropolitan Police whom they could manipulate. As a result, many police officers wonder whether they were fighting a losing battle."

"Perhaps it's not a surprise that many police officers move into security roles," said Alex. "The money can be better in personal security, and the client gets the peace of mind they crave."

"The public can't rely on us to keep them safe from burglars, so more and more have turned to private firms," said Neil. "There are now almost a thousand gated communities in the UK."

"The Security Industry Authority regulates the private security industry," said Grace. "They focus their resources on driving up standards and combating organised criminality by targeting companies or employees that fail to meet required standards. Over three hundred thousand employees currently operate in the UK in around four thousand businesses."

"It's one of the country's few growth industries," said Lydia.

"One can appreciate why officers are leaving us and why the public looks elsewhere for help," said Geoff. "They read headlines claiming we've given up the fight, and the yobs have taken over. They believe we have lost control of the streets. The latest figures on my desk show that an estimated fourteen million incidents of anti-social behaviour occurred last year—one every two seconds. Rowdy and abusive behaviour has been allowed to fester because police have retreated from the streets in the past two decades. The idea there must be a better way has grown from statistics such as those."

"Was there an effort to win universal acceptance it was better to work with these vigilantes?" asked Grace.

"The fact Gus said not everyone is singing from the same hymn sheet tells you that even if they tried, they were unsuccessful, Grace," said Geoff. "Avon & Somerset carried out the necessary surveillance and executed the recent raid on the Manor to bring offenders to face the courts."

"I wonder whether a jury would find them guilty?" asked Lydia.

"What do you think Luke is up to, sir?" asked Neil.

"I'm afraid he's gone rogue, DS Davis," said Geoff.

"His colleague at Gablecross, Tom Spencer, told me yesterday Luke was on an undercover assignment," said Gus. "He'd had to leave his mobile phone at home. The four-person team he was part of used burner phones while they were off the grid. Was that rubbish?"

"Not entirely," said Geoff. "The four-person surveillance team left Portishead four days ago. The phones they were issued with had GPS tracking. So for three days, the phones were where Portishead expected them to be in the Bath and North-East Somerset area. But, they realised they had lost a phone on Sunday evening."

"Luke disabled his GPS tracking," said Lydia, "but why?"

"Have they heard from the other three team members?"

asked Gus. "Did they send someone to the last location they received? What protocol were they using?"

"Surveillance has been curtailed until the situation is resolved," said Geoff. "The other three officers have returned to base. They were unaware DS Sherman had left the area he was covering. The grids in which each officer worked never overlapped to reduce the risk of compromised surveillance. Contact between officers was minimal, but the daily check-in with their handler was sacrosanct."

"So, you're saying Portishead know where Luke was on Saturday evening, sir," said Blessing. "When did they lose the GPS signal?"

"Each officer was supposed to check in at six in the evening," said Geoff. "When DS Sherman failed to make contact, they checked his location. The last signal placed him in the small village of Marksbury, about seven miles from Bath. The western boundary of his grid was Chew Magna, eight miles further west. So his handler believes DS Sherman was heading in that direction at six."

"Luke disabled his GPS or ditched his burner phone," said Alex. "What were his orders if his target was heading beyond Chew Magna?"

"We're not privy to that information, DS Hardy," said Geoff. "Portishead are keeping their cards very close to their chest."

"That can be interpreted in two ways, sir," said Neil. "They can't trust anyone outside their group not to have a mole. Or they messed up and are covering their tracks."

"The Chief Constable stressed that in the past, only criminals have been targeted by vigilantes such as David Scott and his outfit," said Geoff. "There's nothing to suggest DS Sherman is in danger from that source."

"Hang on," said Gus, "Portishead last heard from Luke

at six o'clock on Saturday evening. They haven't got a confirmed sighting of him between when he failed to get in touch and now, which suggests Luke avoided major routes and towns where he might get caught on a CCTV camera. So why would he leave his grid area to follow someone on such a circuitous route to Brent Knoll?"

"I can tell you've got a plausible scenario, Gus," said Geoff. "Take me through it step-by-step. "I'm confused."

"Someone at Larcombe had already identified Atkinson and Newbold as targets," said Grace. "They held them responsible for the deaths of those trapped in the caravan fire. Am I on the right track, Gus?"

"Exactly. David Scott and at least one of his colleagues went to Burnham as soon as they received confirmation of the deaths," said Gus. "Grace and I heard the news from DI Crooks at lunchtime on Saturday. However, the information wasn't released to the media until Sunday at noon. The senior fire officer wanted twenty-four hours grace to attempt to identify the deceased. That proved fruitless because the severity of the blaze had obliterated any ID. The gang members took their documents away before locking them inside the caravan. It could take months to trace the victims' identity from dental records."

"I can't believe the vigilantes were aware of the events that led to the original fire set by Becky Hood," said Lydia.

"Nor can I, Lydia," said Gus. "The murders we were investigating occurred before these people started operating. Becky Hood's mischief-making spurred the Burnham gang into action. They couldn't afford the police to check a fire-damaged caravan to determine whether a crime had been committed. So Atkinson and Newbold decided the best option was to ensure nothing was left worth checking."

"How do you explain what DS Sherman's car was doing in Brent Knoll on Monday lunchtime?" asked Geoff.

"That bit's straightforward if we're right, and Luke was following someone off the grid," said Blessing. "Luke ditched his phone, so there would be no proof he was a police detective if he got caught by the vigilantes."

"If the target he was following had done their home-work, they knew Atkinson's house was in the middle of nowhere. Newbold's property was the better option, with several vantage points for covert surveillance. Luke followed the target to Brent Knoll and parked in the lane where Blessing spotted him."

"That's where your theory falls apart," said Geoff. "If DS Sherman avoided detection, he was in that lane for up to fifteen hours before DC Umeh saw him. Once he'd iden-tified the target and his location, he should have contacted Portishead, using a public telephone if necessary, and back-up would have been despatched."

"Although Newbold's house was easier to keep watch on, surely they wanted Atkinson too?" said Lydia. "We would make two raids at first light. From the little I've heard of Scott and his colleagues, they wouldn't do half a job."

"David Scott is ex-SAS," said Alex. "It's a reasonable assumption everyone in that set-up is ex-military. We're missing something."

"We might not have every piece of the jigsaw yet," said Gus. "However, I feel we're on the right track. I suggest we call Bridgwater Police Centre to ask DS Burgess to visit that leafy lane in Brent Knoll."

"I thought you and the team would want to go, Gus," said Geoff. "I know what a tight bunch you are."

"If you came with us, it might stop us from getting into hot water, Geoff," said Gus.

"I can't do anything without clearing it with Kenneth," said Geoff. "He would need to phone his counterpart at Portishead too."

"What was Kenneth doing this morning?" asked Gus.

"A session with the local MP, followed by a lunchtime meeting with the PCC."

"Leave a message with Vera Butler," said Gus. "That buys us four or five hours. Then, I'll call Jill Crooks to ask her to do similar. It's bound to take a while for the message to get relayed to everyone involved."

"It beats a morning stuck in the office," said Geoff. "We'll leave as soon as we've made our calls."

When they got downstairs to the car park, it was plain Neil and Lydia intended to take the same passengers as yesterday. Geoff nodded towards his car.

"I've seen the alternative transport," he said. "You two had better come with me."

"Do we still have clearance to use the facilities at Burnham, Gus?" asked Grace.

"Jill Crooks arranged for us to be welcome for up to five days. So we'll find a scattering of staff there today. Perhaps our presence will put a dent in their PCC's view the building is far too big for the town's needs."

Geoff Mercer followed Gus's suggestion that they cut across the country and approached Highbridge via the A38.

"There's not a lot in it, Geoff," he said. "Fifteen minutes at best, and I saw a sign warning of lane restrictions on the motorway from midnight last night. Unfortunately, Neil and Lydia would have flashed past too quickly to read the sign yesterday."

"We'll pass the junction to Brent Knoll that Neil took yesterday, Gus," said Grace.

"That's all we're going to do until we confirm the lie of the land," said Geoff. "Can we call Atkinson and Newbold to see if they're home?"

"A cold call? They'll let it go to voice mail, Geoff," said Gus.

"I'll shut up and drive," said Geoff. "I haven't been at the sharp end for a while."

They arrived in Burnham by a quarter to eleven. Alex and Neil came five minutes later.

"You'll never guess, guv," said Neil.

"Lots of cones, Neil?" asked Gus.

"Loads, guv, and not a scoop of ice cream between them. I see Kurt Burgess has made it in already."

"No sign of DI Crooks, though, Gus," said Grace.

"Jill didn't think she could persuade her immediate superior to let her skive off for the morning, Grace," said Gus. "She said she'd be here in spirit."

Geoff Mercer led the CRT team inside the station. He had only managed to give the desk sergeant his rank before they were whisked into the squad room. Status has its privileges.

Kurt Burgess joined them at once and introduced himself to Geoff Mercer.

"Show me where these two jokers live, DS Burgess," said Geoff.

"There's only one narrow lane in and out to Paulie Atkinson's place, sir," said Kurt, indicating a spot on a map on a side table.

Several photographs of the property and its occupant were posted on the wall above the map. Kurt moved to the next table, which contained a similar layout.

"Jonny Newbold lives here, the detached house on the

left-hand side of the cul-de-sac. There are open fields behind the property, sir. Newbold will be on his toes before we've parked the cars if we arrive mob-handed."

"Where was it that DC Umeh thought she spotted DS Sherman's car?" asked Geoff.

"In this lane, on the left-hand side of the road through the village, sir. I don't have photographs, I'm afraid. Although, we could risk sending a drone to do a fly-over."

"Avoiding Atkinson and Newbold's properties like the plague, I hope," said Geoff.

"We wouldn't alert Newbold that way, Geoff," said Gus.

"Where does the lane lead to?" asked Geoff.

"It used to be a farm, sir," said Kurt. "The outbuildings are almost derelict now, but the main house is habitable. The farmer, John Sedgewick, still lives there. He's in his late eighties, and his son, John, farms on the outskirts of the village."

"We saw him yesterday," said Neil.

Geoff Mercer studied the maps for thirty seconds.

"We can't wait for more information. The only other access to the lane leading to the farm is by trudging three-quarters of a mile across the fields from Edithmead. What's that word mean, here, on the map?"

"A rhyne, sir?" asked Kurt. "It's a drainage channel. You might call them something else in Wiltshire."

"A ditch?" suggested Neil.

"When you grow up with them, it's easy to assume everyone knows what you are talking about," said Kurt. "I'm a country boy, and rhynes are artificial, water-filled channels you find on the Somerset Levels. They're like a network of wet hedges to mark the boundary of fields and stop livestock escaping."

"I came across the word while I lived in the county, Neil," said Grace. "The Rivers Rhine and Rhone have the same origin."

"Forget the history for now," said Geoff. "Who looks after them?"

"The Somerset Drainage Board, sir," said Kurt.

"Get in touch," said Geoff. "We need to borrow a vehicle for an hour."

"They have an office in Highbridge, only a five-minute drive from here, sir," said Kurt.

"Happy days," said Gus. "We can get four of us into the lane without alerting anyone."

"I have my uses," said Geoff. "Gus, Alex, and Kurt will accompany me. First, we'll need something to make us look legitimate. Any suggestions?"

"You should be able to get wellington boots, over-trousers, and hi-viz waistcoats from supplies held in this building, sir," said Grace. "Even though it's only semi-operational, they should be prepared for anything."

"The Drainage Board have agreed to let us borrow a seven-seater transit van, sir," said Kurt. "As long as we're careful."

"Lead on, DS Burgess," said Geoff. "You know your way around this building better than me. Find me a pair of over-trousers that will accommodate my expanding waistline, and you can drive."

Ten minutes later, they were kitted out and driving into Highbridge. The transit van was ready and waiting in the yard outside the SDB building. Geoff was confident the white van and its logo would fool Jonny Newbold and anyone else who saw it entering the lane. The stile marked on the map at the far end of the lane gave quick access to the drainage channels. It was the obvious place for the SDB to park to pay a visit.

Kurt drove them out of the yard. Within minutes they were turning off the A38 and heading into the village of Brent Knoll. Gus was worried about what they would find.

"The car's still there," said Alex as they entered the lane, "but I can't see a sign of Luke."

"Drive to the end of the lane, DS Burgess," said Geoff. "We'll all get out there, and then you stay with DS Hardy. Keep your eyes peeled and intercept the farmer if he comes out to see what's going on. Then, Gus and I will walk back to the car and check it out."

"I don't like the look of it, Geoff," said Gus as they made their way cautiously towards Luke's car.

"A lot of time has passed, hasn't it?" said Geoff. "DS Sherman may not have been in the driver's seat when your young lady spotted the car yesterday."

"Luke was in Marksbury, driving towards Chew Magna on Sunday before his GPS tracker got switched off," said Gus, "His car is now parked ahead of us. I can't see someone leaving it here to advertise they were in Brent Knoll. No, let's follow our thinking on the timing of the news release. Larcombe Manor heard the news, planned their response, then sent a team to deal with Atkinson and Newbold."

Geoff stopped two yards from Luke's car.

"They were followed here by DS Sherman, arriving early evening. Seven o'clock at the latest."

"Luke didn't report in at six," said Gus, "which means the team passed him before then. He realised they were leaving his grid, turned off the tracker, and followed. We know they zig-zagged their way across country to avoid detection. So it makes sense to me too that they reached here by seven on Sunday evening."

"If the target realised they had a tail, they could have attacked DS Sherman after nightfall. That's almost forty hours ago."

Gus walked to the front of the car and placed a hand on the bonnet.

"Stone cold," he said through gritted teeth.

Geoff Mercer took a pair of white nitrile gloves from his pocket.

"The keys aren't in the ignition, Gus," he said. "I can see a holdall on the back seat—a few bits-and-bobs in the tray between the front seats. Hang on. The keys look to be on the floor in the passenger-side footwell."

Geoff tried the passenger door.

"Locked," he said.

"Just as well I brought this from supplies, then," said Gus, producing an extendable steel baton. He gave the passenger window a sharp rap and knocked enough broken glass onto the passenger seat to let Geoff slip his hand inside to unlock the door.

Geoff opened the door, leaned inside, picked up the keys, and hesitated.

"Go on, Geoff," said Gus. "It has to be done."

Geoff pressed the key fob, returned to the back of the car, and opened the boot.

"That's a relief," said Geoff.

The boot was empty.

"Kenneth didn't think Luke was in danger from Scott and his mates," Gus said. "We have to hope Newbold or one of his cronies didn't stumble across Luke, thinking he was staking out the gang. He wouldn't last five minutes with that lot. We can't relax yet."

"Call DS Hardy," said Geoff. "Burgess can collect us. Then, I need to return to the police station to contact Portishead and put them in the picture."

They were in the transit van two minutes later, heading towards the A38. As Kurt waited at the crossroads for a break in traffic, they could hear sirens to their left.

"It looks like an incident team approaching on blue lights, sir," said Kurt. "Uniformed officers, a forensic van, and by the looks of it, detectives too."

"How did Portishead learn of the car's location?" asked Geoff. "See if you can turn this van around without causing another incident, DS Burgess."

As Kurt entered the lane, several faces turned towards the Somerset Drainage Board van. A uniformed officer raised a hand, indicating he wanted Kurt to stop, then strolled forward to stand by the driver's window.

"You can't go any further, sir. I'll help you reverse into the main road."

"We're not budging," said Geoff Mercer.

"I appreciate you have a job to do, but the ditches will have to wait," said the officer.

"We're not here to check the ditches, constable," said Geoff. "I'm DS Mercer from Wiltshire Police. Take me to your leader."

The constable trotted back to the group of men by the car.

Geoff grinned at Gus. "I've always wanted to say that."

Geoff and Gus got out of the van. A familiar face came to meet them.

"Do I have you to thank for breaking my window, guv?" asked Luke.

"We were worried about you, Luke," said Gus. "What the heck's going on?"

"Did you see anyone you recognised yesterday lunchtime, DS Sherman?" asked Geoff.

"I wasn't here, sir," said Luke. "I was getting the third degree at Portishead. At least they let me have a good night's sleep before they started grilling me. Then, I got an earful from the other three guys I'd been working with. I've got plenty of bridges to mend if I get the chance. Yesterday was a long day, but I had it coming."

"What prompted the cavalry charge this morning?" asked Gus. "Who tipped off Portishead that Atkinson and Newbold were missing?"

"Anonymous phone call, guv," said Luke.

"How did it all start?" asked Gus. "We know you disabled your GPS and followed someone from the area you covered."

"I've seen enough pictures of the blue transits they use, guv," said Luke. "They were heading west, but I had no idea of their destination. I wanted to see whether they were on a mission."

"Why didn't you simply let them go, DS Sherman?" asked Geoff. "You could have reported the sighting to your handler. Then, a senior officer would have decided to have them followed outside your area by another team."

"I haven't covered myself in glory, sir. I appreciate that," said Luke. "They must have realised someone was following them."

"Recriminations are for another time, Geoff," said Gus. "Let's concentrate on why these characters took Luke out of the game for an hour or two. What time did you arrive here on Sunday evening, Luke?"

"Just before seven, guv. The blue transit turned into Church Lane, further into the village. This leafy refuge was my only option. I didn't realise it then, but Church Lane comes out again onto the main road. That enabled the four-person team to cover both sides of their target's property. Of course, I wasn't aware who the target was at that stage. I hoped to learn who they were targeting and maybe follow them when they left."

"Jonny Newbold was their target," said Geoff.

"I hadn't heard of him, sir. But, before we left this morning, Portishead told me about him and his partner-in-crime, Atkinson."

"So what happened next, Luke?" asked Gus.

"I had two visitors an hour after I parked here," said Luke. "One distracted me by urinating in the hedge close to the front of my car. I didn't want to let him know I was watching; suddenly, his accomplice opened the rear door, and I felt the cold steel of a gun barrel behind my left ear. He ordered me to release the bonnet, and the other guy removed the alternator. I was told to sit tight until half-eight if I didn't want trouble. Then, they took my phone, secured my hands to the steering wheel, and threw the keys onto the floor. The guy with the gun told me he knew I wouldn't take long to get free. They didn't want to hurt me, just incapacitate me long enough for them to conclude a bit of business."

"No wonder they didn't bother sending a team to Atkinson's place," said Geoff. "He must have been driving to Brent Knoll for a meeting with his mate."

"Yes, sir, I realise that now," said Luke. "I sat in the car, struggling to get my hands free. I watched several cars pass the lane's entrance. A Range Rover drove past at eight-fifteen. I never heard a thing after that until the blue transit sped past me as I walked to the end of the lane. I still had a ten-minute walk to the Red Cow to make my phone call. I can't tell you which direction they took. Portishead thinks they returned to base."

"Which way did you have to go for the pub?" asked Gus.

"Left," said Luke. "I passed a cul-de-sac on my left, perhaps one hundred and fifty yards from here. The Range Rover was parked on a driveway. Everything was quiet. No neighbours were running around outside, wondering what the commotion had been. The team must have been in and out in seconds, then bundled their targets into the transit van and sped away."

"What time was this?" asked Geoff.

"Sunday evening, just after half-past eight. A car picked me up at ten."

"Didn't you mention any of this to your handler?" asked Geoff.

"On Sunday night, I couldn't confirm the people in the blue van had done anything other than putting my car out of commission. I didn't see anything. I didn't know who Atkinson and Newbold were. The man with the gun's warning could have referred to anything."

"What did Portishead plan for today?" asked Gus.

"They wanted to check my car for clues," said Luke. "We brought a mechanic to get it mobile again so I can drive back for another debrief. A second team went to the cul-de-sac to effect entry to Newbold's house and check out Atkinson's vehicle. A third team has travelled to Atkinson's house from Taunton."

"Did the guy with the gun have an accent?" asked Gus.

"North of the border, guv, but I can't specify a region."

"David Scott, I'll bet," said Gus.

"In the meantime, Scott, or whoever it was, has had a forty-hour start on us," said Geoff. "They captured the two gang leaders, and we know what happens to violent criminals who disappear like that. So we're looking for bodies."

"Back to Burnham Police Station, Geoff?" asked Gus.

"I think that's best," said Geoff. "I'll start making calls to London Road and Portishead. I suggest your team works with DS Burgess to determine where these rascals might have taken Atkinson and Newbold."

Chapter Five

FIFTEEN MINUTES LATER, they rejoined the others in the squad room in Burnham. Geoff Mercer told them Luke Sherman was safe. He then updated them on what happened after they left.

"I'll leave a message for the Chief Constable to keep him in the loop," said Geoff after he'd finished. "When I get back, I hope you have ideas about where we start our search."

Geoff Mercer disappeared into a nearby office to make his call. Gus looked to his team for suggestions. "Some of you haven't exercised your brains this morning," said Gus. "Time's ticking."

"We didn't sit on our hands while you were gone, Gus," said Grace. "Lydia told us in detail what they discovered on Monday afternoon. Kurt found a journey made by a fishing boat that left Burnham at eleven-thirty on the night of the twenty-eighth of August in 2006. The trip wasn't near any known fishing grounds, and the boat returned before dawn. Kurt explained there was a shelf running for several miles close to the centre of the Bristol Channel. The spot where the fishing boat stopped and turned to start its inward journey is where the water depth changes from forty feet to between seventy and one hundred feet. That's where Kurt is confident the gang buried Gavin and Sylvia Tilson."

"James Devine would have taken the fishing boat out for Atkinson and Newbold in 2006," said Gus. "He had graduated to middle-management until today. We need to find him and bring him in for questioning."

"Are we sure other gang members weren't at that meeting in Brent Knoll, guv?" asked Alex.

"Luke didn't mention seeing several cars in that cul-de-sac," said Gus. "Newbold's car must have been in his garage if Atkinson could park his Range Rover on the driveway. So Carr, Devine, and Ellis are still out there, but I don't know how long."

"Geoff Mercer was concerned about the length of time since Atkinson and Newbold were taken, guv," said Alex. "Surely, the three men you mentioned would be aware something was up when their leaders hadn't been in contact?"

"You don't have a dog and bark yourself, Alex," said Gus. "Those three men manage the gang's day-to-day business affairs. If Atkinson and Newbold felt the need to get involved every five minutes, then those three would have cause to worry. So the longer they go without having their bosses bothering them, the better. It means Atkinson and Newbold are satisfied with how everything's going. If not, then watch out. Remember what happened to Adam Wilson."

"We have addresses for Carr, Devine, and Ellis, sir," said Kurt. "Can we justify bringing them in for questioning?"

"Luke told us raids on Atkinson and Newbold's properties were underway or imminent, guv," said Alex. "If the gang were still in the dark and heard a whisper this morning, they'll assume the police came to arrest them."

"That's possible," said Grace. "If we visit Devine's place, we can tell him lawyers are looking after Atkinson and Newbold's interests, not the hired help. We could persuade him he would receive a lighter sentence if he told us what he knows."

"Suggest he gets his retaliation in first, guv," said Neil.

"It's worth a try, guv," said Lydia.

Geoff Mercer returned from the office.

"Kenneth was already with the PCC, as I feared. With luck, Vera can persuade Kenneth to contact Portishead before he drives home to complain about not being given the full picture. So, we'll stay here this afternoon, but Vera said Kenneth wants everyone back in the office tomorrow. He wants to meet with us at some point too, Gus. So, what have we got?"

"We thought we'd pay James Devine a visit," said Gus. "We can dangle the carrot of a lighter sentence in return for co-operation. We can prove he took a fishing boat into the Bristol Channel hours after the last sightings of Gavin and Sylvia Tilson. We'll suggest the evidence points to him having killed them."

"Do you think Devine will swallow that?" asked Geoff.

"We can only prove *someone* took a boat out that night, sir," said Kurt. "Devine will know our chances of finding anything after all this time are slim to none. Let alone evidence to connect him, or anyone else, to the murders."

"If Devine is unaware the police didn't take his bosses into custody, you could hint that Atkinson and Newbold were already naming names, guv," said Blessing.

"I fail to see how this approach helps in our search for the gang leaders' bodies," said Geoff.

"We can't be certain they're dead," said Lydia.

"We're not going back to the office without a result of some sort," said Gus. "If we can get James Devine to crack, it will allow us to draw a line under the deaths of Gavin and Sylvia Tilson."

"I'll take the lead," said Geoff. "How many of us should go, Gus?"

"The Portishead cavalry arrived in Brent Knoll mob-handed, Geoff. My team has nothing to do, so let's try shock tactics on Mr Devine. Kurt, you have his address. Take us to him."

Two cars soon prepared to leave Burnham Police Station for Marine Drive. Kurt jumped into Geoff Mercer's car while Gus and Grace got in the back. The other three travelled with Neil.

James Devine opened his front door to find eight people on his doorstep. He looked upset rather than surprised.

"DS Mercer, Wiltshire Police," said Geoff. "My colleagues and I wish to have a friendly chat. Is it convenient?"

"They've taken Morgana," groaned Devine.

Nobody was any the wiser.

"Perhaps we'd better come inside, sir," said Geoff.

"It's a pity you couldn't find this many coppers with nothing to do last night when I called you," said Devine,

Geoff looked to Gus for help.

"Maybe you should start from the beginning, James," said Gus.

Everyone filed into James Devine's living room. A loose description of where the thirty-seven-year-old bachelor appeared to leave most of his rubbish. A glass-topped table next to a black leather settee was covered in empty lager cans, takeaway cartons, and cigarette butts.

Blessing wondered how long it had been since the curtains had been open.

Lydia's nose was assaulted by stale body odour, cannabis, and something she preferred not to think about.

Neil thought if these were the trappings of a senior gang member, you could keep them.

"They took Morgana," said James.

"So you say, James," said Gus. "Who took Morgana, and why?"

"I don't know. When I was walking home from the pub last night, I saw her leaving the Sailing Club. So I came straight here and called the police. Theft doesn't feature high on your priority list, according to the media, so I wasn't surprised when there was no response. I never expected them to send this many coppers from a neighbouring county."

"Who, or what, is Morgana?" asked Geoff Mercer.

"My fishing boat," said James.

"Have you had her long?" asked Gus.

"Twenty years," said James.

"Can someone take me back to my car? I need to drive to Bridgwater," said Kurt.

"What on earth for, DS Burgess?" asked Geoff.

"He wants to check the GPS signal, sir," said Blessing. "To see if it matches the one from twelve years ago."

James Devine slumped back on his settee.

"Doesn't anyone care that someone stole my fishing boat?" he cried.

"We'd like to help you find it, James," said Gus. "Why the rush, anyway? You don't need it to earn a living as a fisherman."

"When did you last speak to Paulie or Jonny?" asked Neil.

"I might have seen them in a pub on Saturday night. Who says I know them, anyway?"

"Let's not play games, James," said Gus.

"Where were you at around midnight on Friday night?" asked Alex.

"Hard to remember that far back," said Devine.

"Anywhere near Berrow Road?" asked Lydia.

"I've got no cause to go there," said Devine.

"I'm surprised Paulie and Jonny rely on Ben Mulligan to do their dirty work," said Alex.

"Ben? He's not working for anyone. Last I heard, he was on his way to Combwich."

"So, we might find his body in a field, like Adam Wilson?" asked Alex.

"No comment," said Devine.

"Who decided to torch the caravan, James?" asked Gus.

"That had nothing to do with me," he said.

"You've guessed we know what happened twelve years ago," said Geoff. "You were asked to drop two packages in the Bristol Channel. It's no good protesting your innocence. We established your journey through the GPS tracker on your precious fishing boat. We have you bang to rights. Who gave the order to kill Gavin and Sylvie?"

"I can't tell you that. It's more than my life's worth," said Devine.

"You wondered why we were called in," said Geoff. "Our colleagues from Portishead are extra-busy at present. They could already be taking statements from Paulie and Jonny. Their lawyers will earn their corn covering your bosses' backsides and playing the blame game. You're running out of time, Devine. Your best bet is to tell us everything you know."

"No comment," said Devine.

"Better start talking now, James," said Gus. "If you wait for DS Burgess to return with news about the Morgana, it will be too late. Why do you think she was taken, anyway?"

"It wasn't another delivery of illegal immigrants, was it?" said Neil. "Of course not. If that were the case, you would know who took her out, and there would be no cause to call the police."

"I can see why you would panic, though, James," said Alex. "Is there a delivery planned for later this week?"

"No comment," said Devine.

"We'll wait for DS Burgess to return from Bridgwater then," said Geoff.

"There's no point in all of us hanging around here, sir," said Neil. "Do you want us to drive to those other two addresses? So we can see how Jack Carr and Gary Ellis feel about what's on offer?"

"Good idea, DS Davis," said Geoff. "Mr Freeman can go with you."

James Devine looked agitated. Grace noticed his hand shaking as he lit a cigarette.

"I need guarantees," said Devine. "They can't learn it was me that spoke out."

"They won't hear a word from us, James," said Geoff. "You have my word."

"If you take me to the local nick, they'll hear about it," said Devine. "They have people in their pocket who live nearby."

"In that case, we'll call DI Crooks in Taunton," said Gus. "She can arrange for someone to collect you in an unmarked car. You'll feel better after getting it off your chest."

Gus made the call on his mobile and told Neil they should leave. Alex and Lydia followed them outside.

"Jill Crooks will have someone here inside thirty minutes," said Gus. "She's also sending local uniformed officers to collect Carr and Ellis."

"I've updated Kurt, guv," said Alex. "He's five minutes from Bridgwater. He hopes to join us at the station within the hour. I'll ask Kurt to forward whatever evidence he finds about the Morgana's latest voyage to DI Crooks."

"I'll keep DS Mercer in the loop," said Gus. "When he's waved goodbye to Devine, he can bring Grace and Blessing to join us at the station."

"Where can we look next, guv?" asked Lydia.

"DS Mercer wants to know what happened to Atkinson and Newbold, guv," said Alex.

"DS Burgess is one step ahead of you," said Gus. "That's disappointing. Perhaps your minds are half on your upcoming holiday. Kurt worked out the crew that whisked away Atkinson and Newbold used the Morgana to mirror that journey from 2006. We're not dealing with amateurs. Luke was impressed with how these people plucked high-ranking criminals from their homes without a trace. Not a single body has ever been found. I believe Scott and his colleagues wanted to show Portishead they are way ahead of them."

"Blimey," said Neil. "What sort of intelligence do these people have access to?"

"How long will Luke stay on that assignment, guv?" asked Lydia.

"Luke suspected his superiors wouldn't be happy with

his actions on Sunday evening," said Gus. "He'll return to Gablecross."

"At least DS Mercer was wrong about Luke going rogue, guv," said Lydia. "I didn't believe he could do that for a minute."

Gus hoped Neil was right.

Geoff Mercer brought Grace and Blessing back to the squad room just after two o'clock.

"James Devine is on his way to Taunton," said Geoff. "I am confident DI Crooks will get enough from him to scupper those final human trafficking routes."

"DS Burgess will be with us shortly, Geoff," said Gus.

"Good. By the way, I noticed the Somerset Drainage Board van in the car park," said Geoff. "They'll want it back."

"We'll get onto that, sir," said Alex. "It slipped our minds."

Alex and Lydia were leaving the squad room when Kurt walked in.

"Wait five minutes, you two," said Geoff. "You might want to hear this."

"I think you all want to hear it," said Kurt. "The Morgana left the Sailing Club and sailed to the same spot as it did on the twenty-eighth of August, twelve years ago. The profile of the journey was so similar it was spooky."

"We already worked that out, Kurt," said Neil. "You've got to get up early in the morning to get one over on this team."

Alex and Lydia disappeared to the car park. Grace and Blessing looked puzzled.

"Nice try, Neil," said Gus, patting him on the back.

"So, Atkinson and Newbold have joined two of the people they had murdered at the bottom of the sea," said

Geoff. "Poetic justice. Let's hope Devine names the person who killed Gavin and Sylvie Tilson. Meanwhile, Portishead must use every tool at its disposal to arrest these vigilantes. They may have provided Avon & Somerset Police with the wherewithal to take down a criminal gang, but they can't be allowed to continue operating outside the law."

"When Lydia brings Alex back from the Drainage Board yard, I suppose we can head home," said Grace. "Everything that needs to be done now is outside our brief. We need to let Taunton and Portishead get on with it."

"We've got loads of updates to the Freeman Files," said Blessing. "That will keep us occupied tomorrow."

Gus wasn't sorry to be returning to the Old Police Station office. They had tackled problems in the past two days that were only loosely connected to the murders of Mark Fennell and Helen Roker. If he couldn't put their killer behind bars, Gus had hoped perhaps he could discover who murdered two people to tie up loose ends.

Now, as they prepared to leave Burnham-on-Sea, he had to accept someone had snatched that dream from under his nose. Together with Kurt Burgess, they had identified Paulie Atkinson and Jonny Newbold as the men behind the murders, even if they ordered someone else to pull the trigger.

The Crime Review Team had only been thwarted twice so far in their quest. The first was Grant Burnside, the sixty-five-year-old patriarch from Swindon, and now two gangsters who moved from London to terrorise the North Somerset coast. On each occasion, a mysterious outfit was responsible. A group that even a level-headed detective such as Luke Sherman considered to be like a modern-day Robin Hood.

It was a bitter pill to swallow for Gus Freeman. He

couldn't accept David Scott was a heroic fighter against tyranny and organised crime.

Alex and Lydia soon made it back to the squad room. Grace and Blessing gathered together the items borrowed from supplies and returned them. Geoff Mercer signed them out at Reception at ten minutes past three.

"I suggest you follow us across country," Gus said to Neil and Alex. "Those roadworks on the M5 will be there for days."

"I should reach the office with Blessing by half-past four, guv," said Neil. "Can we leave the paperwork until the morning?"

"Gus suggested you follow me, DS Davis," said Geoff. "I expect to arrive at our destination at ten to five."

"Got it, sir," said Neil.

"You can drive direct to Chippenham, DS Hardy," said Gus.

"Thanks, guv," said Lydia.

Geoff dropped Gus and Grace by the CRT parking bays and checked his watch.

"Almost to the minute," he said as Neil drew up behind him.

"You need to get out more, Geoff," said Gus.

"I enjoyed today," said Geoff. "Don't forget to speak on my behalf tomorrow when we face the Truelove inquisition."

Geoff watched Grace and Blessing drive away from the car park.

"How do you do it, Gus?" he asked.

"Do what?" asked Gus.

"You've knocked more sharp edges off Grace Packenham in a couple of weeks than London Road managed in three months."

"You always insisted she was a good officer, Geoff. So far, she's been a pussycat, but I know she has claws because they were all I saw while working at London Road. So I'm forever watchful."

Geoff laughed.

"I'm off home," he said. "I'll wait a second until you get that Focus started. It looks on its last legs."

Gus hoped his faithful friend hadn't heard. She started first time, and he followed Geoff out of town and into Devizes.

Gus spotted Suzie's car ahead as he entered the lane leading to the bungalow. She must have got away from work at five o'clock on the dot. He flashed his headlights. Suzie turned through the gateway and parked under the rambling roses. Gus drew up alongside her second later.

"Perfectly in unison," she said. "Did you have a good day?"

"You win some, you lose some," said Gus. "I'll fill you in after we've eaten."

"Do normal services resume again in Burnham tomorrow?" asked Suzie.

"All wrapped up as far as we're concerned," said Gus. "I hope you're hungry. We didn't stop for a bite all day."

"I didn't see Geoff Mercer at London Road today. He was briefing you at nine, wasn't he? Where did he disappear to after that?"

"Geoff fancied a trip to the coast. I know this is the interrogation you promised before we left home. But there's nothing for us to do. So, forget about work for an hour. Let's get cooking."

After eating a hearty meal and loading the dishwasher, they relaxed on a settee in the lounge.

"Are you sitting comfortably?" asked Gus.

Suzie sipped her cup of coffee and nodded.

"Then I'll begin."

"Well," said Suzie when Gus had finished describing the day's events. "Will Portishead find enough evidence to bring this crowd to book?"

"Hard to tell," said Gus. "They've only operated on our patch once that we know about, back in 2014. We only tackle cold cases, so unless we discover another occasion where they intervened, it's none of our business."

"You must have been shocked to bump into Luke Sherman," said Suzie.

"I was mighty glad we didn't find his body in the boot of his car," said Gus. "I hope Gablecross give him a challenging case when he rejoins them from this assignment. After that, Luke doesn't need time to ponder whether the grass is greener elsewhere."

Wednesday, 10 October 2018

GUS WAS eager to spend much of the day updating his digital files in the office.

They had covered a lot of ground on Monday before getting ordered home. Then the snap decision from Geoff Mercer to continue the investigation yesterday morning meant admin had been brushed aside.

Suzie was making breakfast as he emerged from the shower.

"Cereal and yoghurt this morning," she said.

Gus wasn't looking for an argument. He poured his coffee and prepared to tuck in.

"So, you expect a summons from Kenneth later?" she asked

"Geoff reckoned he wanted to see both of us," said Gus. "I'm hoping we can get everything ready to take a completed case folder with me when I get the call. If it were down to me, I'd prefer not to hear from him until tomorrow."

"He's under pressure," said Suzie. "The local MP raised fresh concerns about the county's performance, according to the rumours flying around London Road yesterday afternoon. No doubt the PCC waded in with more demands, adding to the doom and gloom."

"More, better, every day, with less," said Gus.

"I couldn't have put it better," said Suzie. "When did you think of that?"

"We've lived with it for the past decade. So when Geoff was rallying the troops yesterday morning, I wondered how long it would be before our jobs disappeared. In their place, private security would be for those who can afford it, and something akin to the National Guard dealing with criminality among millions who can't."

"That would be unthinkable, Gus," said Suzie. "It doesn't sound like a country where I want our child to grow up."

"We can only continue following my six-word mantra for so long," said Gus. "Something has to give. There could soon be more groups, such as the one Luke seems taken with, which operate outside the law. Blessing questioned whether a jury would find them guilty if brought before a court. Organised crime has a stranglehold on parts of the country, and the public doesn't see us making headway in breaking their grip. If a bunch of vigilantes remove even part of the threat those criminals pose, they could be viewed as heroes, not villains."

"Time to get ready for work, I think," said Suzie. "I'm going to make it my mission to make the world a better place today, and I hope you are in a more cheerful mood tonight."

"You'll probably hear on the grapevine if I'm with Kenneth this afternoon and likely to be home late. As it's Wednesday, we'll be dining with the newly-engaged couple in the Lamb. I promise to be my usual cheery self by then."

They kissed on the doorstep five minutes later before walking to their cars.

"Make the most of your final journeys in your Focus, darling," said Suzie. "We're hunting for its replacement at the weekend."

"I shall be sad to see her go," said Gus.

He arrived in the Church Street car park without incident thirty minutes later. Although he was last to arrive, Gus couldn't hear the usual hubbub of conversation as he rode in the lift to the first floor.

When the doors opened, he saw the tops of five heads. Everyone was hard at work updating their elements of the Freeman Files. Gus sat at his desk, fired up his computer, and opened his notebook. If he stuck at it for four hours and his phone stayed silent, his reports would be done and dusted.

A shrill ring broke the silence just before ten o'clock.

"Freeman. How can I help you?"

"Morning, Gus. Jill Crooks here. We had a productive session with James Devine yesterday. It's not often things go our way, and with a different lifestyle, Devine would have continued with 'no comment' until we grew tired and had to let him go."

"What have I missed?" asked Gus.

"Devine didn't get out of bed until ten minutes before you arrived on his doorstep. As you know, he'd spent the evening drinking before he noticed his fishing boat leaving, and it appears Devine continued drinking when he reached home. He needed something to do while waiting for the police to respond to his cry for help. If he'd been a sober law-abiding citizen, he would have got up at a reasonable hour and discovered his precious Morgana was back at its mooring."

"Did anyone see the boat return?" asked Gus. "Did we get CCTV pictures of the people who took it to sea?"

"I warned you the coverage in Burnham was problematic, Gus," said Jill. "I'm told the system experienced a glitch for ten hours from eleven o'clock on Monday night. Nobody can explain it."

"I think I can," muttered Gus. "What's on the menu today?"

"Another extended interview with Devine," said Jill. "Meanwhile, Kurt Burgess is somewhere near Combwich with a team carrying out an extensive search for the remains of Ben Mulligan."

"Did Devine give you directions?" asked Gus.

"He swears he wasn't involved, but we did get him to narrow down the date when Mulligan disappeared. The last time Devine saw Ben alive was just over a month ago."

"Another wasted life," said Gus. "Thanks for the information, Jill. Goodbye."

Gus sighed and noticed the others had paused in their labours.

"The Morgana was returned to her rightful place," he said. "We were lucky James Devine wasn't the sort to go for an early run."

"Another body too, guv?" asked Neil.

"Ben Mulligan," said Gus. "Atkinson and Newbold didn't keep anyone on their books who couldn't dance to their tune."

"They're no longer a threat, guv," said Blessing.

"Coffee, guv," asked Lydia.

Gus nodded.

He watched Grace get up to join Lydia in the restroom. Some things were moving in the right direction.

Once they had returned with the drinks, the comfort break was over. Everyone resumed working on their digital files. Gus studied his notebook. At this rate of progress, he could finish by early afternoon.

"How are the rest of you getting on?" he asked as eleven o'clock beckoned.

"We had the least input, guv," said Neil. "Blessing, and I will be done by twelve."

"Good. In that case, I have two jobs for you. First, pay a visit to the bakery on the high pavement and buy a selection of cakes. My treat, as we won't be seeing one another for a fortnight. Then, start clearing the decks of the Fennell and Roker cases when you've done that. We might not have anything to put on the wallboards in their place, but the office won't look like a tip when we return to work."

"Got it, guv," said Blessing.

Grace, Alex, and Lydia told Gus they would be up-to-date by half-past one.

"No problems, Grace?" asked Gus.

"No, Gus," she replied. "Blessing knows I like chocolate. If the bakery doesn't offer a vegan option, she can pick up a bar from the newsagents next door."

"I meant with the work, Grace, but it's good to know you're flexible," said Gus.

While Neil and Blessing were shopping, the phone rang again. This time Gus groaned when he realised it was Vera Butler.

"Tell me the worst," he said.

"Can you be in Kenneth's office at two sharp?" asked Vera.

"I have every chance," said Gus. "Pray the roadworks in Seend haven't returned."

Vera laughed and ended the call.

Gus heard the lift returning from the ground floor. Time for coffee and a cake.

"Alex. Join me by the Gaggia. It's our turn to do the honours."

"No problem, guv," said Alex.

Neil and Blessing exited the lift, bearing gifts as Gus and Alex entered the restroom. Soon, everyone was taking another well-earned break.

"I knew you would enjoy the Chelsea bun, guv," said Neil.

"It reminds me of my schooldays, Neil."

"Didn't the chalk affect the taste, guv?" asked Neil.

"Chalk and slates were what my father used, Neil. We had progressed to pen and paper."

One by one, the team finished their contribution to the files, and Gus had a completed folder ready to deliver to the Chief Constable.

"I hope everything goes okay, Gus," said Grace.

"We all do," said Alex. "It was a team effort sanctioned by DS Mercer."

"Well said, Alex," said Gus. "Perhaps you three can help Neil and Blessing with the tidying up. I don't expect to be back this afternoon, but please remain in the office until I call. I'm sure the Chief Constable will want me to pass a message to you. What type of message, I'm not sure."

Chapter Six

GUS HEADED for the lift with his folder and drove out of the car park. The team had done well to give him forty minutes to get to London Road. Even with every traffic light at red, once he reached Devizes, Gus was bounding up the stairs to the admin area by five to two.

"I had every faith in you, Gus," said Vera.

"So did I, Mr Freeman," said Kassie.

"Have you done the refreshment run, Kassie?" asked Gus.

"I can get you a coffee, Mr Freeman, but all my fancies are gone."

"Not to worry. I had a Chelsea bun earlier," said Gus. "A shop-bought item; it wasn't a patch on yours."

Kassie blushed.

"Geoff went in to Kenneth's office a couple of minutes ago, Gus," said Vera.

"I'll tell Kenneth his clock's fast," said Gus.

"That only works once, Mr Freeman," said Kassie as she handed him a coffee.

Gus tapped on the Chief Constable's door and waited for the invitation to enter.

Kenneth Truelove was standing by the window. He glanced at the clock—one minute after two.

"Cutting it fine, Freeman. Something else you make a habit of, eh?"

Gus placed the large folder on Kenneth's desk.

"Returned with interest, sir," he said.

Kenneth returned to his desk and sat down.

"Give me the highlights, Freeman," he said.

"We established Gavin Tilson murdered Mark Fennell and Helen Roker, sir," said Gus. "Fennell, Webber, and Hood distributed drugs in the Chippenham area for decades. Their supplies came from South Wales in the latter part of their career, with Tilson as the middle man in Burnham-on-Sea. Tilson worked for Shane Prosser from Cardiff."

"I've heard of the late Mr Prosser," said Kenneth. "I didn't realise he had links on this side of the Bristol Channel."

"Tilson stashed drugs bound for Chippenham in a caravan owned by Fennell," said Gus. "Two London gangsters, Paulie Atkinson and Jonny Newbold, sought to change the focus of the gang's operations after Prosser died. Drugs weren't as profitable as human trafficking. They put the squeeze on Tilson; and ordered him to eliminate Fennell. Roker's name was added to the hit-list later to keep Webber and Hood in line."

"DS Mercer informed me you made an arrest on Saturday morning," said Kenneth. "How was that connected to the murders?"

"Grace and I arrested Becky Hood, Helen Roker's sister. Becky was fed up with her husband's drug dealing, so she attempted to damage the caravan beyond repair by setting fire to it. The Burnham gang made sure the caravan was destroyed to cover their tracks. They were using the caravan to hide illegal immigrants. We arrested Becky Hood for murder. Subsequent investigations in Burnham on Monday proved it was a second fire that killed the three people inside. Atkinson and Newbold were responsible for that fire. We haven't identified the arsonist as yet. DI Crooks is working that case now."

"Did you forget the reason for your trip to the seaside in the first place?" asked Kenneth.

"No, sir," said Gus. "DI Crooks told me on Saturday morning the person we believed killed Fennell and Roker had disappeared, with his wife, on Monday the twenty-eighth of August 2006. Thanks to DS Burgess from Bridgwater, we located their burial site. A fishing boat owned by another gang member, James Devine, ferried the bodies to the middle of the Bristol Channel and dumped them. Devine is now in custody, helping DI Crooks with her enquiries."

"Did Devine play any part in either of these deaths?" asked Kenneth,

"He was detained overnight in Bridgwater for drunk driving back in 2006, so he couldn't have murdered anyone, but he was back in Burnham the following day to take the boat out at midnight. Devine denied having anything to do with the caravan fire, and DI Crooks continues to interview him as we speak. I don't believe it was Devine or any of the gang's minions who murdered Tilson and his wife. Atkinson and Newbold were violent thugs. I suspect one of them was responsible."

"The conversation I had with DS Mercer before you

arrived suggests we won't see those gentlemen in court anytime soon."

"Which brings us to the question of DS Sherman and his presence in Burnham-on-Sea."

"What did you make of that, Freeman?" asked Kenneth. "A little out of character based on everything I've heard. The man was as solid as a rock while under your wing."

"I can't take any credit for that, sir," said Gus. "Luke was a dependable type before he joined our team. The man beside me wouldn't have put his name forward if he'd been flaky."

"Nobody from Portishead has been in touch to deliver a fulsome apology for their behaviour," said Kenneth. "I contacted them last week, at DS Mercer's request, to pave the way for your team to pursue the broader Fennell enquiry on their patch. At that time, my counterpart could have mentioned they had a covert surveillance team nearby."

"I would have expected them to let us know DS Sherman was on that team," said Geoff. "We didn't need to know the details of his assignment, but as subsequent events proved, if you bump into a friend, or colleague, in an unexpected place, you can't help wondering what they're doing there. It's human nature."

"Maybe it would have been better if Portishead had informed you *who* they were watching, sir," said Gus. "Atkinson and Newbold weren't on their radar on this occasion. DS Davis had the sense to abandon his unplanned sortie into bandit country on Monday afternoon. He assumed he and DC Umeh had stumbled on a stakeout of our gang by Avon & Somerset. A natural response when spotting a police officer in an unmarked car less than two hundred yards from the home of a dangerous criminal."

"I ordered you to return to base as soon as I got the call," said Kenneth. "I didn't know what was happening, and it seemed the safest option. When I called Portishead, they claimed to be unaware of any surveillance sanctioned within the Burnham and Highbridge area. Mercer called me on Tuesday to tell me DI Crooks had the same blank looks when she asked her superiors for an explanation. Can you enlighten me further today?"

"The surveillance team's role was to track operatives from Larcombe Manor, sir," said Gus. "It was put in place after the abortive raid several weeks ago when they found the place empty. Luke spotted a van from the Manor driving through Marksbury on Sunday evening and followed it to Brent Knoll, just outside Highbridge. He should have reported in, but he didn't. Geoff and I don't fully understand his motives."

"I admit I was concerned," said Geoff. "Luke reckoned he opted to switch off the tracking system on his phone in case he got caught. The best chance of his handler finding him if something had gone wrong was if that tracker was still traceable. Luke found a hiding place in the village, yet his target found him inside an hour."

"Luke told us they removed the alternator, tied him to his steering wheel, and warned him not to leave the car once he'd freed himself," said Gus. "They took his burner phone with them, which meant he had a half-mile walk to the nearest pub to call Portishead. Why not walk down the lane to the farmhouse? He could have ignored their request to stay put, and uniformed officers would have been sent. Then, even if they were too late to prevent the raid on

Newbold's house, they would have been hot on the trail of the blue transit."

"Perhaps DS Sherman was unaware of the farm," said Kenneth.

"I'm not sure how much Luke knew about Brent Knoll, sir," said Gus. "I can see why he headed left when he searched for somewhere to make the call. He had driven from the A38 turn-off and would have noted the buildings on the main road into the village. However, even on a Sunday evening, country villages have general stores open all hours, and you can't walk anywhere without bumping into a dog walker. Why not just knock on the door of the first house he came to anyway? No, I agree with Geoff. It's a concern. Luke took the time to walk through the village, noting where a Range Rover was parked. Yet, he claimed never to have heard of Atkinson and Newbold."

"Did his behaviour seem odd to you over the next thirty-six hours?" asked Kenneth.

"Without question, sir," said Geoff. "Luke maintained he had a good night's sleep before facing questions. He had to have held something back. Why didn't someone collect his car until Tuesday? No, the whole thing feels wrong to me. Are senior officers at Portishead incompetent, or did DS Sherman deliberately delay the investigation into the kidnapping of Atkinson and Newbold?"

"If DS Sherman believed the van he was following was up to no good, he should have given that information to his handler when he called on Sunday night," said Kenneth. "Although he had no proof an attack had occurred, he saw the van leaving Brent Knoll at high speed. That should have been enough to alert suspicion at HQ. Yet they waited until Tuesday morning and an anonymous tip-off."

"That phone call came from Larcombe Manor," said Gus. "They'd had a clear day with Atkinson and Newbold to decide how to get rid of the bodies. But, as DS Davis pointed out, they have superior intelligence. So it was no surprise when DS Burgess told us he could have laid the profile of Morgana's journey on Monday night on top of the trip in August 2006, and you wouldn't spot the difference."

"We have to take action, sir," said Geoff. "This case had already uncovered a police officer who believed they made more of a difference working in the private sector."

"Heavens, Mercer," said Kenneth. "Is that hidden in this folder? Why didn't you consider it a highlight, Freeman?"

"DC Annie Drew works for a business linked to the charity, sir," said Gus. "She helps domestic and sexual abuse victims and locates missing persons. Other employees are security personnel. Annie Drew left the force soon after the Fennell murder. There were issues with DI Jim Francis. You'll find a separate report on that situation too, sir. After a decade in a safeguarding role on Brentwood, Annie returned to the area, and another ex-copper, Callum Wood, offered her a job."

"It gets worse, Freeman," said Kenneth. "Leave the folder with me. I'm glad I've got two weeks while you are out of my hair. You can't lift any more stones so that something rotten crawls out. So close the office from tonight, and pray I can sort this unholy mess before you return."

"I can only apologise, sir," said Gus. "We don't do it deliberately."

"We know, Gus," said Geoff.

"I don't know why you're excusing him, Mercer," said Kenneth. "What did you think you were playing at, taking them to Burnham-on-Sea on Tuesday? My instructions were for you to explain why I took the decision I did on Monday, and get them to complete the paperwork, whether the investigation was concluded or not."

"I used my initiative, sir," said Geoff. "We achieved a positive outcome. Well, apart from our concerns about DS Sherman."

"Two vicious criminals died at the hands of a group of vigilantes, and the Avon & Somerset Police were made to look stupid."

"There is that too, sir," said Geoff.

"I think we're finished," said the Chief Constable. "We'll speak again on Monday at noon."

Gus called Grace as he left the office and told her everyone could go home.

Geoff Mercer walked with him to the top of the stairs.

"I presume our next meeting will see you get your next cold case, Gus," he said.

"Or my marching orders," said Gus.

"Should we practice keeping in step," asked Geoff. "I could be joining you."

Wednesday, 10 October – Sunday, 21 October 2018

LYDIA LOGAN BARRE and Alex Hardy took full advantage of the extra time they had to prepare for their trip to Dubai. Their flight from Bristol International had been booked for six weeks, but with no real clue how long they would be tied up in Burnham-on-Sea, Lydia had feared they'd be packing at the last minute.

Grace's phone call left Alex and the others wondering what had happened when Gus presented their final report on the Fennell and Roker case. Instead of hearing the high-lights of Gus's discussions with Geoff Mercer and the Chief Constable, they heard nothing.

Grace told them Gus said they could go home as soon as they'd tidied the office. But, with an uncertain future for the Crime Review Team, how could anyone enjoy their holiday now?

Alex and Lydia drove to the long-stay parking zone beyond the airport on Saturday morning. After transferring to the terminal by bus, they checked in, and although their flight was delayed by fifty minutes, any frustration disappeared when they landed in Dubai seven hours later. The forecast for the next two weeks was for wall-to-wall sunshine, with temperatures in the high thirties centigrade. There was no hint of rain.

Lydia's father, Chidozie, met them at the airport in a brand-new Lexus and drove them to the marina. His partner, Rosa de Vries, greeted them in the foyer when they entered the apartment building.

"Welcome to Dubai," she said. "I know it's much warmer here than you're used to in the UK, but thankfully the humidity drops at this time of year, making the heat more bearable during the day. There's someone upstairs who can't wait to see you."

They made their way to the apartment, and Lydia was reunited with her mother.

Eleanor's flight from Edinburgh had landed twelve hours earlier.

"Your father told me he has news, Lydia," whispered Eleanor. "But he wanted to wait until you arrived before sharing it."

Lydia wondered what her father was planning now.

"Hello, Alex. It's good to see you again," said Eleanor.

Alex and Eleanor hugged one another.

It had taken Lydia so long to find her birth parents; they'd only spent a short time together. One thing Alex had learned was that Lydia's father was full of surprises.

Chidozie and Rosa took them to a prestigious restaurant in the marina that first evening, and as they left, he stopped to look back at the building.

"What do you think?" he asked.

"The food and service were excellent," said Alex.

"It's in a prime position," said Lydia. "I can see why it warrants five stars."

"I've discussed it with Rosa, and we agree it's time for a change of pace. So I'm selling the Lady Eleanor, and we're moving here full-time. Do you remember Lucas Romeijn, our chef? I was right; we couldn't hold on to him for long. Rosa and I loved his food so much that when I heard he had landed the head chef's job here, the obvious solution was to buy the restaurant. It's only a five-minute walk from our apartment, so from the first of November, we'll be able to enjoy his food every day."

"I'll be sad to say goodbye to the Lady Eleanor," said Rosa. "It's where I met your father and fell in love. But, the good news is that I've met the real Eleanor, and I hope we will remain good friends."

Rosa and Eleanor walked back to the apartment arm-in-arm. Lydia was pleased they got on so well.

When they awoke the following day, Alex and Lydia thought the first night of their holiday had been so special that it would be tough to beat. Chidozie and Rosa did their best to prove them wrong. The following two weeks passed too quickly. They visited the beaches and the water parks and enjoyed the stunning scenery and food on offer wherever they went.

As the holiday drew to a close and they were relaxing with a drink at the apartment, Eleanor asked Lydia if they had given any thought to Christmas.

"Would you and Alex like to spend it with me?" she asked.

"We'd love to," said Lydia.

"We don't have that Hog word in Dubai," said Chidozie, "but New Year can be exciting here too."

"Hogmanay, Chidozie," said Eleanor. "The word means a gala day. We Scots have celebrated the occasion since Mary, Queen of Scots, in the sixteenth century."

"Well, if you two want to fly here for New Year, you can watch the Burj Khalifa fireworks. They're spectacular, even if we've only been able to celebrate the occasion for a handful of years rather than five centuries."

Lydia laughed. Was this how things would be every year? A battle between her mother and father for her attention?

"Okay," she said. "I give in. Christmas in Edinburgh and New Year in Dubai. Any objections, Alex?"

"Not one," he said.

All too soon, it was time to fly home. The gap between seeing one another again was only a matter of weeks. Lydia went to the airport with her father to watch Eleanor board her flight while Alex packed their cases back at the apartment.

"What is it you say, Alex," asked Rosa. "A penny for them?"

"Oh, it was nothing to do with the past two weeks, Rosa. We thoroughly enjoyed ourselves. The company has helped, of course. You and Chidozie have been excellent hosts, and I enjoy seeing Lydia spending time with her mother. But, no, it's going back to work on Monday that's bothering me. We may have stirred a hornet's nest on our last case."

"I'm sure everything will turn out for the best, Alex," said Rosa.

"I hope you're right," he said.

Chidozie and Lydia returned from the airport, and Rosa prepared a light meal for the four of them.

"Remember, Lydia," said Chidozie. "No long goodbyes; we'll be reunited soon enough. Why don't you come with us, Rosa? We'll see these young people check in, and then we can start thinking about what we can do with the décor in the restaurant when we take over the reins in just over a week."

"This venture was supposed to signal a change of pace," said Lydia. "Don't you ever want to put your feet up and relax?"

"Change is good, Lydia," said Chidozie. "You have to embrace it."

Two hours later, Chidozie drove them to the airport. Alex and Lydia removed their cases from the boot of the Lexus and said their brief goodbyes. Chidozie and Rosa stood by the Departures entrance and watched until they disappeared from view.

WHEN NEIL ARRIVED home early on Wednesday afternoon, Melody and her mother were busy with a tape measure in the living room.

"Hello," said Melody. "It's not half-past five already, is it?"

"No, Gus called from London Road to say we could start our holiday today."

"That's good. We were deciding what changes we wanted to make in here."

"What's wrong with it the way it is?" asked Neil. "It's only three years since we decorated the ground floor throughout."

Melody's mother tutted.

"Typical bloke," she said.

Neil was about to ask what it had to do with her. He and Melody had to live with it day in and day out. He bit his tongue.

"We've got everything ready in the nursery," said Melody. "For now, I'm happy with the kitchen and the bathroom…."

Neil wasn't happy with the phrase 'for now', as it promised to be expensive.

"… but this lounge and dining room could benefit from a lick of paint."

"Well, that won't take too long," said Neil.

Mother-in-law tutted again.

"Come on, Neil," said Melody. "You can't just freshen the paintwork. We'll need new lighting and carpets, and I can't decide whether this furniture will go with the colour scheme Mum suggested."

Neil groaned. Two weeks of this would be bad enough.

He blamed his friend, Luke Sherman. If he hadn't gone walkabout in Somerset, this wouldn't be happening.

Melody's mother had something to add.

"I hope you're feeling fit, Neil," she said. "It's important for Melody to rest over the final few weeks. She can't take risks with the baby after getting so close."

"You expect me to do the work on my own, is that it?" asked Neil.

"Don't worry, darling," said Melody. "I'll be here to supervise."

"I can't wait to see the progress after you've been at it for ten days," said mother-in-law. "Next week, I'm off to Poole with my girlfriends from the Liberal Club."

Neil hoped the others were having fun. He'd be lucky to have enough energy left for a night out with his mates in Devizes. The return to work couldn't come quickly enough, even if dark clouds were on the horizon.

WHILE NEIL WAS SUFFERING in Devizes, Blessing Umeh arrived at Worton Farm and told Jackie Ferris the news.

"So, you have a couple of days off work," Jackie said. "What's Jamie doing?"

"He's working Monday to Friday," sighed Blessing. "He can't take time off."

"You'll have to make up for it at the weekends," said Jackie with a cheeky grin.

"My mother is ringing tonight," said Blessing. "As if it hadn't already been a bad day."

"Now, now, Blessing," said Jackie. "Maryam's a good sort, and she has your best interests at heart. By the way, will your friend still want to come to dinner tomorrow evening?"

"I forgot to ask," said Blessing.

"Give her a ring now," said Jackie. "Ask her if there's anything she fancies."

Blessing looked at the large clock on the wall. She wondered whether Grace had gone shopping on her way home.

"I'll message her," said Blessing. "She might still be on her way to Easterton."

Grace called twenty minutes later.

"Yes, I'd love to drive over tomorrow, Blessing," she said. "Can you hand me over to Mrs Ferris, please?"

"Grace wants to speak to you," said Blessing.

Jackie took the phone and listened.

"I'm so pleased, Grace. We look forward to seeing you tomorrow."

"She's coming for dinner then?" asked Blessing.

"Yes, Blessing, and she's contacting Monty Jennings this evening to give notice. In four weeks from now, Grace will move in."

"She told me what she would like tomorrow night," said Blessing, pulling a face. "Baked falafel in tahini sauce."

"I think I need to get to the supermarket first thing in the morning," said Jackie.

Blessing giggled and went upstairs to change.

Later that evening, Maryam Umeh rang her daughter. After a quick catch-up on what they'd been doing over the past seven days, she asked about Jamie.

"You've been seeing this young man for several weeks, Blessing," she said. "I might be wrong, but this one feels more important to you. Your father wants to meet him. So I'm to invite you both to have dinner with us on Sunday."

"He's not Nigerian," said Blessing.

"Ah, but he's a military policeman," said Maryam. "That's a respectable occupation. James would wear his dress uniform at your wedding. Your father is most eager to make his acquaintance."

Blessing shook her head.

"It's Jamie, mother," she said. "I'll call him tomorrow, and we'll drive over to Englishcombe for two o'clock."

"Bless you, my daughter," said Maryam.

After she'd ended the call, Blessing realised she hadn't

told her mother she was on holiday. If Sunday wasn't a disaster, perhaps she could arrange to spend time in English-combe. They hadn't gone shopping as they used to since her parents moved south. So the weekdays might not drag so much after all. The weekends would take care of themselves.

IN EASTERTON, Grace Packenham was pacing the kitchen floor. When was Monty Jennings going to answer his phone?

Blessing's text message had arrived just as she reached the checkout in the Co-op in nearby Market Lavington. The die was cast now. She'd listened to Gus Freeman's opinions on Jackie Ferris's cooking and decided he was right. She'd be a fool not to accept her offer. Food was far from being the only reason for her decision, but that was for Grace to know and nobody else.

Life had its ups and downs.

Geoff Mercer hadn't wasted time getting in touch. Her mobile buzzed as soon as she walked through the door of her rented cottage with her heavy shopping. He had an assignment to keep her busy next week. She was to investigate DS Sherman's behaviour; the whole business was hush-hush.

Her phone rang again. This time it was her landlord.

"Sorry I didn't get back to you earlier," said Monty. "Ms Packenham, was it?"

"Yes," said Grace. "I can't settle here, I'm afraid. So I'm moving in with a colleague near Worton. I'm giving you the statutory twenty-eight days' notice."

"Terrific," said Monty. "I've been getting calls from people all week. They can't wait to get home to Europe, thanks to Brexit. I'll have half of my properties standing vacant before Christmas at this rate."

"There are many homeless people out there, Mr Jennings," said Grace.

"More trouble than they're worth," said Monty. "I need hard-working professionals like yourself, not someone on the social. When you move out, the place will be spotless. Six months with one of that lot living there, I'd be facing a huge bill to bring the decoration back up to spec. Still, it's not your fault. You don't want to hear how hard it is to be an entrepreneur."

Grace agreed with him but didn't reply. Monty told her he'd sort the paperwork, and she should hand the keys into his office on November the eighth.

Grace drove to Worton for the Thursday evening dining club on Thursday evening. She met John Ferris for the first time but never had a chance to speak to him. John suddenly remembered a fence that needed repairing on the farm's boundary.

Blessing told Grace about her and Jamie getting an invite to Sunday lunch.

"I'm not sure whether it's an occasion to look forward to or not," Grace had replied. "I've never been with anyone long enough to introduce him to my parents. But, then again, I haven't spoken to them for years."

"When you finally start your holiday, why not drive home and start building bridges?" asked Jackie.

"I don't know," said Grace. "I'm not sure it's what I want."

"What do you think you'll have to do next week?" asked Blessing.

"Geoff Mercer called me yesterday evening," said

Grace. "I'm off to Gablecross for five days. Just somewhere other than London Road to keep me occupied."

"Will you be free next Thursday, Grace?" asked Jackie.

"It might be best to leave things until I move in," said Grace. "I don't know what I'll need to do in Swindon, and I can use my free time the following week preparing for the move. But, then, who knows where we'll be off to when we return to work?"

After Grace drove home to Easterton later that evening, Jackie Ferris cleared the dinner things and waited for John to reappear. Whatever Grace and Blessing got up to over the next two weeks, she would hear about when they were ready to tell her. In the meantime, a ham and cheese toastie would put her back in her husband's good books.

WHEN GUS ARRIVED at the bungalow, he parked and went inside. He had an hour to kill before Suzie would be home. What should he do? They were eating at the pub at eight o'clock, so there was no rush to shower and change.

He threw his jacket over the back of the settee and opened the back door. When he and Suzie sat on the patio the other day, he'd noticed the lawn and the trees and bushes surrounding the rear of the property needed care and attention. The growing season might be over, but English summers and winters had changed. His neighbour had mowed his lawn just before Christmas last year.

Gus mowed the lawn and trimmed the edges. It was a start. He had two weeks to find his lopper and secateurs to get everything under control before taking a trip with the branches and foliage to the recycling centre. While storing the mower in the garden shed, he heard Suzie's car roar into the driveway.

Gus made a mental note to check the rarely used garden bench as he passed by. An hour next week would save it from falling apart by February or March. He wouldn't have time to deal with it then.

"How long have you been here?" asked Suzie, standing by the back door.

"I'm surprised you didn't hear on the grapevine. Kenneth sent us home early. We've blotted our copybook, it appears. So your assertion he knew I didn't do things deliberately was misplaced."

"Oh, I am sorry, darling," said Suzie. "I was spreading the word at local schools today and only spent five minutes at London Road before driving home. So, you took your frustration out on the lawn, did you? That's awfully short for this time of year."

Gus told her the whole story of his day, and Suzie advised him to forget work for tonight. It would be pointless telling him to ignore it for the entire two weeks. She knew him too well for that.

They met Brett and Clemency, had an enjoyable meal, and talked about anything but work. It was the start of a busy fortnight. They drove into Devizes on Thursday, searching for the right family car. Gus braced himself for the horrors that might lay ahead. Sometimes the gods smile down on you when you least expect it.

"We've looked at over twenty cars, darling," said Suzie. "I can't believe I'm saying it, but I must admit the car in front of us best fits our needs."

"If you're happy, I'm happy," said Gus.

After spending an interminable time with the young sales rep, a deal was struck. Finally, Gus could collect his Ford Focus, 2015 reg, five-door hatchback on Saturday morning. The windows had worked perfectly throughout the twenty-minute test drive. Although some reviews thought the model lacked acceleration, Gus knew with a child on board from early next year; acceleration was overrated.

Saturday soon arrived, and Gus parked the Focus under the rambling roses. One item ticked off on the list of things to do during the holiday. Suzie returned from Worton in time for lunch and told him Jackie's news.

"I told Grace it made sense," said Gus. "Blessing and Jamie are fine as they are. I hope Kelechi doesn't make waves."

"Let's get lunch," said Suzie. "Then you can disappear to the allotment."

"Why are you in such a rush? I've got two weeks to fill. You're up to something."

"I've got more sense than to overdo things, Gus," said Suzie. "My time is best spent making a list of jobs I'd like you to do for us before you return to work."

Gus groaned. He wondered which pub Neil was in this lunchtime, watching the football on the big screen. Gus didn't miss the subtle 'us' Suzie used. These tasks were for the three of them, so he had no choice but to comply.

Gus spent the afternoon with Bert Penman in the warm sunshine at the allotment.

Then, as the weather turned wet and windy on Sunday, he and Suzie argued over the order in which he should tackle the lengthy list. Finally, he stood and waved on Monday morning as Suzie drove to work alone. There was a first time for everything.

Friday always creeps up on you sooner than expected. Gus scrapped his trip to the recycling centre to purchase the final few items they needed for the weekend. When Suzie returned to work on Monday morning, the second bedroom was converted into a nursery.

Gus made a sentimental journey to the recycling centre with memories of his life with Tess. The furniture they had bought together and several ornaments relegated to the spare room many years before. They had to go to make way for the sea change that lay ahead.

As the second week of his enforced break brought a freak spell of warm weather, Gus remembered to repair and paint the garden bench. The weather encouraged him to visit the allotment more often, to spend what he sensed would be valuable time with Bert. The list Suzie had prepared was shrinking. Whether he would complete it before returning to work was uncertain. He leaned on his fork, thinking about what might happen on Monday.

"It's not those potatoes you're worrying over, is it, Gus?" said Bert.

"You're very perceptive, Bert," said Gus.

"You've always been a deep thinker since you moved to the village," Bert said. "Nothing beats you, not when you set your mind to it. I never imagined you'd make a half-decent gardener, but you proved me wrong. When they persuaded you to return to work, I thought you wouldn't last five minutes with their new-fangled ways, but you found a way around that problem too. Whatever's ailing you today, you'll master it."

"I'd like to think so, Bert," said Gus.

"That's me done for the day," said Bert. "A pint of cider in the Lamb, and then I'm putting my feet up this evening. Irene has unearthed another TV series she wants us to watch."

"A series?" asked Gus. "I can't remember having enough time to watch a series."

"Me neither," said Bert. "It was first shown five years ago. Irene retrieved it somehow, and I don't profess to understand how. We can watch it when we like, and tonight we're watching three episodes."

"That's a serious commitment, Bert," said Gus. "Three in a row?"

"I'll be asleep before the last episode," said Bert. "Irene will tell me what I missed tomorrow morning at breakfast."

"You've experienced quite a change in the past year, Bert," said Gus. "What with Irene moving in and Brett arriving from Canada. Now, you'll soon have a granddaughter-in-law."

"That's the thing with change, Gus," said Bert. "It happens when you least expect it. So, whatever has you worrying at the minute isn't important. Instead, spend time after I leave for the pub chewing it over, and you'll know what to do before you reach the bungalow."

"Thank you, Bert. You're a good friend," said Gus.

As Bert crossed the allotment towards the gateway, Gus fetched his chair from the shed.

After ten minutes of visiting the different outcomes he thought possible from Monday lunchtime's meeting, Gus put the chair away.

He and Suzie had a whole weekend before he needed to deal with work. So the best way to spend it was together, tackling the few remaining tasks on her list and keeping so busy that he didn't have time to think about Kenneth Truelove and Luke Sherman.

Chapter Seven

BRADFORD-ON-AVON

Thursday, 15 January 2015

TAMMIE KENYON WAS BORN in 1999 and raised in Bradford-on-Avon by her parents, Phillip and Debbie. She attended Fitzmaurice Primary before moving to St Laurence Academy. Her friends described Tammie as full of fun and always up to mischief.

The morning of Thursday, the fifteenth of January, was bitterly cold. Tammie left her home in Northleigh at twenty-five minutes to eight to make the twenty-minute walk to school. Phillip and Debbie Kenyon could only afford one breakfast club session per week, but the benefits were there to see in Tammie's school report they received just before Christmas.

Tammie was last seen alive by a cleaner driving to the Leigh Park Country House Hotel. Karla Bates, fifty-three, who lived near Woolley Grange, told police she left home, drove to work along the B3105 and saw Tammie near the crossroads with the B3109.

"I saw a young girl wearing a short, dark-coloured jacket over her school uniform. She looked about fifteen and was alone, hurrying along the pavement. She had to wait for traffic on both sides of the road to pass before darting across the road ahead of me."

Phillip and Debbie assumed Tammie would walk to school with Alfie Jones, the sixth-form student she'd been seeing for eight months. What her parents didn't know was Alfie had told Tammie the previous weekend he wanted to end the relationship. Alfie needed to ensure he got his predicted grades in the A-Levels he took that summer. Alfie's school report in late December hadn't been as positive as Tammie's. The university place Alfie's parents were pinning their hopes on was in the balance. They put pressure on the young lad to decide where his priorities lay.

Phillip and Debbie had left for work when someone from the school rang to ask why Tammie hadn't arrived for her scheduled session. Debbie listened to the recorded message when she popped home to Northleigh at lunchtime. Her first thought was Tammie must have gone off with Alfie. So she rang his home number, but nobody was home.

Debbie Kenyon left a message for her husband on his mobile. He wouldn't see it until his shift ended, but Debbie was livid. She hadn't objected to her daughter seeing Alfie, despite him being a couple of years older. But skipping school was unforgivable, especially as she and Phillip had scrimped and saved to pay the extra money for the blessed breakfast club.

Debbie returned to work, wondering where Tammie had gone, but she felt she had little choice. Times were hard enough without losing her job to drive around town hunting for her daughter. At five o'clock, she went home to find the house in darkness.

Debbie racked her brain. She rang Naomi Fletcher, Tammie's best friend who lived in Berryfield Road. Why hadn't she thought of that before? Tammie passed Naomi's house on her way to school every day. Perhaps they spent the day together, the little devils.

Naomi's mother answered and called her daughter to the phone. Debbie tutted when Naomi told her she hadn't seen Tammie. The last time they spoke was on Tuesday evening when they walked home after school.

Debbie had her car keys in her hand and was ready to drive to Alfie's home, but suddenly remembered they had never asked Tammie where in Bradford-on-Avon he lived. She was about to call his home number again when she heard Phillip's car pull onto the drive.

"Tammie's not home," she said as Phillip stepped inside the front door. "I've checked with Naomi, but she didn't see her at school. I was just about to ring Alfie."

"You had better do it, Debs," said Phillip. "I'd say something I regret. I'll get changed, and we'll drive to collect her if that's where she is."

When Phillip left their bedroom, he found Debbie sitting on the stairs.

"She's not there either?" he asked.

"Alfie said he ended it at the weekend," said Debbie. "Why didn't she say anything?"

"Are you sure he doesn't know where she is?" asked Phillip. "We need to report this. Tammie's been missing for almost twelve hours."

"Tammie was keen on Alfie," said Debbie. "I'm sure the last thing she wanted was to stop seeing him. She was her usual bubbly self when she left home this morning. If she were depressed, we would have noticed, surely?"

"Tammie's too level-headed to do something stupid, Debs," said Phillip.

He said the words to reassure his wife, but there were so many instances of teenage girls taking their own lives over something that seemed trivial to grown-ups. These days, the stuff that went on in schools was nothing like what Phillip and Debbie had faced. Bullying, fat-shaming, pressure to conform, nothing made sense anymore. Kids had stepped in front of a train because someone laughed at the trainers they wore. If you didn't wear the latest fashion, you were cancelled.

Debbie continued hugging her knees, sitting on the stairs as Phillip rang the police.

At first light on Friday morning, the search began. Uniformed officers retraced the steps Tammie should have taken from Northleigh to St Laurence, asking if anyone had seen her.

Karla Bates was already hard at work when they patrolled near the crossroads with a photograph of the missing teenager. Few cars were on the B3105 at half-past seven in the morning, and even fewer pedestrians. Police didn't find any eyewitnesses.

As they drew closer to the school, the search proved hopeless despite the increased traffic volume and pedestrians. How would anyone recognise one young girl in school uniform among over a thousand students?

As the light began to fade on Friday afternoon, Miss Beverley Metcalf took her dog, Missy, for a walk along Leigh Road. The retired shop assistant wanted to get back indoors as soon as possible. The wind had picked up, and rain threatened.

Missy pulled Miss Metcalf along the narrow pavement, then disappeared through the metal bars of a gate at the entrance to a field. The elderly lady couldn't hold onto the lead, and Missy bounded across the ploughed field and disappeared into the darkness.

She stood by the gate and called for her Jack Russell terrier.

Missy returned carrying a black shoe in her mouth.

"What on earth have you got there?" asked Beverley. "Put it down at once."

Missy wasn't keen on letting go of her new toy. Miss Metcalf studied the padlock on the metal gate and realised she was in trouble. A few years ago, she would have stood on the middle bar and swung her leg over the gate, dropping to the floor easily on the other side. But, at sixty-six years of age, it was more likely she'd end up in an ambulance and be on her way to the Royal United Hospital in Bath if she attempted that tonight.

A young man on a bicycle stopped to ask if he could help. His front light enabled Beverley to look more closely at the shoe Missy still held.

"It looks quite new," she said.

"Size four or five, perhaps," said the young man. "It reminds me of my sister's school shoes a few years ago. Practical, but not stylish. They're not cheap either."

"I expect it was young lads messing about," said Beverley. "They took it from a poor girl and threw it over the hedge."

"We're a long way from the nearest school. My name's Neville, by the way. Neville Robinson. Do you think your dog would let me grab that lead? I can lift her over the gate, and you can get off home. It's too cold to be hanging around for long tonight."

"Thank you, Neville," said Beverley. "That would be a great help. Be careful, though. Missy is a nipper."

"You're Miss Metcalf, aren't you?" said Neville. "You worked in the cake shop in town for years. My mother would send me in with the right money to get cakes for our tea on Saturday afternoon."

Neville soon clambered over the gate. Missy darted five yards away and stopped. Neville wasn't in the mood to play games. He placed a size eleven trainer on Missy's lead, and she was going no further. Miss Metcalf told Missy to behave, and Neville escaped unscathed when he returned Missy to her owner.

"I never cycle in the winter without a decent pair of gloves," he said. "Thank goodness."

Missy had discarded the black shoe in the mud by the gateway. Neville stooped to pick it up.

"I wonder what happened to the other shoe?" he asked.

"Missy covered most of the field after she got away from me," said Beverley. "It could be anywhere. That's if it's in the field."

"As you said, it's almost new," said Neville. "I reckon it's worth a phone call."

"To the police, d'you mean?" asked Miss Metcalf. "Oh, heavens. I won't sleep tonight."

Neville left Miss Metcalf and Missy as they walked back along Leigh Road to her cottage. He cycled in the opposite direction, and when he arrived home, he called the police.

On Saturday morning, police searched the field on Leigh Road. A second black shoe, size four and a half, was discovered under a hedge. On the other side of the hedge was a clump of trees, their bases surrounded by thick brambles.

When officers probed the brambles with long poles, they

found Tammie Kenyon face down, still wearing her short dark overcoat. Her body was lying one hundred yards from where they had discovered the second shoe.

DI Julie Kemp had hoped to enjoy the weekend with her ten-year-old daughter, Emily. Julie's ex-husband, Vince, had dropped their only child off last night at eight. They had argued, as usual, because Vince was meant to arrive by six.

"You're never home on time, Julie," he'd said. "You spend more time working now than you did when we were married. I thought I'd save myself having to sit outside the house waiting for you to get home. It's not fair on Emily."

Julie didn't want a slanging match in front of their daughter. Vince and his new partner, Josie, were better placed to look after Emily during the week. She hadn't objected to the arrangement and made every effort to make their precious weekends memorable.

After Vince left, she and Emily ordered pizza and snuggled together on the sofa, watching the second How To Train Your Dragon movie. Then, this morning, her boss called as they were about to leave for the railway station. The shopping trip to Bath had to be cancelled; uniforms had found the body of a missing schoolgirl. Julie was the only Detective Inspector available to lead the investigation.

As Julie ended the call, Emily's crestfallen look broke her heart.

"I'm sorry, poppet," said Julie. "I'll make it up to you."

She knew how empty that gesture sounded and steeled herself for the next phone call.

Emily was standing beside her mother when Vince accused Julie of not being fit to be a mother. Why should he disrupt his plans for the weekend so that Julie could go to work? He was adamant she needed to drive Emily to his place because he'd been drinking last night.

When Julie delivered Emily to Vince's front door, his partner answered the doorbell.

Emily ran indoors and went to her room.

"You're asking too much of us, Julie," moaned Josie. "We deserve a life of our own."

"A murdered schoolgirl is a tragedy, not an inconvenience," snapped Julie. "I'd do anything rather than speak to her parents in a couple of hours. First, I have to collect my colleague, who was planning to watch the rugby this afternoon, then we're going to a field to attend the murder site."

Julie left Josie on the doorstep, turned on her heel, and walked to her car. DS Alan Quinn lived on the other side of town, so almost an hour had passed since receiving the call when they reached Leigh Road.

"Not hard to see something's up," said Alan Quinn.

A uniformed officer was trying to keep traffic moving on the narrow country road. Several vehicles were parked on the verge near the gateway to the field.

"The gate's unlocked," said Julie. "That Land Rover must belong to the farmer. Whoever the Crime Scene manager is, he's managed to get the forensic team's vehicles closer to the action."

"I'll get out and chase them up, boss," said Alan. "We're playing catch-up without walking across two fields."

"Excuse me, Sergeant," said Julie. "It was hard enough cutting short my weekend with my daughter without you having a dig."

"Sorry, boss. I wasn't thinking."

Alan got out of the car and soon found a uniformed sergeant who had been a familiar face in town for twenty years; they were in safe hands. Two minutes later, Alan returned to the car to tell Julie they could drive into the field, keeping to the left-hand side until they reached the perimeter tape. Then, they had to walk to the corner of the field where the body lay.

Julie zipped her coat to the neck before retrieving a white protective kit from the boot.

"A cold one this morning, boss," said Alan.

He had thrown a bag into the back seat when Julie picked him up and was soon into his hooded jacket over trousers and boots. Once they were ready, they headed toward the action, following anti-contamination stepping plates laid down by the forensic team.

"The Crime Scene Investigators have done the right thing," said Alan. "They've got the ubiquitous blue tent keeping them warm. The photographer's in there now, by the looks of it."

"I think you'll find the tent is to prevent further degradation of the murder scene," said Julie. "I didn't recognise one of the cars on the grass verge back there. We must have a newbie from the coroner's office inside."

Sergeant Eddie Stokes, the Crime Scene Manager, had gone on ahead while they donned their protective clothing. He greeted them at the door to the tent.

"Hang on a tick, ma'am, until our resident David Bailey here has finished recording everything for posterity. The poor lass has been on the ground for a while. Flies and maggots, don't wait for an invitation in the post. I hope you aren't squeamish."

"This isn't my first rodeo, Sergeant," said Julie.

She wasn't going to tell Stokes it was only her second murder investigation, but she'd seen more than enough dead bodies during her career. Julie had learned to cope with finding people their neighbours hadn't seen for several months. The victims of high-speed car accidents were just as tough to deal with, but children, well, that was a different matter.

The photographer nodded at her when he left the tent. She tried to remember his name, but it wasn't David Bailey. Julie took a deep breath, ventured inside and looked around.

A female forensic team member was finding it difficult to find clues amongst the brambles. After her initial foray, she would have to get someone to remove the spiky vegetation and take it to the lab. Once the area was clear, it was essential to sieve the soil beneath for evidence. Her male colleague was brushing dirt away from Tammie's body.

Julie knew the tiniest scrap recovered by the man who knelt before her could prove vital. She noticed a diminutive lady in green protective clothing standing by a table on the opposite side of the tent.

"I'm DI Kemp, the SIO. Have you viewed the body yet?" she asked.

"Shobna Patel, forensic pathologist. I arrived only five minutes before you."

"In that case, there's no point asking for the cause of death," said Julie.

"All in good time," said Mrs Patel. "I've noted the volume of blowflies and maggots. Experience tells me the body has been here for approximately forty-eight hours."

"Tammie Kenyon died on her way to school then," said Alan Quinn. "I'm DS Quinn, by the way."

While the forensic duo continued their painstaking work, Julie Kemp studied the victim. Tammie's hair was dark and shoulder-length. After two days on the cold, damp ground, it was matted and streaked with mud. Until Shobna

Patel got to work, they wouldn't see Tammie's face, but there was very little blood evidence.

"No visible wounds," said Mrs Patel, "I think it unlikely to be a shooting or a stabbing."

"You can read minds, too?" asked Julie.

She was sure Mrs Patel gave a hint of a smile at that remark, despite the mask covering the lower half of her face.

"The killer dragged your victim here from the adjacent field," said Shobna. "I can't confirm whether she was dead or alive at that point."

"Tammie Kenyon," said Alan Quinn. "This young girl is Tammie Kenyon. Her parents reported her missing on Thursday evening."

"The attack took place in the next field," said Shobna. "I noticed something odd about how the grass on the other side of the hedge was disturbed. So I asked the photographer to get as many pictures of it as possible."

"A cyclist reported seeing a school shoe by the gateway," said Julie. "A dog found it somewhere in the field and took it to her mistress."

Shobna Patel nodded her head.

"That explains it," she said. "The victim was only wearing one shoe when her killer started to move her to a better hiding place. They placed their arms under her shoulders and walked backwards, letting the victim's heels drag along the ground. That was when she lost the second shoe. You'll find a marker at that spot."

"We need to check the field more closely," said Julie. "The attack started elsewhere."

"Why would Tammie enter the field in the first place, boss?" asked Alan.

"She met someone she knew, a boyfriend, school friend,

teacher, travelling salesman," said Julie. "Who knows? Whoever it was, they covered a fair bit of ground to reach that marker. We must ensure a fingertip search is carried out before we lose vital evidence."

"If the killer's clothing was in close contact with Tammie's overcoat, we might get fibres or hair, boss," said Alan.

Shobna Patel shook her head.

"You don't know how tall the attacker was, Detective Sergeant. You are six feet tall, are you not?"

"Six feet, one inch, ma'am," said Alan. "The extra inch is important."

"I am under five feet tall and weigh the same now as when I left school thirty-five years ago. It would be simple for you to drag me backwards without transferring anything useful to your clothing. I'll check under the arms of the victim's coat for skin and fibres. I'd be surprised if the killer didn't wear gloves on a bitterly cold January morning."

"You insist on referring to Tammie as the victim," said Alan.

"That's because she is a victim, DS Quinn. I've worked as a forensic pathologist for many years in different parts of the country and never allowed myself to get personally involved. I want to deal with facts, nothing more."

Eddie Stokes returned to the tent and spoke with the two forensic crew members.

Julie Kemp intercepted him as he left and passed on the request for a fingertip search.

"I agree. We need to be thorough, ma'am," he said. "The lass deserves nothing less. These two will join the others outside in a few minutes. Do you need them for anything?"

"I shall require assistance turning the body, Sergeant,"

said Mrs Patel. "There's only so much I can determine in her current position. However, I've noted her size and physique, and your photographer has taken shots of everything I asked."

Eddie Stokes returned with two burly uniformed officers.

"They know where not to put their big feet, ma'am," he said.

Tammie Kenyon's body was turned under the watchful eye of Mrs Patel.

"Thank you, gentlemen," she said. "Now, to determine the cause, mode, and potential time of death."

DI Kemp and DS Quinn stood and watched while Shobna Patel set to work.

"The minor cuts and abrasions to the face are attributable to the brambles into which the victim was thrown," she said. "Vermin contributed to the other post-mortem injuries we can see. I'll confirm everything when we get the body back to the mortuary, DI Kemp, but I believe the victim was strangled. Look at the bruising on the neck. No other wounds are present, so I don't believe we're searching for a weapon. If you pushed me for a time of death, I would venture between seven and eleven the morning she disappeared, but don't hold me to it."

"Thank you, Mrs Patel," said Julie.

"The sooner we get this one back to the mortuary, the better," said Shobna. "Can either of you detect an odour that feels foreign to you?"

"Just the normal stench of death," said Alan Quinn. "You never forget it."

"Now that I can see Tammie's face, it's clear she didn't wear make-up," said Julie.

"Some schools ban lipstick and eyeliner on the premises," said Shobna. "At least until students reach the sixth form."

"That applies to boys and girls at my children's school," said Alan.

"Even so," said Julie, digging Alan in the ribs. "Most girls would wear deodorant or perfume. We'll ask her parents. How can you distinguish one smell from another?"

"I caught a whiff of something when I studied the marks on her neck more closely. Ah, I think I know what it might have been."

Mrs Patel asked Eddie Stokes whether he'd call back the two uniformed officers.

As they entered the tent, Alan Quinn could see the puzzled look on their faces as Shobna drew close to them and sniffed. The younger man blushed when she asked what deodorant he used.

"I don't recall the brand name, ma'am. My mother gets it for my sensitive skin."

His colleague stifled a laugh.

Shobna Patel tutted.

"You might benefit from using something yourself, constable," she said.

The two officers left the tent, and Shobna Patel turned to Julie.

"I wondered whether there was a transfer between one of those two and the victim's clothing when they turned her over. But I caught a different odour, something unrelated. I'll have to give it more thought when I carry out the post-mortem."

"The scent of a perfume doesn't last long, does it?" asked Alan Quinn.

"Between one and thirty days, Detective Sergeant," said

Mrs Patel. "A scent will last longer if you spray it on clothing. Textiles are better than skin for scent retention."

"Some perfumes can stain your clothing, though," said Julie.

"Your forensic people will be here for days, DI Kemp," said Mrs Patel. "I'm sure you wish to notify the parents. When Sergeant Stokes is ready, I'll ask him to arrange to transport the body to the mortuary. I would expect the PM to take place on Monday morning. No doubt I'll see you both there."

Julie realised Shobna Patel was right. They were getting in everyone's way. She returned to where she'd parked the car and discarded her protective clothing. Alan soon joined her; he had stopped to chat with Eddie Stokes.

"It can pay to have an experienced hand on a case like this, boss. Because he's lived in Bradford all his life, Eddie could give me background on the father, Phillip Kenyon."

"How far is Northleigh from here?" she asked.

"Half a mile, boss," said Alan.

"Let's get it over with," said Julie.

While Julie broke the news, Alan watched the father's reaction. According to Eddie Stokes, Kenyon was an easy-going individual who wasn't prone to violent outbursts. However, Alan sensed the man sitting across from him with an arm around his wife's shoulder was full of anger.

Debbie Kenyon blamed herself for her daughter's death. She should have driven Tammie to school on a Thursday when she attended the breakfast club sessions. It was just one day a week in term time, and in January, apart from the cold weather, it was dark, especially along that first stretch of road near the Leigh Park Country House Hotel.

Debbie blamed herself, too, for not asking Tammie how things were going with Alfie Jones. What sort of mother had she been if her daughter didn't feel she could talk to her about getting dumped by her boyfriend?

Phillip Kenyon asked how Tammie had died.

Julie Kemp knew hearing she'd been strangled wasn't enough. Kenyon was desperate to learn whether his only child had been raped. After she answered his question as briefly as possible to save Debbie further pain, Kenyon stood up.

"Did he interfere with her?" he pleaded.

Alan Quinn decided to intervene and motioned to Phillip Kenyon to sit down.

"We have to await the results of the post-mortem, Mr Kenyon."

"Can we see her?" he asked.

"We can arrange for that to happen," said Julie. "There are procedures to follow, as I'm sure you understand. A colleague will visit you this afternoon. You will have lots of questions; it's only natural. The Family Liaison Officer will help you with those questions, and she will let you know how the investigation is going. If you need extra help at any stage, we can contact Victim Support. They can have someone available twenty-four seven."

They left Debbie and Phillip Kenyon sitting in the lounge.

"Tammie's death has shattered them," said Alan.

"Unless he's the world's best actor, Phillip Kenyon didn't murder his daughter," said Julie. "However, we need to do it by the book. Let's get to the station and list the people we need to interview. Who's in the frame for the FLO role?"

"Bonnie Adamson, boss," said Alan. "She's got the right temperament."

"She'll need it," said Julie. "Phillip Kenyon looked ready to explode."

"You noticed it too, boss. I still don't think he did it, but we must ensure he doesn't get close to whoever did."

Julie and Alan spent the rest of the weekend setting up interviews and identifying potential suspects. The number of criminals in a small town like Bradford-on-Avon didn't fill one side of a sheet of lined paper, but access to the road where contact was first made meant they could be dealing with a larger catchment area.

On Monday morning, Alan Quinn collected his boss from her home, and they drove out to the morgue at Flax Bourton. The results were in line with what they expected, death by strangulation. Despite clothing having been removed, there was no clear evidence of a sexual motive for the murder.

"Tammie's attacker removed clothing from the lower half of her body," said Shobna Patel when she spoke with them afterwards. "Her trousers and underwear were recovered from the scene. Although she was half-naked, Tammie had not been raped."

"There's something you're not telling us, isn't there?" asked Julie. "Why use the term 'clear evidence' in your report?"

"The victim was sexually active, DI Kemp," said Shobna. "Not unheard of in fifteen-year-olds in this day and age. It's possible there was attempted penetration on Thursday morning, but I found no trace of semen or tissue damage indicative of force."

"So, the killer may have tried to have sex with Tammie but couldn't perform. Is that what you're saying?" asked Alan.

"Hard to tell, DS Quinn," said Shobna. "After forty-eight hours on frozen ground, it was impossible to determine that degree of detail from the body. It would be pure speculation."

"Why would he remove her clothing unless he intended to go further," said Alan.

"It adds another dimension to our investigation," said Julie. "We need to talk to people who knew Tammie, particularly her friends. The list we have at present is short."

From the outset, this case was difficult for Kemp and Quinn. Long hours on the frozen ground had destroyed evidence that might have helped Shobna Patel. In addition, the cold weather kept people indoors on Thursday and Friday, which meant that dogwalkers like Beverley Metcalf walked their dogs close to home.

On short winter days, a leisurely walk across the fields was off the menu. So, Tammie's body wasn't found for forty-eight hours. After they returned from Flax Bourton, Alan Quinn was concerned they had no motive, no obvious suspect, and no leads.

"We must stick to the tried and tested routine, Alan," said Julie.

Chapter Eight

Monday, 19 January 2015

BONNIE ADAMSON HAD SPENT Sunday afternoon with Debbie and Phillip Kenyon and passed on information about the break-up with Alfie Jones and the names of Tammie's best friends.

Alan thought they had found their first suspect, but Alfie explained why the relationship ended when interviewed. His parents believed they had persuaded him to break up with Tammie to concentrate on his schooling. Alfie said he was happy to let them think that, but the truth was Tammie was moving too fast. She kept wanting sex with him, and he wasn't her first lover by any means. Tammie had convinced herself Alfie loved her, and they would get married. Unfortunately, that wasn't on the cards as far as Alfie was concerned.

When Julie Kemp asked Alfie where he was on Thursday morning, he said he left home at half-past eight, walked to school with his mate from next door, and spent the morning in the company of over a dozen fellow students of Chemistry and Physics. The teachers confirmed that Alfie hadn't been out of their sight at any time.

Naomi Fletcher and several of Tammie's schoolfriends gave similar replies about who Tammie went out with and what she was like. Julie Kemp asked if Tammie had argued with anyone. Were there any strangers outside the school in the days before the murder? Everyone seemed to know the names of the boys Tammie had been with. She got on with everyone, which made it impossible to think of anyone who wished her harm. Nobody had noticed any strangers near the school.

Karla Bates called the police station on Monday evening. She'd worked a shift at the Leigh Park Country House Hotel, and a customer had mentioned police activity in the field off Leigh Road. When Karla asked a colleague about it, she began to wonder whether the girl she'd seen on Thursday morning was Tammie Kenyon.

Julie Kemp and Alan Quinn interviewed Karla Bates at home the following morning.

Alan showed Karla a photograph of Tammie in her school uniform.

"Gosh, yes, that's the girl I saw," said Karla. "How dreadful for her family."

"Can you tell us what happened, from when you left home until you reached work, Karla?" asked Julie.

"It was still dark here in Woolley Grange when I came out of my front door. So, I put my headlights on. I pulled out of the driveway onto the main road and drove along the B3105. I spotted a girl wearing a short, dark-coloured jacket over a school uniform. The same school colours as in the photo you just showed me. She looked a couple of years older than that photo, say, fifteen or sixteen. There was nobody else on the pavement near her. It was hard to tell whether she was late for something and running; or just eager to cross the road the second she spotted a gap in the traffic."

"You didn't see anyone following her?" asked Alan.

"No, dear," said Karla, shaking her head. "As I neared the crossroads, the traffic volume caused me to slow to a crawl. The young girl could see she had a chance to dash across to Leigh Road, and after she'd reached the pavement, I accelerated again and turned into the gateway to the Hotel a few seconds later."

"Did you see anyone hanging around on Tammie's side of the road?" asked Alan.

"I didn't look back, I'm afraid. I was concentrating on the road ahead."

"Have you ever seen Tammie before?" asked Julie. "She would have been walking that route every Thursday morning during term time."

"I didn't recognise her when you showed me the photo," said Karla. "I see children in uniform from St Laurence all the time. Who doesn't in Bradford-on-Avon?"

"Karla Bates must have been the last person to see Tammie alive, apart from her killer," said Alan as they drove back to the station. "I know weather conditions and length of time before the body was discovered means the time of death was tricky to determine, but Tammie never left Leigh Road alive."

"One thing Karla mentioned could help us," said Julie. "Although she had to slow down at that crossroads, the number of vehicles involved couldn't have been many that early in the morning."

"We can appeal for drivers who travelled on the B3109

and B3105 between seven-thirty and whatever time last Thursday morning."

"That's the problem, Alan," said Julie. "We know Tammie left home in Northleigh at seven thirty-five and was less than halfway to school when Karla Bates saw her. So when did Tammie enter that field, and how long was it before her killer left?"

Alan arranged for signs to be erected on both sides of the crossroads, asking motorists for information. Julie ensured the appeal was also relayed to local media, and they waited in vain for someone to call the tipline number with anything remotely useful.

"What did we expect," moaned Alan. "It was cold and dark. Half of those drivers probably didn't clear their windscreens before leaving home. Their vision would have been impaired."

"Several had a cup of coffee in one hand or were fiddling with the radio," said Julie. "Five days in, and we've got nothing."

Alan wanted to take another look at Debbie and Phillip Kenyon.

"Why?" asked Julie. "Their alibis checked out. Both of them were at work all day. Witnesses placed them exactly where they said they were."

"Debbie told us she came home at lunchtime, listened to the recorded message from the school, and returned to work. Why didn't she raise the alarm at once?"

"She left a message on her husband's phone and tried to get hold of Alfie," said Julie. "Would our response have been immediate to news that a kid skipped school?"

"Convenient that Kenyon doesn't have access to his phone during a shift," said Alan. "Also, why didn't Debbie know Alfie's mobile number or where he lived?"

"Relationships at Tammie's age can be brief," said Julie. "I dated three guys in a fortnight one summer. Before you ask, I wasn't as free with my favours. With Emily, I wouldn't expect to hear that sort of detail until she was ready. Although, I hope that won't be for a few years yet."

Later that week, Julie received reports on Tammie's mobile phone and laptop. She dropped the information on Alan's desk.

"A fat lot of use that was," she said. "Tammie had a new phone at Christmas. We've only got a list of contacts we could have prepared ourselves and a handful of messages. We interviewed most of them already."

"So, nothing controversial," said Alan. "I hoped we might get lucky and find death threats or a brief message, such as KYS. Unless we get an eyewitness who has been on a skiing holiday that saw two people on Leigh Road, we're stuffed."

Thursday, 14 January 2016

DI JULIE KEMP appealed for new information on the anniversary of Tammie's death. Naomi Fletcher retraced what was believed to be her best friend's footsteps on that fateful morning.

Debbie Kenyon told a Wiltshire Times reporter: "It's disappointing because every day when we wake up, we always hope something will turn up to help solve the mystery. We can't understand why Tammie was killed. What had she done to deserve to die?"

Phillip Kenyon added: "I'm certain Tammie knew her killer, and they live locally. You could walk past them daily on the streets, speak to them, and not realise they're hiding a dreadful secret."

"If anyone suspects a family member might have been responsible, please contact the police," said Debbie. "If the police haven't established a motive for Tammie being targeted after a year, then no young woman in town is safe."

"You could have done without that comment, boss," said Alan Quinn.

He was phoning Julie Kemp from Salisbury the following morning. After the investigation came to a halt, they were reassigned to other cases, and in September, Alan relocated to Salisbury with his family.

"Every detective has at least one case that haunts them, even after they've handed in their warrant card," said Julie. "How are things at Bourne Hill?"

"Hectic," he replied. "Do you think Debbie Kenyon has a point?"

"We haven't heard of any dead bodies being discovered this morning," said Julie. "I think we've avoided the Wiltshire Times dubbing our killer the Anniversary Assassin."

"Good to hear you haven't lost your sense of humour, boss," said Alan. "Happy New Year."

"You too, Alan," said Julie. "Bye."

Sunday, 8 May 2016

IMOGEN HENDERSON LEFT her home on Springfield Avenue at seven-thirty for her usual Sunday morning run. The willowy, seventeen-year-old sixth-form student was a natural athlete. Unlike other girls her age in town, she wasn't suffering from a hangover. Imogen had gone to bed at ten, just as she did every day of the week.

Imogen lived in a four-bedroomed detached property with her parents, Steve and Elaine, and Zack, her thirteen-year-old brother. It was Zack's turn on Sunday to take Rebel, the family dog, for a walk. Rebel was the only one stirring when Imogen crept from the house by the back door. He got up, placed his paws on Imogen's shoulders, and she pushed him down before he slobbered all over her face.

"I won't be long, Rebel," she whispered.

Imogen did a few exercises at the side of the house to warm up before heading for Woolley Street. It was a familiar routine, a slow section to start, and then she planned to stretch her legs on her way to Woolley Grange.

When she reached the junction with the B3105, she would turn right and run towards Holt Road. The traffic was always busy at that junction, and it was where Imogen took a breather before jogging along the pavement beside the main road into the town centre. Another right turn brought her back to Springfield Avenue and completed the circuit of two and a half miles.

Imogen wasn't aiming to shave seconds or minutes off her average time. She enjoyed thirty minutes of exercise every week, which she spent alone—a time when she could forget about exams, university, and the pressures of being a teenager.

When she spotted Woolley Grange Country House Hotel up ahead of her, Imogen thought about what she might do when she reached home at around quarter past eight. She had study work to catch up on, ready for school tomorrow, but, as usual, she'd have to go to church with the others. But, never mind, she could squeeze a couple of hours studying into the afternoon.

Zack was never out of bed before ten on a Saturday, but on Sunday, he was under orders to be up by eight to take Rebel for a long walk. So everything was geared toward when the family left home to make the two-minute drive to Christ Church, high on the hill at the top of town.

You could see the spire from miles away if you were interested. Zack wasn't. At thirteen, he couldn't tell his father he preferred a lie-in. His sister was even less keen on attending church services. As Zack lay in bed, he wondered whether Immie had much to confess.

The sound of conversation along the corridor told him Mum and Dad were on their way downstairs. If he didn't move soon, there would be ructions. Zack made for the bathroom and emptied his bladder. He took a quick shower, looked out of his bedroom window to check the weather was fine and grabbed a t-shirt and shorts from a drawer. His trainers were by the back door where he'd chucked them when he got in yesterday evening.

Steve and Elaine heard Zack thumping down the stairs at pace.

"If you got up earlier, you wouldn't need to rush," said his mother.

Zack looked for his sister, but she wasn't home yet. So, fine, he'd make his breakfast. After two slices of toast, washed down with a glass of milk, he was ready to leave. Rebel was already standing, tail wagging, by the back door. Zack shouted goodbye as he went.

At the latest, he and Rebel had to be back by half-past ten when Dad would probably order him to shower again, and Mum would insist he wore a white shirt and tie. With his black trousers and shoes, he looked like a pupil from an expensive public school, not an ordinary student from St Laurence. Thank goodness none of his classmates ever went to church.

Zack and Rebel went in the opposite direction to Imogen. He preferred to head for the town centre and visit the playing fields near the Tithe Barn. Then, if Rebel were up for it, they would walk along the canal footpath for a while. The weather was set fair, and they had two hours to kill.

Steve Henderson looked at the kitchen clock.

"Did you hear Immie leave this morning, darling?"

"I thought I heard her moving around at seven or a little later. Why?" asked Elaine.

"It's unlike Immie to run longer than forty minutes," said Steve. "Even if she bumps into a friend on her circuit."

He got up from his chair and headed for the front door.

"I hope you'll put a top on before you step outside, Steve," said Elaine. "It's Sunday, and it's not seemly for a middle-aged married man to parade around in shorts and flip-flops."

Steve dashed upstairs for a t-shirt and a pair of sandals. He grabbed his car keys.

"I'll try Immie's circuit in reverse," he shouted to Elaine, who was still finishing her coffee. "Perhaps she's pulled a muscle."

Elaine heard the car leaving the garage and placed her empty cup on the draining board. What a lot of fuss for a teenager who preferred running to boys. Elaine thought it was about time Imogen pulled something other than a muscle. She went upstairs to shower and dress, ready for church.

Steve Henderson returned home after twenty-five

minutes. Elaine was sitting in the lounge reading the newspaper.

"You should have a word with Abbas at the newsagent, Steve," she said. "That lad who delivers the papers is getting later and later. Is Imogen not with you?"

"I drove along her usual route," he said. "I couldn't see her anywhere. I stopped a couple of times to ask if someone had seen a young girl running. I chatted with people out with their dogs or couples enjoying the sunshine. None of them had seen Immie. A chap cutting a high hedge in Woolley Street told me he was getting his steps and cordless hedge trimmer from the shed at around twenty to eight. He saw Immie run past his driveway."

"Perhaps she decided to take a different route, Steve," said Elaine. "Although, she's a creature of habit, that one. Should we be worried?"

Steve didn't want to think about what could have happened to their daughter. Elaine had been battling cancer eighteen months ago when that other young girl was murdered. His wife had come through that ordeal, but Steve had been home alone on the evening when the police detective had appeared on local TV with the parents. Elaine hadn't heard the chilling warning that young women in Bradford-on-Avon were in danger.

Steve told himself Immie was a sensible girl. She could run fast enough to escape, given the opportunity. Anyway, most of the roads she used for her run weren't quiet, leafy lanes far away from people and places, and in May, Immie was running in broad daylight.

"Steve?" asked Elaine. "Should we be worried?"

"I'd better phone the police," he replied.

Steve made the call, and two uniformed officers drove to

Springfield Avenue within fifteen minutes. He repeated everything that had happened this morning.

"So, your daughter left here at half-past seven, and you would expect her to reach home by eight-fifteen."

"Eight-thirty at the latest," said Steve. "I've driven the route myself. She's not there, I've already told you. So why aren't you going to look for her?"

"I don't suppose she took a mobile phone with her?" said the constable.

"Don't you think I would have called her if she had?" said Steve.

"Good point, sir," said the PCSO. "Does she have any friends on the way? Somewhere she might have popped in for a coffee. She could turn up outside the house in two minutes."

"Boyfriend's place?" asked the constable.

"Imogen doesn't have a boyfriend," said Elaine.

"We have the route you believe Imogen would have taken," said the constable. "We'll take a look. I'm sure there's a reasonable explanation, sir. We'll be in touch."

"But if she wanders through the door after we leave, you will ring the station, won't you, sir?" said the PCSO.

Steve nodded. Elaine sat quietly in her Sunday best, clutching her handbag to her chest.

Zack arrived home with Rebel at twenty-to-eleven. He burst through the back door, full of apologies.

"Sorry, I'm late. I got chatting with some boys in my year by the Tithe Barn. Rebel ran off, and we had to chase him across the field. I can still get ready in time."

"Immie's missing," said Steve. "The police are looking for her."

"Of course they are, Dad," said Zack. "Look, I said I was sorry."

Zack kicked off his trainers by the back door and walked into the lounge to find his mother crying.

"You're not kidding," he said.

"No, Zack," said Steve. "We won't be going to church today."

The family's torment lasted until sunset. After an initial check of the route Imogen usually followed yielded nothing, the officers returned to the police station, where they bumped into Eddie Stokes in the car park. He had popped in to catch up on his paperwork and was looking forward to having the next two days with a rod in his hand on the riverbank.

"Why the long faces, lads," he asked.

"We received a report of a missing girl, sarge. She went for a run early this morning and never returned."

"Whereabouts?" asked Eddie.

"Woolley Street, out to the Grange, and back into town."

"Eighteen months ago, I was out that way for another missing girl," said Eddie. "The fish will have to wait. Let's get inside and start rounding up a few more uniforms. We need to search field by field along that route. I don't like the sound of it."

Imogen's fully-clothed body was found in a field three-quarters of a mile from her home at a quarter to seven. There had been no attempt to conceal the body.

DI Julie Kemp had spent the weekend with her daughter, Emily, and was driving home after dropping her off at her father's house. Vince and Josie were now married. Not that it had seen any reduction in hostility when they met.

Since Alan Quinn's transfer to Bourne Hill, Julie had teamed up with DS Tony Wyvern, a thirty-seven-year-old Bristolian who was married with one daughter. Tony was watching TV with Sally and fifteen-year-old Nicole when his mobile phone rang.

"Curses foiled again," he said. "Work calls."

"Again," said Sally.

Tony walked into the hallway and listened to what the duty sergeant had to say. A forensic team was on its way to a field four hundred yards on the right past The George gastropub on Woolley Street. A teenage girl's body had been found in the far left corner.

"Got it, sarge," said Tony. "Is DI Kemp on her way?"

"No reply. I've left a message."

Julie had left her phone at home for the short trip to and from Vince's house. She picked up the message when she reached home. Then, she turned around and headed out the front door with a sigh.

DS Wyvern had already arrived at the murder scene on Woolley Street. He parked on the grass verge opposite the gateway to the field. There was only one narrow pavement on this stretch of road, and only an idiot would block it. Tony wondered who owned the single car on the opposite side.

He recognised the figure of Eddie Stokes one hundred yards away in the corner of the field. Everything would be running like clockwork. Tony stood inside the gateway and donned his protective clothing. Time to join the party. The familiar sight of people in similar gear greeted him as he stayed close to the field's perimeter. Inside the blue tent, he caught a glimpse of someone in green clothing.

Tony heard a faint shout. Julie Kemp had parked behind him, crossed the road, and hurried to catch up. She was tucking her hair inside the hood of her white jacket.

"Are we dealing with another one, Tony?" she asked as she pulled on a pair of nitrile gloves.

"Another one, boss? I was told a girl failed to return from a run, and uniforms found a body. I thought it was a suspicious death."

"While you were still working in Bristol, a young girl was murdered not far from here. A couple of fields over, close to Leigh Park."

"You didn't catch the killer, I take it?" asked Tony.

"Not even close," said Julie. "We couldn't establish a clear motive, and every convicted sex offender and pervert on our radar proved to be squeaky clean. We made various appeals, but nobody came forward with information. If a mother, wife, or girlfriend suspected a male member in their household of being responsible, we never heard a whisper."

Eddie Stokes booked them in and told them who else was present and the current state of progress. As Tony Wyvern expected, Eddie had his finger on the pulse. They moved to the tent entrance, where a short, middle-aged lady in green met them.

"Good evening, DI Kemp," said Shobna Patel. "We meet again."

"I wish we hadn't, Mrs Patel," said Julie. "No offence."

"None taken," said Shobna. "Who do we have here?"

"DS Wyvern, ma'am," said Tony.

"Step inside my office," said Shobna. "The victim was seventeen years of age. As you can see, she has vivid bruising to the neck but no other visible injuries. Her parents told the police their daughter left home at half-past seven this morning for a run. I was in Bradford visiting my sister when I got the call. A thorough search of the fields on either side of the road started in the early afternoon. They discovered the body at a quarter to seven. I always carry my equipment in the car, so I can reach the scene and start work by ten minutes past seven."

"When do you think she was killed?" asked Tony.

"Normally, I would shake my head and tell you not to be silly young man," said Mrs Patel. "However, the victim wore a GPS running watch. She used it to track distance, pace, heart rate, and calories. The model in question also has a function that automatically alerted her when she completed each mile. The first beep on her logged route never came. When we upload the activity from this morning's run to a PC, we'll be able to follow her progress on a map of the route. In addition, we'll see the exact time at which she stopped running. That spot was three-quarters of a mile from where she set out, which means even without the details from the watch, I would suggest her attacker interrupted her run between seven-forty and seven-forty-five."

"Time of death was twelve hours ago, give or take," said Tony.

"I can't see how it could be much less," said Mrs Patel. "I'll know better once I've got her to the morgue."

"Any signs of sexual activity?" asked Tony.

"You've glanced towards the body on several occasions, Detective Sergeant. You will have seen the victim's upper clothing pushed up to expose part of her left breast, and her shorts and underwear have been disturbed. All will be revealed when I perform the autopsy."

"There are no signs the victim was dragged from the gateway to where we're standing," said Julie. "She's still wearing her running shoes."

"I didn't see any tyre marks, boss," Tony said.

"This is a large field," said Julie, "and the low wall beside the pavement would allow drivers and pedestrians to see people struggling, even in this far corner. The killer must have persuaded the victim to come here, and then they strangled her."

"The ground is dry and rutted further into the centre, boss," said Tony. "I suppose it's possible a vehicle was involved."

"Forensics will gather all the evidence they can," said Julie. "We need to break the news to the parents. Did you find anything else significant so far, Mrs Patel?"

"The victim was fully-clothed and in excellent physical health. She wore a white sports bra, red singlet, red shorts, and white briefs. A rainbow-coloured hairband secured her ponytail. Her watch was on her left wrist. As for her footwear, they are a pair of size six Nike Revolution trainers, with no inner sock."

"You've been close to the body?" asked Julie.

Tony Wyvern looked at his boss. Where was she going with this? When did she meet this Mrs Patel anyway?

"Those were very different conditions, DI Kemp," said Mrs Patel. "The body had been exposed to the elements and vermin for several days. Many different odours were battling for supremacy when I viewed the victim. As you will recall, one of the two officers who turned the body for me was also wearing deodorant. Rigor mortis commences after two hours and can last until thirty-six hours after death. It takes around twelve hours for a human body to be cool to the touch and twenty-four hours to cool to the core. In other circumstances, we use clues such as these to esti-mate the time of death. Today, the calculations are much simpler."

"I appreciate all of that, Mrs Patel," said Julie. "Stop prevaricating. Did you notice anything odd?"

"The victim had been running for ten minutes, DI

Kemp. Perhaps you could determine whether she wore perfume or deodorant when she exercised. Most women would have showered when they reached home and applied it then. It's expensive enough without wasting it. If you discount the possibility of scent being applied to her body or her clothing, I'll consider what I've included in my notes and make the information available. I won't keep you from informing the poor girl's parents any longer."

With that, Mrs Patel returned to the blue tent.

"I'm glad we cleared that up," said Tony. "I didn't understand half of it."

"She insists on referring to Imogen as the victim rather than using her name," said Julie. "Exactly how she did things eighteen months ago. Mrs Patel annoyed Alan Quinn then, and it's getting on my nerves now. She mentioned a faint whiff of a smell on Tammie Kenyon's body that seemed out of synch. Why she did that, I don't know. It could have been the uniformed officer's deodorant, but I sensed she caught a scent earlier this evening. She was alone in the tent with the body, taking measurements, studying the bruising to the neck."

"Transfer, d'you mean? She thought the killer wore a powerful enough deodorant that lingered on the victim's body. How long before the first body was discovered?"

"Tammie Kenyon died on Thursday morning, and Shobna Patel performed her initial examination of the body on Saturday morning."

"What are your initial thoughts now we've seen the body, boss?" asked Tony. "When you arrived, you asked whether we were dealing with another one. Could it be the same attacker?"

"Did you think Imogen had been raped?" asked Julie.

"No, boss, there would have been much more evidence

of a struggle. If I were a betting man, I'd say her clothes were disturbed after death."

Julie Kemp sighed.

"Follow me to Springfield Avenue, Tony. Let's get it over with."

Chapter Nine

JULIE AND TONY changed out of their protective suits at the side of the road and drove back along Woolley Street into town. It was half-past eight when Julie rang the front doorbell. She heard a woman's anguished scream inside, and seconds later, Steve Henderson opened the door.

"My wife is convinced if the police send detectives, it's always bad news," he said.

"DI Kemp and DS Wyvern, Mr Henderson," said Julie. "May we come in?"

"Have you found my sister?"

A young lad looked down at Julie from the top of the stairs. He was a couple of years older than her daughter, Emily.

"Go to your room, Zack," said Steve Henderson.

He showed the two detectives into the lounge, where Elaine Henderson was already in bits, and Julie hadn't said a word. Steve sat beside his wife and held her close.

"I'm sorry," said Julie.

Several minutes passed before she could explain where Imogen was found.

"I drove past her while driving home," said Steve. "I never thought to stop and search the fields. So why would Immie go there? Perhaps if I'd stopped, I might have got to her in time to save her."

"That's not possible, sir," said Tony. "The pathologist reckons the attack occurred less than fifteen minutes after Imogen left home."

"She was dead before I started to wonder where she was," said Steve. "We expected her to walk through the back door at about a quarter past eight. When she didn't, we didn't panic."

"Who would have wanted to kill Imogen," cried Elaine. "Are you telling us everything?"

Julie understood the way Elaine's mind was working. So she decided to cut to the chase.

"Imogen's murder was planned," said Julie. "She was strangled, and the attack was controlled and ferocious. We do not believe Imogen was the victim of a sexual assault, despite the fact some of her clothing had been disturbed."

"What do you mean, planned?" asked Steve.

"The killer must have watched your daughter over several weeks. They knew her movements on Sunday mornings and waited in an isolated spot on Woolley Street waiting for her to run past."

"Did your daughter wear perfume?" asked Julie.

"Not for school or when she was running, like today," said Elaine. "Imogen would use deodorant every day, but she had a natural beauty that only required a minimum of make-up."

"Did Imogen have a boyfriend?" asked Tony.

"Absolutely not," said Elaine. "I wished she would show more interest in boys."

"Was your daughter gay?" asked Julie.

"How dare you?" shouted Elaine. "I won't listen to such disgusting nonsense."

"We noticed the hairband she was wearing," said Julie.

"Imogen had a dozen badges, stickers and wristbands supporting various causes. Our daughter was intelligent and took an interest in the world around her. We raised her to be a Christian sympathetic to the struggles of others who hadn't yet turned to the Bible for guidance."

"Did Imogen have many friends?" asked Tony. "Had she fallen out with anyone?"

"Immie was popular at school," said Steve.

"With her teachers, Steve," said Elaine. "Her phone is in her bedroom. You can trace her small circle of friends through that."

"Is it password-protected?" asked Tony.

"Yes," said Elaine. "But we only allowed her a phone if we had access to it. Steve can unlock it when you're ready to leave."

Tony Wyvern didn't think they'd find anything useful on the phone if the parents monitored every conversation.

"What about a laptop or tablet?" asked Julie.

"I won't allow one in the house," said Elaine. "The internet is the Devil's playground."

"But Imogen had a phone," said Tony.

"She wanted to make and receive calls," said Elaine. "We weighed the risks and decided once Imogen was sixteen, we could trust her to stay on the straight and narrow. But perhaps we were mistaken."

Julie wanted to get out of this house before getting into trouble. Where did they find these people? Imogen's father didn't seem to be quite as much of a zealot or as biased as her mother, but this case was becoming more complex with every step.

Imogen Henderson was the polar opposite of Tammie Kenyon on the evidence they'd seen. So if the same person killed both teenage girls, they couldn't be accused of having a type. Julie heard Tony telling the parents what would happen next. The post-mortem would likely occur the next day, and they could arrange to see their daughter. A Family Liaison Officer would be in touch in the morning.

Steve Henderson listened intently and asked questions every grieving parent asked. His wife remained seated, staring into space, with her hands folded in her lap. Tony accompanied Steve upstairs to Imogen's bedroom. They took far longer than necessary to pick up a phone.

Julie knew her colleague would be having a casual chat with the father while absorbing everything about Imogen's room to gauge the true character of the victim. You couldn't always rely on the parents. Julie took advantage of the break to ask her own questions.

"You said Imogen was popular with her teachers, Mrs Henderson. Was there any teacher in particular?"

"Imogen was at the top of her year in most subjects, Detective Inspector. I find teachers are always happiest when teaching students who want to learn. So many children seem to think the world owes them a living and education isn't a fundamental requirement for achieving their goals. I attend parents' evenings for both my children. Steve has always been too busy with work. I don't recall a particular teacher taking an undue interest in Imogen. Every teacher spoke of her in glowing terms. She could have achieved so much, and now some pathetic low-life has robbed her of the opportunity."

"We'll do our utmost to find her killer, Mrs Henderson," said Julie.

Steve Henderson and Tony Wyvern returned to the lounge. Zack appeared in the doorway behind them and ran to be with his mother.

"We'll be in touch," said Tony. Julie stood, and they left the room together.

Steve Henderson followed as Julie and Tony headed for the front door. He stood on the step outside and half-closed the door behind him.

"Do you think it was a hate crime?" he asked.

"Were you aware of your daughter's sexual orientation, Mr Henderson?" asked Julie.

"We never discussed it. Immie was a young seventeen if you know what I mean? She was an attractive young woman. The fact she didn't have a string of boyfriends might have surprised me if I didn't know how determined she was to get the predicted A-star grades that would get her into Cambridge University. There would be plenty of time for boys later. At least, that was what I thought until this evening. I'm beginning to wonder whether I knew my daughter at all."

"We're sorry for your loss," said Tony.

Julie could have kicked him where it hurt when she heard that hackneyed phrase.

Steve Henderson returned inside and closed the door.

"Back to the station?" asked Tony, standing with his hand on his car door.

"I need a clear head," said Julie. "Let's sleep on it. We'll hear the time of the PM when we reach the station in the morning. The schedule for the rest of the day will have to dovetail with that."

"Righto, boss. See you first thing."

Monday, 9 May 2016, onwards

THE AUTOPSY CONFIRMED Shobna Patel's initial observations.

Imogen Henderson had been strangled in the corner of the field off Woolley Street. Her voice box had been flattened against the spinal column, and there were also signs of congestion across the centre of the neck muscles. There were no signs of a sexual assault.

When Julie and Tony returned from Flax Bourton, they knew they had their work cut out to find the killer. The attack had occurred in broad daylight, one hundred yards from the road and less than half a mile from Woolley Grange Country House Hotel. So far, they had just one eyewitness—the man cutting his hedge at a property close to the junction with the B3109.

"What did we get from the phone?" asked Julie.

"We have contact numbers for fourteen friends," said Tony. "Twelve of those are school friends in the same year; only two of which are male. In addition, two teachers provided Imogen with a mobile number, which is increasingly rare. One is her PE teacher, Mrs Oram, who is retiring this summer. The other is the Head of Year 12, David Sayers. He's forty-two, the same age as Steve Henderson."

"Married?" asked Julie.

"Engaged to a Languages teacher at the school, Matthew Cotton, twenty-eight."

"Was that it?" asked Julie.

"Apart from her parents and grandparents, yes," said Tony.

"I can understand why those two teachers weren't

concerned that people might suspect inappropriate relationships," said Julie.

"If Sayers had been straight and sent a photo of his bits to Imogen, Elaine would have died of shame."

"A strange woman, that one," said Julie. "So far, I can't see religion playing a part in her daughter's death. When we've interviewed those few friends, and the teachers, perhaps we'll have a different opinion."

"With so few friends, did that mean she attracted a lot of enemies?" asked Tony.

"For the first time since I became a detective, I can't use social media to learn about a victim."

"That might not be true, boss," said Tony. "All these students will have accounts; you can bet on it. They could provide us with useful information. Her friends couldn't bully or slag her off online or on her phone, but they could have talked about her behind her back."

"Good thinking. Get someone to trawl through those names and highlight any reference to Immie or Imogen Henderson. I wonder whether she had interests outside of school besides running?"

"Is there a church youth club?" asked Tony. "That's the only organisation I can see Elaine letting her daughter attend."

"I spoke with Bonnie Adamson when I arrived, " Julie said. "She was on her way to Springfield Avenue. Bonnie told me Eddie Stokes had suggested she did a house-to-house and had a quiet chat with the neighbours to see if there were any rumours."

"He's got uniforms on Woolley Street doing a more comprehensive search for eyewitnesses. Eddie said you got nothing from the message boards back in 2015. Is it worth placing one by the entrance to the field this time?"

"I'm sure it can't do any harm, Tony," said Julie. "We need to try everything."

One by one, the initial interviews were scheduled and completed.

Imogen's school friends, although few, were united in their grief.

"Immie touched the lives of everyone she met," said one.

"I can't believe we won't see her again," said another.

The emotional responses convinced Julie Kemp that despite her mother's fears, Imogen had friends she could count on, both male and female.

Rosemary Oram was the first teacher they spoke to, just after she blew the final whistle for a hockey match.

"Gosh, I'm getting too old to keep up with these young girls," she said as she joined Julie and Tony to sit on a grass bank beside the school playing fields. "What was it you wanted to know?"

"We were interested to note that Imogen had your mobile number," said Julie.

"We attended the same church," said Rosemary. "I've known Elaine since we were at school. I was Imogen's godparent. Games aren't the only subject I teach here. I cover Religious Education too."

"Religion was important to Imogen then," said Tony. "Did she come to you for guidance on other matters?"

"My door is always open to all my students," said Rosemary. "I'm not sure what you're driving at?"

"We haven't found a motive for Imogen's murder," said Julie. "Every student Imogen considered a friend spoke very highly of her. Not one of them could point at someone at school with whom she'd argued. That included students, teachers, and parents."

"Imogen was particular in her ways," said Rosemary. "She saw the world in black and white. The boys and girls you've spoken to were white. I don't mean the colour of their skin. I mean that everyone else outside that small clique was considered black. I've known her mother for longer than I care to remember, and it would be impossible for Imogen and Zack to grow up without acquiring some of Elaine's idiosyncrasies. Imogen rejected the more extreme views, but she was single-minded in her ambition of getting to Cambridge and achieving a first-class degree. Nothing could be allowed to stand in her way. So, she identified the right people to allow into her life; those who were serious and studious. They didn't have to believe in God, but anyone who Imogen thought fell short of the high standards she set didn't exist in her world. She wouldn't engage in conversation with them. It would be time wasted."

"That in itself would have antagonised some fellow students," said Tony. "Are you telling us that you and David Sayers were the only teachers Imogen spoke to?"

"I'm not aware of anyone in a position of authority that would say they felt Imogen didn't pay them due respect. Oh, I see; Imogen must have had David's phone number. The Head of Year is an important role in which David leads and manages the progress and pastoral provision for our Year 12 students. He's passionate about his subject and is a strong classroom practitioner who can engage pupils. So I'm not surprised Imogen considered him a mentor and someone she could confide in."

"Well, she *was* hiding something," said Tony.

"I'm not sure what you mean," said Rosemary.

"Imogen was gay, wasn't she?" he said.

"Heavens, no," said Rosemary. "Is that why you think she was killed?"

"Elaine was adamant we were mistaken," said Julie. "Imogen wore a rainbow-coloured hairband the morning she died."

"I thought you were better trained than that," said Rosemary. "Yes, I've heard boys at school pass comments about several of the girls. This year's bunch is no different to the boys at school with me. If they ask a girl out and she refuses, then they must be gay. If they take a girl out and she doesn't give them what they want, she's frigid or a lesbian. That story is as old as time."

"So the hairband was merely a way of showing support for the gay students and teachers at the school?" asked Tony.

"A rather simplistic explanation, but yes," said Rosemary.

"Imogen never had boyfriends, even before she became fixated on the goals she'd set," said Julie.

"I'm sure you've learned Imogen was immature, not physically but emotionally. I watched her develop from eleven when she came here. Because her parents sheltered her from the worst elements of modern life, Imogen avoided adding to the long list of unwanted teenage pregnancies. But, like her classmates, she flirted with boys when she was thirteen or fourteen. I'm sure, in time, she would have found the perfect partner. A boy who loved to run and who cared about others less fortunate. A young man who paid more than lip service to diversity and tolerance."

"Guys like that are thin on the ground," said Tony.

"You have to look in the right place, Detective Sergeant. Imogen would have found the time to do that once she'd completed her education. I didn't marry until I was thirty-eight. Everyone's in such a rush these days, and it's no surprise that so many marriages fail."

Despite spending a fair amount of time with Rosemary Oram, they didn't discover anything that pointed to a potential motive or suspect.

The next day, Julie and Tony interviewed David Sayers. They stood in the corridor outside his office until he finished a telephone conversation.

"Good afternoon, Mr Sayers," said Julie. "I'm DI Kemp. My colleague, DS Wyvern, and I are interviewing those closest to Imogen Henderson."

"You flatter me," said David Sayers. "The news of Immie's death was a terrible shock. She had so much she wanted to achieve, and I was positive that young woman would make a lasting contribution in whichever field she eventually chose."

"Many students have a clear vision of where they're going," said Julie. "I knew I was joining the police from the age of twelve. A local detective visited our school to warn us of stranger danger. There had been sightings of a man outside the school gates, and one morning someone was spotted lurking among the trees close to the tennis courts. Mr Godsell was mowing the grass on the main field, but when he stopped the mower and ran to where he'd seen the man, the intruder was no longer on the school premises."

"You wanted to make a difference, I presume," said David. "Immie was interested in climate change, the plight of refugees, and so much more. We often spoke about which direction a particular degree course would lead her. But, sadly, she hadn't made up her mind about what to study."

"Do you attend Christ Church?" asked Tony.

"Not me," said David. "The last time I set foot in a church was when my parents had me christened. After that, I never felt the need to go back."

"Did you ever meet Imogen outside of school?" asked Julie.

"On a couple of occasions. But I was with Matt, my partner. It wouldn't have been appropriate to be seen alone with a student."

"Were these social occasions?" asked Tony.

"Imogen and a handful of her friends joined Matt and me at a café in town when we got engaged. An informal afternoon tea since neither of us drinks alcohol. I only recall speaking to Imogen off the premises outside the railway station. We were on our way into Bath one evening for a spot of late-night Christmas shopping, and Immie was walking her dog."

"Was she alone?" asked Tony.

"It wasn't unusual," said David. "Immie wasn't the gregarious sort. Our train was due in five minutes; therefore, we couldn't chat for long. I asked how she was, and Immie seemed glad I stopped. I thought I saw someone in the shadows moving out of sight around the corner. Whether Immie got closer to the station because it was well-lit and had more people around, I don't know."

"Imogen may have had a stalker?" asked Tony.

"I couldn't possibly say. I didn't see more than a shadow."

"Your role means you provide emotional, spiritual, and social care to sixty-odd students. Is that a fair assessment?" asked Julie.

"When they all turn up, it's close to that number," said David.

"Imogen only had a small circle of loyal friends," said Julie. "Who did she fall out with from her year group? Who might have followed or approached her last December? We are talking about last Christmas, aren't we, when you and Matt Cotton saw her at the station?"

"I don't recall anyone Immie fell out with," said David. "It's hard to fall out with someone you have zero connection with. But, yes, it was last December."

"Can you remember where Imogen was on January the nineteenth this year?" asked Tony.

"That's very specific," said David. "I'd need to check."

He got up and walked to a three-drawer filing cabinet beside his desk. After searching a folder, he sat down again.

"Immie was at home recovering from an emergency appendectomy," he said.

"Where were you at a quarter to eight last Sunday morning, Mr Sayers?" asked Tony. "Just for elimination purposes?"

"We're never out of bed that early on a Sunday, Detective Sergeant. Matt and I deserve to take advantage of every hour recharging our batteries before we resume battle with the children on Monday morning."

Julie and Tony walked through the maze of corridors to the school's main entrance and stopped outside in the car park.

"You didn't seriously consider Sayers was responsible?" asked Julie.

"No, but he was a bit smug. I wanted to remind him we were dealing with a murder. What about the other question?"

"January the nineteenth? You wondered whether the killer planned to attack Imogen on the anniversary of Tammie's death. The sighting at the railway station could have been preliminary scouting to establish her routines."

"Appendicitis only delayed her death if that was the case," said Tony.

"Look at it as a positive, Tony," said Julie. "Whatever the trigger was for our man to murder Imogen, it was personal."

"We have no names in the frame, boss. Neither teacher suggested a student who took issue with Imogen over anything. Are we more certain now the two murders were carried out by the same person?"

"Both victims were strangled," said Julie. "There was a significant degree of planning for each attack. Although neither girl was raped, there were indications the killer wanted sexual intercourse. So it seems more likely than not."

"Are we looking for a teenage boy, boss?" asked Tony.

"Could someone her age have strangled Tammie?" asked Julie. "I doubt it, somehow. If a young lad had moved Tammie's body, it would have been covered in evidence. But, unfortunately, there was no transferred DNA to identify, and Shobna Patel didn't find any trace of semen."

"Point taken, boss. A young lad and his first time and all that."

"Quite," said Julie. "Imogen was older, taller, fitter. A sixteen or seventeen-year-old doesn't fit the attacker's profile in my head. When we get back to the police station, can you follow up on the social media angle? Let's see if that's uncovered anything."

"Okay, boss," said Tony.

Julie went to her office and called Eddie Stokes.

"Did anything come from the house-to-house, Eddie?"

"I'm afraid not, ma'am. Steve and Elaine Henderson have lived in that house for a decade. They've never fallen out with anyone, but few had a good word to say about the wife. They call her Aunty Elaine because she's anti-everything. Most considered Steve a decent bloke who spent as much time at work as possible to avoid being home. Imogen was snooty but not as intolerant as her mother. Zack can be moody at times. The most popular member of the household is Rebel, the dog."

"What about Woolley Street?"

"Two guys were standing by a blue van near the gastropub on Sunday morning. That was around eight o'clock. Half a dozen near neighbours mentioned seeing that. The landlord had paid a couple of lads to take away an old upright freezer. We spoke to everyone involved, but they were too busy to see anything happening several hundred yards along the street."

"Anything from passing pedestrians or motorists?" asked Julie.

"Not a sausage, ma'am," said Eddie. "I'll get someone to fetch those message boards later in the week. They're just cluttering the pavement. Sorry, we can't offer anything positive."

Julie wondered whether this case would prove as fruitless an exercise as Tammie Kenyon's. Tony Wyvern popped his head around her office door just as she was getting ready to go home.

"What do you know about incels, boss?" he asked.

"I know it stands for involuntary celibate," said Julie. "People who define themselves as incel say they lack a sex life despite wanting to be in a relationship. A website offered support for lonely people who felt left behind twenty years ago. Has this come from trawling through the social media accounts of students from the school? Please don't tell me one of the teachers defines himself that way."

"One of Eddie's guys widened the net to include people who lived within a five-mile radius of the town."

"Initiative like that will get them out of uniform in a flash. You'll need to watch your back, Tony."

"Yes, boss. Anyway, since the days when that website gained popularity or notoriety, incel beliefs morphed. Some forums are full of self-pity. Some are dominated by grievance. It's mostly men participating in these forums, and they share an unfulfilled sense of entitlement to sex that women withhold from them."

"Did this guy find a likely candidate living in Bradford-on-Avon?" asked Julie.

"He hasn't identified anyone yet, boss. It's not as easy as taking down a name and address from their profile and sending a car round to pick them up. A forum can have as many as ten thousand active members hiding behind fake names. The threads they post can advocate violence against women, but you can't say the whole of the incel subculture is violent. You might think these people are deluded, but the overriding view Eddie's guy got was that they truly believe their fate is sealed from birth by forces beyond their control."

"When I joined the police, the old-timers would tell me about the good old days," sighed Julie. "There might have been a lot wrong with how we operated back then, but it was far easier to spot a criminal. Those old coppers really *did* arrest people carrying a bag of swag over their shoulder."

"As for students with active social media accounts who attended the school or had just left, they've gone back to posts from Year 7 and found nothing, so far, to indicate any antagonism against either of our victims."

"Hard to believe with online bullying being in the news so often that these teenagers appear squeaky clean," said Julie.

"Oh, I wouldn't go that far, boss," said Tony. "Not everyone from the school escapes criticism or discrimination. It's shocking to read stuff from kids using derisive terms for those who classify themselves as transgender or non-binary. Most of it is uninformed rubbish."

"We must keep digging to discover whether any of it disguises a grain of truth," said Julie.

"We don't have many leads to follow, boss," said Tony. "Are you heading home?"

"I need to finish the weekly shop this evening," she replied. "I have a busy weekend planned with Emily."

"Have fun, boss," said Tony. "We intend to. Sally and I have the house to ourselves. Nicole is staying with one of her friends."

Despite events over the following weekend, the investigation led by DI Julie Kemp into the two murders ground to a halt. Over two years later, she and Tony Wyvern were working out of the Trowbridge police station. But, as with so many investigations, time and resources took their toll.

Chapter Ten

Monday, 22 October 2018

"WAKEY, WAKEY, SLEEPY HEAD," said Suzie. "You can't be late on your first day back."

Gus rolled out of bed and headed for the bathroom. Why hadn't Suzie let him finish that dream? It had involved Bert Penman and a giant cauliflower.

When he reached the kitchen, the waffle maker was two minutes from producing his breakfast—plenty of time to choose which fresh berries to top them with and pour a coffee.

"Was it because we had a busy day and a late night?" asked Suzie. "Or aren't you looking forward to what you'll hear when you get to London Road?"

"I've got to sit through stories of 'what we did on our holidays from the team first. Just like when I was eight at junior school, the first day after the long summer break."

"I hope you listen closely or take notes," said Suzie. "I want to hear all about it tonight."

Gus sighed. It was going to be a long day.

They left the bungalow at twenty-five past eight, and he followed Suzie through the gateway into the lane. He didn't hit anything because there had been several opportunities to practice with his new car. Unfortunately, two weeks wasn't nearly enough for the work to be completed on London Road, so they took the detour without a second thought.

Suzie disappeared with a wave, and Gus joined the Monday procession into town. Nobody seemed rushed this morning, which suited his mood just fine.

Gus parked his Ford Focus at the end of the row. Neil had arrived before him, but it was only five to nine. Perhaps the others weren't desperate to return to work either. So he rode up in the lift alone and was greeted like a long-lost friend.

"Morning, guv," said Neil. "You have no idea how glad I am to see you. Melody and her mother gave me a list of decorating jobs as long as your arm. Unfortunately, I didn't get a chance for a pint with my mates until last Thursday."

"Did you get everything done?" asked Gus.

"I thought I'd finished on Thursday afternoon, guv," said Neil. "But when mother-in-law dropped by on Saturday, she convinced Melody the rooms I didn't re-decorate now look shabby in comparison. Melody reckons I can forget about the weekends between now and Christmas."

"You want everything ready for the baby, Neil," said Gus. "And the smell of fresh paint will have gone by the New Year if you get stuck in."

"I was hoping for sympathy, guv," said Neil. "I suppose you put your feet up for two weeks."

"Hardly, Neil," said Gus. "I replaced my old car with a newer model, worked hard on my allotment, and had a general clear-out in the garden and indoors. The spare bedroom is now the nursery."

"Glad to hear I wasn't the only one," said Neil. "Sounds like we've got company."

The lift returned to the ground floor, and Alex, Lydia and Blessing emerged one minute later.

Neil shared his war stories with the others while Gus re-acquainted himself with the Gaggia. He listened to Blessing telling the others that she had introduced Jamie to her parents. Lydia asked whether this meant a wedding was on the horizon. Blessing said it was still early days. They were enjoying being single at present. Although, when she took Maryam to Bath shopping, her mother insisted on looking at a selection of hats.

Gus soon learned that Chidozie Barre was selling his bar restaurant in Rotterdam and moving to Dubai full-time. He was glad Lydia had found her birth parents again, and by the sound of things, Alex and Lydia had their Christmas and New Year activities sorted well ahead of time. He hadn't given the matter of his first Christmas with Suzie a second thought. It hadn't been a factor in the recent past.

"No sign of Grace this morning?" he asked.

"Did you know she accepted Jackie's offer of a room, guv?" asked Blessing.

"Suzie told me," he replied.

"Grace spent the first week at Gablecross on a special project," said Blessing. "Because she wasn't sure whether she'd be able to get to Worton on Thursday evening, Grace told Jackie she'd give the Thursday Dining Club a miss. When she moves in, a vegan alternative will be on the menu every night."

"Ooh," said Lydia. "A special project. I wonder what that's about?"

"Mr Mercer told her not to breathe a word," said Blessing.

"I wonder what's keeping her today," said Alex.

"I suggested she used her one-week holiday to get in touch with her family," said Blessing. "Perhaps they locked her in the tower and won't let her out until she agrees to become a lawyer like the rest of her family."

Gus thought it more likely Grace was with Geoff Mercer right now, stirring the cauldron ahead of his lunchtime session with the Chief Constable.

"We could tell what you did while you were away, guv," said Lydia. "How on earth did you persuade Suzie to let you stick with a Ford Focus?"

"It was a joint decision," Gus complained. "Five years younger than my old jalopy, and Suzie's happy it will suit our needs in the springtime."

"I don't remember reading of any window problems with that model, guv," said Neil.

"That wasn't high on our list of concerns, Neil," said Gus. "Space and economy were more important features."

"Has anyone heard from Luke while we were away?" asked Alex.

"Not a dicky bird," said Neil.

"I hope he didn't get into trouble," Blessing said.

Gus wasn't one to wish the time away, but the sooner he could leave for London Road, the better. Sometimes, the gods look down on you and answer your prayers. His phone rang.

"Gus? Geoff Mercer, can you meet us in my office in half an hour?"

Saved by the bell. Gus searched his desk for folders before remembering they had delivered the final reports on the last case. There was nothing for it; he had to face the music.

"I may be some time," he said to the team as he headed for the lift.

Gus drove his bright new Focus out of the Crime Review Team parking bay without incident and eased into traffic on Church Street. Light rain dappled the windscreen as he drove to the outskirts of town. As he climbed Caen Hill towards Devizes, the rain stopped, and he convinced himself there was nothing to worry about.

Accessing the visitors' car park at London Road was getting easier. The new strip of fresh tarmac signalled the progress made in the past month. Or lack of progress, depending on your point of view. Traffic cones disappeared into the distance, which annoyed everyone and highlighted how much further that narrow strip had to go before things returned to normal.

Gus hunted further and further from the main entrance for a space, eventually reversing into one close to the Hub building. Tess used to chastise him for taking the trouble to reverse the car when parking. Gus argued that he preferred to drive straight out when he returned to the car, especially in unfamiliar places. The world would be a dull place if everyone thought the same.

As he crossed to the main building, the sun was peeking through the dark clouds. Was that a good sign? Once inside the door, Gus spotted a familiar face, The young constable that had played a prank on him a while back. He still looked as if he should be at school, but a policeman's life is not a happy one, and Gus sensed early signs of someone who realised he was fighting a losing battle.

Gus signed in, nodded to the youngster, and headed upstairs to the mezzanine.

"It's like marriage, lad," he called out. "The first ten years are the worst."

When he reached the admin area, Vera Butler heard his voice and was poised, ready to intercept him.

"Welcome back, Gus," she said. "Amazing Grace is with Geoff Mercer. I thought I'd warn you. As for Kenneth, he left for an urgent meeting with the PCC. He told me he expected to be back for your get-together."

"As long as he hasn't got someone from HR with him," said Gus.

"Don't be silly. We don't get rid of our best people. Not by choice, at least."

"Kassie has news," said Vera.

"News rather than gossip," said Gus. "That makes a change. So, did the sartorial makeover bring positive results?"

"Almost immediately," said Vera. "While you were planning a trip to the seaside, Kassie was being wined and dined by a young doctor."

"Divya Yadav had a word with her husband, is that it?" asked Gus.

"The good doctor works long hours in Swindon, but he has a healthy appetite."

"That's enough," said Gus. "I don't think I want to hear any details."

"A healthy appetite for food, Gus," said Vera. "Watch out. Geoff's standing at the end of the corridor. You had better join him."

"Wish me luck," said Gus, "and tell Kassie I'm pleased for her."

Geoff spotted Gus crossing the room and returned along the dark corridor. Gus hurried to catch him.

"Come on in, and sit down, Gus," said Geoff. "Grace

has completed her investigation. We want to bring you up to speed."

Grace looked up from the folder she was reading and smiled. Why did that always unnerve him, Gus thought as he took the only other chair in the room.

"I asked Grace to work from Gablecross during the first week of the CRT's holiday," said Geoff.

"Tell me something I don't know," said Gus. "Blessing told everyone as soon as we returned to work this morning. She didn't know what Grace was asked to do while there, but it wouldn't take a genius to work out it was related to Luke Sherman."

"I spent time in Swindon and Portishead, Gus," said Grace. "Several officers I worked with in the past were prepared to give me a fuller picture of what was going on than the party line from the top brass."

"The top brass wanted to brush the whole incident under the carpet, I presume," said Gus.

"That's about the size of it, Gus," said Geoff. "However, Grace has learned that things went deeper than we thought, even after speaking with Luke in Brent Knoll."

"Why don't you run through what you found from the beginning, Grace?" asked Gus.

"The die was cast several months ago," said Grace. "Luke and his partner, Nicky, had lived together for some time, and Luke's career only caused a slight niggle in their relationship. Luke worked more regular hours in the months before you needed an armed bodyguard during one of your early cases. Weeks later, you made him a full-time team member, and things changed. Despite that, he and Nicky felt settled enough in their relationship to get engaged. Over the following months, matters deteriorated, and the niggle became an excruciating pain. Nicky told

Luke he'd become more and more distant with each successive case, and it was clear he thought more of dead people than he did of him. There was no way back after that."

"I remember when Luke arrived in the office after the fight with Nicky," Gus said. "He told us they'd grown apart and accepted Nicky's criticism that his work had always come first. But, unfortunately, Luke couldn't see that situation changing, so the break-up was inevitable."

"It was obvious Luke was troubled," said Geoff. "He soon came to me, wanting a transfer. So you and I discussed what we thought we could do to stop him leaving, and I must admit, I thought the move to Gablecross was the best workaround."

"Luke could tackle a variety of cases in Swindon rather than digging into unsolved murders," said Gus. "I hoped we might see him return to the team once he'd got the wanderlust out of his system. When I met Tom Spencer at the Waggon & Horses, I thought a new relationship might cement Luke's presence in Wiltshire, and if that was the case, the door could remain open for the foreseeable future."

"I made matters worse by assigning Luke to the joint operation with Portishead," said Geoff. "If Luke hadn't suddenly become available, Rick Chalmers would have continued to flip-flop between various undercover tasks with Hampshire & Dorset or Avon & Somerset. Rick had been on the botched Larcombe Manor raid, so it made more sense for him to join the surveillance group. Instead, I opted to send Luke."

"You can't blame yourself, Geoff," said Gus. "Rick had spent weeks chasing illegal immigrants on the south coast, and then he played hide-and-seek among the trees near

Larcombe. He needed a rest, even if he probably spent his two weeks holiday drinking lager and eating fast food."

"I spoke with DS Spencer at Gablecross, Gus," said Grace. "The signs were there in Luke's behaviour, but nobody picked up on them and reported them back to London Road."

"When I spoke to Tom on Luke's phone while we were in Burnham, it was obvious they were close," said Gus, "He said how much he missed Luke since he went undercover."

"It appears those feelings weren't mutual," said Grace. "DS Spencer said their physical relationship had never been an issue. It was new and exciting, but Luke always seemed distant in other areas, as if his mind was elsewhere. At first, Tom accepted that after ending a long-term relationship, Luke might still have been thinking of Nicky. Maybe it was too soon to expect Luke to commit. However, Tom was prepared to bide his time because he felt a connection with Luke unlike anything he'd felt before."

"Did Tom ask Luke what was troubling him?" asked Gus.

"He intended to, but Luke got the call to join the surveillance team working in Somerset," said Grace. "We both know all there is to know about that business. However, you don't know what happened while you were on holiday."

"I imagine Luke wasn't popular with the top brass at Portishead," said Gus. "Nor with the other surveillance team members, which he abandoned. The last thing the Chief Constable said to me was he hoped to sort the unholy mess before we returned to work."

"I was in a meeting with former colleagues at Portishead the Thursday before last when the rumours filtered through. Luke spent several hours with his team leader and briefly spoke to the Avon & Somerset Chief Constable afterwards. These meetings followed several discussions following the debrief we heard about while in Burnham. Luke drove to Gablecross the following morning."

"Grace returned from Portishead and delivered the results of her investigation to me on Friday afternoon," said Geoff. "I read her report and passed it straight to Kenneth, as he instructed."

"As soon as I arrived here this morning, I received a call from DS Spencer," said Grace. "When Luke reached Gablecross that morning, he visited ACC Rebecca Gregory's office. After that meeting ended, DS Sherman cleared his desk and left without speaking to Tom Spencer or his colleagues. Rebecca Gregory contacted the Chief Constable as soon as Luke left."

"What happened next?" asked Gus. "Did Kenneth get Luke to come here and persuade him not to be reckless? Where is Luke now?"

"I'm sorry, Gus," said Grace. "My involvement ended on Friday afternoon. Don't forget, I was on holiday last week. The fact this was all news to you shows that Suzie didn't hear a whisper on the grapevine last week either. The Chief Constable kept a tight lid on things."

"Kenneth didn't even tell me he'd heard from Rebecca Gregory," said Geoff Mercer. "I'm as much in the dark as you."

"It strikes me Kenneth has landed us in a greater unholy mess than we were before," said Gus. "Our meeting should be fun."

"I hope you won't do something stupid, Gus," said Geoff. "Well, that's it. You're as much in the picture as the rest of us now. Grace can drive to the Old Police Station and join the rest of the team. Unless you have anything to ask?"

"I won't spoil the others' enjoyment, telling you what they got up to, Grace," said Gus. "You look refreshed and rested. I suppose you've started preparing for your move to Worton?"

"That won't take me more than a weekend, Gus," said Grace. "I travel light. Blessing persuaded me to get in touch with my family against my better judgement. My father was unimpressed when I told him I was one of the youngest women in the country to become a Detective Inspector. He left me alone with my mother while he cleaned his guns. My father frequents half a dozen game shooting sites in Lincolnshire. As for my mother, she was only lucid for part of my visit. None of my brothers lives at home these days, and my mother didn't recall any of them asking after their sister. A Jacobean hall can be a chilly place in winter. It was decidedly frosty when I left to drive home to Wiltshire."

"I'm pleased you think of it as home," said Geoff. "Where's Kassie with the refreshments? We haven't long before Kenneth summons Gus and me to his presence."

"I'll leave for the office now, sir," said Grace. "Kassie has trouble making my drink the way I like it."

Grace collected her things and left.

"Far be it from me to suggest that was a deliberate act on Kassie's part," said Geoff. "At least with Grace gone, I can order two sticky buns without hearing Grace tutting in the background."

"Forget your stomach, Geoff. We've got far more serious matters to discuss. Has Luke quit his job? If so, what are we doing about it, and where is he off to next?"

Geoff didn't get a chance to answer. A sharp rap on the door announced the arrival of Ms Trotter with her trolley.

"Amazing Grace has gone, thank goodness," said Kassie. "No sticky buns today, Mr Mercer. I've got a new recipe for Chester cakes from my young man, Noah Edwards."

Gus watched as Kassie revealed her latest offering.

"Irish origins, I believe, rather than Welsh, Kassie," said Gus. "In some parts of the country, they call them the fly's graveyard. Don't let the name put you off, Geoff. I'm sure they taste better than they look."

"Just one this week, please, Kassie," said Geoff.

"What about you, Mr Freeman?" asked Kassie.

"I over-indulged with the chocolate biscuits while on holiday," said Gus. "Suzie says I need to cut back on the cakes."

"You know I'll check with DI Ferris when I visit her office, don't you, Mr Freeman?"

"In that case, I'll take one, Kassie. Perhaps Mr Mercer might decide to share half with me in a minute or two."

"Noah Edwards?" asked Geoff. "Where have I heard that name?"

"Noah's a junior doctor at the Great Western Hospital in Swindon," said Kassie. "He's playing rugby for the town this season."

"Of course," said Geoff. "The club's just up the road. I'm surprised you haven't found him before."

"Noah didn't move from Chester until August, Mr Mercer. He trained with the First XV and was told the same night that he was certain to play whenever his work allowed."

"Wasn't he selected for the Welsh Under-12 and Under-14 sides?" asked Geoff.

"That's him," said Kassie.

"I imagine he's a big unit, Kassie," said Gus.

"A number eight, Gus," said Geoff.

"That's where he plays, Mr Freeman," said Kassie. "I saw your eyebrow raise."

"I have so much to learn about many sports," Gus sighed. "The terminology can get me into all kinds of trouble."

Kassie was soon on her way, and Geoff Mercer didn't take long to polish off his cake, wherever it came from.

"Are you going to eat that?" he asked, eyeing Gus's slice of Chester cake.

"I grabbed a napkin from Kassie's trolley," said Gus. "Wrap it up and stick it in your drawer for Ron."

"If he doesn't drop by this afternoon, I'll eat it," laughed Geoff. "We must keep our sense of humour intact, or we'd be lost. Come on; the witching hour has arrived."

They left Geoff's office, trudged along the dark corridor, and crossed the admin area to Kenneth's office. Geoff tapped on the door and entered. Kenneth Truelove was sitting at his desk.

"Welcome back, Freeman," he said. "I hope you took full advantage of the break?"

"I tried, sir," said Gus. "I've been back three hours, and I'm not liking anything I've heard so far."

The Chief Constable gestured they should take a seat.

"I wish I had good news, Freeman, but once ACC Gregory told me DS Sherman was hell-bent on throwing his career out the window, there was little I could do. His mind was made up. In fairness, Sherman's conduct whilst working with Avon & Somerset placed me in an invidious position. They wanted him punished for his actions. By handing in his warrant card and quitting on the spot, he helped me avoid any unpleasantness."

"Where is he now, sir? What are his intentions? Will he move into private security?"

"Calm yourself, Freeman," said Kenneth. "You know where he's gone."

"Larcombe Manor?" asked Gus. "How can he work alongside the man who killed Grant Burnside and the people who sanctioned the hit?"

"He's one of many who believe we've given up the fight," said Kenneth. "I'm afraid you'll just have to accept that we've lost him, Freeman."

Gus wasn't sure that he could.

"We have his mobile number," he said.

"Useless," said Geoff. "Luke left it with DS Spencer when he went to Portishead and never collected it. His new bosses will provide him with all the kit he needs. Luke Sherman has gone to ground, and we cannot contact him."

"Time to draw a line under the matter, Freeman," said Kenneth. "That's an order which applies to the rest of your team, too."

"We're a detective down," said Gus. "When do I get a replacement?"

"DI Packenham will stay with you until the New Year," said Geoff Mercer. "I've warned DS Chalmers he might fill in for DS Davis and yourself when you take paternity leave."

"Discussions on a permanent replacement for Luke Sherman will have to wait," said Kenneth. "We're under pressure from the PCC due to our perceived drop in performance levels across the board. He recognises we have some outstanding sectors, but the axe is hovering."

"It won't be aimed in your direction, Gus," said Geoff.

"A good point at which to introduce your next case,

Freeman," said the Chief Constable. "We can't relax because the killer may have more victims on their list."

"A potential serial killer?" asked Gus. "Where are we off to this time?"

"Bradford-on-Avon," said Kenneth. "The first young girl died in January three years ago. Tammie Kenyon was fifteen and lived with her parents, Phillip and Debbie. Tammie attended St Laurence Academy in the town. Everyone described the only child as full of fun. Tammie left home in Northleigh at twenty-five minutes to eight to walk to school for a breakfast club session. Tammie was last seen alive by a cleaner driving to the Leigh Park Country House Hotel. Karla Bates told police she saw Tammie at the crossroads close to her place of work. Tammie was alone, hurrying along the pavement, before dashing across the road in front of Ms Bates' car. Tammie's parents were at work all day, so her disappearance didn't become apparent until later that evening. They checked with her boyfriend and best friend to see whether Tammie was with them, but they hadn't seen her all day."

"Trowbridge Police sent officers to start the search at first light on Friday morning," said Geoff. "They retraced the steps Tammie should have taken from Northleigh to St Laurence, asking if anyone had seen her. At that time of the morning, it was dark and bitterly cold. They drew a blank."

"Later that day, a dog-walker found a school shoe," said Kenneth. "Rather, her dog found it in a field off Leigh Road."

"Is that close to the girl's route to school?" asked Gus.

"Tammie had to walk along that road to reach the school. A passing cyclist stopped to help Miss Metcalf, the dog-walker, retrieve her dog and the shoe. Neville Robinson had the presence of mind to call the police as soon as he got home. The field on Leigh Road was searched the following morning. The second shoe turned up in that search, and the officers found Tammie Kenyon, face down, one hundred yards further on."

"How did Tammie die?" asked Gus. "Who handled the investigation?"

"Tammie was strangled," said Geoff. "DI Julie Kemp ran the investigation, and DS Alan Quinn was her second-in-command."

"Shobna Patel, a forensic pathologist, attended the scene," said Kenneth. "The attack began close to where they found the second shoe. Missy, the dog, picked up a shoe when she was racing around the field, so we don't know when or where Tammie lost it. Mrs Patel found marks on the grass that indicated the killer dragged Tammie a hundred yards to the next field to hide the body. When Mrs Patel carried out the autopsy, she confirmed the cause of death was strangulation. Despite Tammie's trousers and underwear having been removed, there was no clear evidence to suggest a sexual motive for the attack."

"That was a blessing for her parents," said Gus.

"Her parents were unaware that Tammie was sexually active," said Kenneth. "Shobna Patel couldn't rule out a possible attempt at penetration, but the body exhibited no tissue damage indicative of force."

"The attacker removed her clothing," said Geoff.

"We can't say that categorically, Geoff," said Gus. "Tammie could have removed them herself, then changed her mind. Did they have any suspects at this stage?"

"An ex-boyfriend, Alfie Jones, eighteen, but his alibi was rock-solid. Tammie's best friend, Naomi Fletcher, could name several of the boys with whom Tammie was intimate. Still, as the days passed, it became clear to Kemp and Quinn they lacked a motive, as nobody could identify a single person who might have wished Tammie harm."

"What about the eyewitness?" asked Gus.

"She contacted the police two days after the body had been found," said Kenneth. "Karla Bates couldn't add to what I read you earlier. Karla confirmed the girl she spotted by the crossroads was Tammie Kenyon. The girl had dashed across the road to reach the pavement on Leigh Road. Nobody was chasing her or waiting for her on the other side."

"Is that it?" asked Gus. "What else did they try?"

"They appealed for information in the press and placed boards beside the spot where Tammie was last seen. Nothing came from either approach. They eliminated the usual suspects. DI Kemp appealed for new information on the anniversary of Tammie's death, and Tammie's best friend helped reconstruct Tammie's journey in 2015. Once again, Julie Kemp's efforts proved fruitless."

"When was the next attack?" asked Gus.

"On a warm Sunday morning in May," said Kenneth. "Imogen Henderson, seventeen, left home in Springfield Avenue at seven-thirty. She planned to complete her usual Sunday morning run before the family went to church. Imogen lived with her parents, Steve and Elaine, and Zack, her thirteen-year-old brother."

"How far did she run?" asked Gus.

"Two-and-a-half to three miles," said Kenneth. "Zack left home with the family dog after his sister had been gone for thirty minutes. Dad started to wonder where she was at half-past eight. He jumped into the car and searched the route, expecting to find an injured runner. Nobody along the route had seen anything untoward, so Steve Henderson called the police, and uniformed officers started the search. Sergeant Eddie Stokes, who had been Crime Scene Manager on the Kenyon case, got involved. He suspected foul play and increased the number of boots on the ground. Imogen's body was discovered in the far corner of a field between Woolley Street and Woolley Grange."

"Where's that in relation to the first murder site?" asked Gus.

"A couple of fields across," said Geoff Mercer. "Half a mile at most."

"Did the same team of detectives investigate?" asked Gus.

"Several team members were the same," said Kenneth. "DI Kemp was in charge. Eddie Stokes was the Crime Scene Manager, and Shobna Patel conducted the post-mortem. She was in Bradford-on-Avon on Sunday evening and responded to a call to the murder scene. Julie Kemp had DS Tony Wyvern working with her this time. DS Quinn had transferred to your old patch at Bourne Hill."

"What were the highlights of the murder scene?" asked Gus.

"The victim had vivid bruising to the neck but no other visible injuries. The thorough search of the fields on either side of the road started in the early afternoon. The body was discovered at a quarter to seven. Mrs Patel told detectives that Imogen's running watch had features which would enable her to confirm the time of death. Imogen's run was interrupted between seven-forty and seven-forty-five."

"A similar methodology, so far," said Gus. "An early morning, well-planned attack, followed by manual strangulation. Any signs of sexual activity?"

"Imogen's clothing had been disturbed, not removed," said Kenneth. "Nothing found. Mrs Patel confirmed Imogen was a virgin."

"By the sound of it, we have two women from different backgrounds who attended the same school. The attacks took place in isolated spots at different times of the year. The killer didn't leave evidence on the neck or anywhere else, so we assume they wore gloves. Fine, in January, but odd in May unless gloves were a necessary piece of kit in their line of work. I presume nobody saw anything along this stretch of road?"

Kenneth nodded.

"Imogen was popular, never fell out with anyone, and nobody could understand why someone wanted to hurt her?"

"A familiar story, Gus," said Geoff.

"Please tell me there was something we could get our teeth into?"

"Mrs Patel mentioned a faint smell on Tammie Kenyon's body that seemed unusual for a girl who never wore make-up to school," said Kenneth. "She had a similar experience viewing Imogen's body on Sunday evening."

"Was Mrs Patel able to identify this scent?" asked Gus.

"No," said Kenneth, "and it could simply have been transfer from an officer's deodorant on Leigh Road when they turned Tammie's body. However, that wasn't the case at the second site. Shobna Patel recorded her findings, but the detectives never found a suspect to test the theory."

"Did they follow standard lines of enquiry in both cases?" asked Gus.

"They planned to follow a similar schedule to the Kenyon case," said Geoff. "But after they broke the news to the parents, they realised just how different the two girls were."

"Tell me more," said Gus.

"Imogen would use deodorant daily, but a minimum of make-up," said Kenneth. "Tammie wore far more make-up when she wasn't at school. Imogen was a sixth-former, and the rules were more relaxed. When the subject of boyfriends was raised, Elaine Henderson was adamant her daughter showed no interest in boys, which seemed to concern her. DI Kemp asked Elaine if her daughter was gay. That opened a can of worms. Elaine Henderson has rather puritanical views. The internet was off-limits in the house, and Imogen didn't even get a basic mobile phone until she was sixteen. Steve and Elaine had access to that phone at all times. Tammie had access to social media, and her parents didn't monitor her activities as closely as they might have. Their short lives couldn't have been much different."

"What attracted the killer to these two girls?" asked Gus. "I'm not seeing a pattern."

"Steve Henderson admitted his daughter was driven in her ambition to gain acceptance to Cambridge. However, he believed Imogen pushed the idea of a boyfriend aside until she had achieved her goals."

"I don't suppose anything useful came from the mobile phone?" asked Gus.

"Mum, Dad, grandparents, two teachers, and a dozen schoolfriends in her contacts," said Kenneth.

"Teachers?" asked Gus. "Tess was always wary of giving a phone number to a student,"

"Imogen's godmother, Rosemary Oram, was one of those contacts. The other was Head of Year 12, David

Sayers, who was engaged to Matthew Cotton, also a teacher."

"Another dead end," said Gus.

"Kemp and Wyvern interviewed the students but found nothing to suggest there was anyone who hated Imogen enough to kill her. Most said she was snooty, which confirmed her father's assertion that Imogen didn't mix with people because she didn't want distractions. Rosemary Oram was a churchgoer who'd known Elaine Henderson since they were at school. She was adamant Imogen wasn't gay."

"What made DI Kemp think it in the first place?" asked Gus.

"A rainbow-coloured hairband on the body," said Kenneth.

"Is that all?" said Gus.

"Mrs Oram told them Imogen supported a wide variety of good causes," said Kenneth. "When they spoke to David Sayers, he raised the possibility of a stalker. Just a glimpse when Imogen bumped into him and his partner near the railway station. That occasion was in December 2015. DS Wyvern asked if Sayers could recall where Imogen was on January the nineteenth. Sayers told him she was recovering from an emergency appendectomy,"

"Wyvern wondered whether the killer planned to strike on the same day as Tammie Kenyon," said Gus. "Interesting."

"Kemp was certain the same person carried out the two murders," said Kenneth. "Both victims were strangled, and there was significant planning for each attack. Neither girl was raped, but there were signs the killer intended to have sexual intercourse."

"Although, in both cases, the lack of DNA evidence

suggests they couldn't perform," said Geoff Mercer. "After a couple of weeks, the team had few leads to follow."

"The investigation hit the buffers," sighed Gus. "Kemp and Wyvern were destined to get assigned to other cases with more chance of a result."

"Not at that point," said Kenneth. "There was another attack on Sunday, the sixteenth of May. Seven days after Imogen Henderson's murder."

Chapter Eleven

"ESCALATION IS NEVER A GOOD SIGN," said Gus. "Another attack, one week after an eighteen-month gap, is unusual."

"It was unsuccessful, thank goodness," said Geoff.

"DI Kemp always believed the victims knew their attacker," said Kenneth. "That's why she focussed on their schoolfriends, teachers, and ancillary staff. The Hub also provided the names of likely offenders within a ten-mile radius of the town. Everyone who came into contact with Tammie and Imogen outside school was also briefly considered a possible suspect."

"One by one, they were discounted," said Geoff.

"What made the third girl different?" asked Gus.

"She was fifteen and attended King Edward's School in Bath," said Kenneth. "Her parents had moved from Bristol to Bradford-on-Avon towards the end of 2015. Because of his work, her father didn't want his daughter to find it difficult to make new friends or be bullied. So, he looked for a good school in the city where his wife worked."

"The fog is clearing," said Gus.

"DS Tony Wyvern's daughter, Nicole, was the girl who was attacked," said Geoff.

"Tony and Sally Wyvern were enjoying a weekend alone, while Nicole stayed with a school friend, who also lived near Bradford-on-Avon," said Kenneth. "Her friend's father had collected Nicole on Friday evening from her home near Maplecroft, Leigh Road West. After spending Friday and Saturday night sleeping at a house in Great Cumberwell, Nicole was due to be collected by her parents."

"A balloon went up somewhere," said Gus.

"Sally Wyvern had booked a round of golf with three work colleagues and wasn't due home until early afternoon. She had left at eight o'clock for Bowood. Tony had agreed to fetch Nicole as soon as she was ready to come home; however, an urgent call from Polebarn Road saw him driving to Trowbridge ten minutes later. When Nicole called home at eight-thirty, she got no reply and started to walk home."

"Risky, given the circumstances," said Gus.

"Nicole and her friend argued," said Kenneth. "She didn't want to hang around the house all day as planned. But, unfortunately, the girl's parents were still in bed, so Nicole took a fifteen-minute walk instead."

"If it was the same attacker, they hadn't stalked Nicole for weeks, establishing a routine as they had with the others," said Gus. "Perhaps it was an opportunist attack by someone on that list the Hub produced."

"That argument didn't convince Sally Wyvern," said Geoff. "She feared the killer was aware her husband was part of the team investigating the latest murder and had tried to assault Nicole as a warning. She suggested Julie

Kemp should check with her ex-husband, Vince, to see whether any strangers had been seen near their home. Sally thought DI Kemp's daughter, Emily, who was now attending St Laurence Academy, would be the next target."

"Where did the attack take place?" asked Gus.

"Nicole had left Great Cumberwell and was heading for the A363. She intended to follow the pavement on the right-hand side of the road almost to her front door. Nicole sensed someone behind her as she rounded a bend in the lane, under a row of oak trees."

"An isolated spot, not visible from the road," said Geoff.

"The trees also screened the pair from golfers on the Cumberwell course," said Kenneth.

"Did Nicole's attacker speak to her? What happened next?" asked Gus.

"Nicole tried to run, but her attacker grabbed the rucksack on her back and dragged her to the ground. She was face-down on a grass verge with her attacker straddling her, pinning her arms under her chest. They were too strong for her. She seized her chance when she felt her attacker shift their weight to force a hand between her legs. Her assailant was slightly off-balance, and Nicole thrashed from side to side, freeing her arms. Then she pushed herself onto all fours, kicked out, and heard a yell of pain. She didn't look back but ran like blazes to the main road."

"Did her attacker attempt to follow?" asked Gus.

"The A363 wasn't busy at a quarter to nine on a Sunday morning," said Kenneth. "However, there was always a chance a car or a pedestrian would appear at any moment. Nicole wasn't followed and ran home, locked, bolted the door, and waited until her mother returned. Tony Wyvern was tied up with a stabbing at an all-night party in Westbury until five o'clock."

"So, Nicole was unable to give a description?"

"She could hear them panting and grunting while they struggled on the grass verge. Nicole told her father she kept her eyes tight shut during the ordeal because she didn't want to see their face. When her attacker tried to interfere with her, they placed a hand on her neck, holding her down. Nicole was positive they wore a leather glove on that hand."

"Anything else?" asked Gus.

"When Nicole kicked out, she wasn't sure whether she contacted a shin or a knee, but the yell it produced was high-pitched. Nicole said it felt good to have hurt them."

"We'll speak to her again if her parents don't mind," said Gus. "If it was the same attacker, Nicole's the only person we know who has lived to tell the tale."

"Well, those were the highlights, Freeman," said Kenneth. "DI Kemp and DS Wyvern continued investigating the murders while another pair of Trowbridge detectives hunted for the person who attacked Nicole Wyvern."

"Then, everything ground to a halt, and the detectives moved to different cases," said Gus.

"You might discover Nicole's attack was unrelated to the two murders," said Kenneth. "Either way, there have been no further attacks."

The Chief Constable closed the folder and handed it to Gus.

"Give it your best shot, Freeman," he said, " and remember what I said earlier."

Gus realised they were ending their session far sooner than usual. No bacon baps or chicken wraps today. Geoff Mercer looked mortified.

"What?" asked Kenneth. "Can't I take an afternoon off for once?"

Gus and Geoff left him buttoning his jacket and left his office.

"Good hunting, Gus," said Geoff as they reached the top of the stairs.

"We might need to try a different approach with this case, Geoff," said Gus. "I can't see the wood for the trees at present."

Gus trotted down the stairs, left the main building, and crossed the car park to his Ford Focus. As he prepared to drive onto London Road, Kenneth Truelove's car eased in front of him and disappeared towards the town centre with a wave.

As Gus joined the queue of traffic heading out of Devizes, he wondered how Kenneth could treat the loss of an excellent detective in such a casual manner. After all, Wiltshire Police had invested a great deal of time and money getting Luke to the position he held ten days ago. But suddenly, they were content to write it off, tell his colleagues to forget him, and move on.

The closer Gus got to the Old Police Station office, the angrier he became. Finally, when he turned into the Church Street car park, he looked at the four cars in the Crime Review Team spaces. Who was he kidding?

He had suffered the same fate as Luke had almost four years ago. After devoting nearly forty years of service to the force, they'd shown him the door. The only person who hadn't forgotten him and moved on was Kenneth Truelove. Whatever the make-up of the team upstairs, it wouldn't exist without Kenneth persuading him to have another crack at what he did best.

Gus parked beside Neil's car, grabbed the folder, and joined his team. They had another double-murder to solve.

"Back already, guv?" asked Neil. "Is that a good omen or not?"

"The Chief Constable had a half-day," said Gus. "Grace, is everyone up to speed?"

"Yes, Gus," she replied. "Nobody enjoyed hearing what happened to Luke, but it is what it is."

"I received strict instructions that the matter is closed," said Gus. "If you want to get something off your chest, do it now."

"I'm not happy we can't contact Luke to tell him how we feel, guv," said Lydia.

"Lydia speaks for all of us, guv," said Blessing. "Luke was a friend, as well as a colleague. It doesn't seem right. It's as if he no longer exists."

"You're preaching to the converted, Blessing," said Gus. "But, as Grace points out, it is what it is, and this team cannot change that. We must draw a line, move on, and do what they pay us to do, which is to investigate cold cases."

Gus waved the folder he'd brought from London Road.

"Two young girls strangled, eighteen months apart," he said. "Followed by what could have been either an attempted murder, a copycat, or a random sexual assault one week after the second murder."

"A tangled web," said Lydia.

"First, I'll take you through the key events," said Gus, "and then we'll discuss the best way to organise our investigation."

"Where did these attacks take place, guv?" asked Alex.

"Bradford-on-Avon," said Gus. "Blessing, can you call Divya, please? We need a large street map of the town. I suggest the scope of our detailed area maps should extend three miles outside the town boundary."

"Were these attacks more recent than our usual cold

cases, guv?" asked Neil. "Are we investigating what the press called the Morning Murders?"

"Two girls who attended the same school," said Alex. "That was only a couple of years ago when I worked at Gablecross."

Gus spent the next hour running through the headlines. When he'd finished, Lydia removed the crime scene photos from the folder and attached them to the wallboards. Blessing told Gus that Divya had promised she could collect the maps on her way to work in the morning.

"DI Kemp still works at Polebarn Road, guv," said Neil. "I remember seeing her name on an office door when we were there several weeks ago."

"DS Wyvern's still there too, Neil, according to the folder," said Grace. "Alan Quinn has been promoted to Inspector at Bourne Hill. So we shouldn't have trouble getting to speak with them."

"Let's not arrange interviews just yet," said Gus. "Although the detectives involved carried out a thorough investigation, based on everything I've read in the folder, they couldn't establish an irrefutable motive for these attacks. Every line of enquiry proved a dead-end, which meant they didn't identify a single possible suspect."

"How do you suggest we tackle this case, Gus?" asked Grace.

"I want to concentrate on the fields where the attacks took place," said Gus. "Is it possible the killer was connected to those locations?"

"If those fields belonged to the same farmer, surely DI Kemp and her team would have realised it, guv," said Lydia. "You reckoned they carried out a solid investigation."

"There's no record of any farm labourers being interviewed, guv," said Alex. "The only mention of a farmer was when the police searched the field on Leigh Road after the shoe had been found."

"They needed someone to unlock the gate for the forensic crew to transfer equipment closer to the action," said Neil. "I don't remember seeing that farmer's name in the murder file, guv."

"That's an angle we can pursue, Gus," said Grace.

"Fair enough," said Gus. "Add that to the flip chart."

"I noticed with the Imogen Henderson case they paid scant attention to social media," said Blessing. "That usually offers a wealth of background information."

"In fairness, Imogen's parents barred her from accessing the internet, Blessing," said Lydia. "Or at least her mother did. However, DI Kemp asked that someone scrutinise the accounts of anyone relevant. Is there a report on that in the appendix?"

"Yes," said Alex. "I was flicking through items that might not have been included in the highlights. For example, DC Anderson trawled through Facebook, and although Imogen didn't have an account, girls and boys from her school referred to her from time to time."

"Bonnie Anderson was Family Liaison Officer on the Tammie Kenyon case," said Neil. "She looks to be a jack-of-all-trades."

"Tammie Kenyon had several social media accounts, with plenty of friends or followers," said Lydia. "It's shocking some of the stuff kids post on social media for the world and his wife to see, isn't it?"

"Why wasn't Tammie's account closed?" asked Gus.

"Often, the family keep an account for a loved one open for years," said Blessing. "I'm not sure whether I like that or not."

"Did Bonnie Anderson uncover anything that might help us?" asked Alex.

"When you were at school, did you have a nickname, Alex?" asked Lydia.

"If I had, I wouldn't tell you," said Alex. "Why?"

"Nicknames were used a lot in the posts Bonnie Anderson recorded," said Blessing. "There were clues within the various accounts that allowed DC Anderson to identify the boy, or girl, being criticised, or drooled over. Teenage kids can be cruel. Bonnie highlighted one nickname she couldn't attribute to anyone from the school. Whoever it was, they were a figure of fun."

"Perhaps it was a grown-up," said Neil. "Someone well-known in the town. They shouldn't be hard to find. Male or female?"

"Bonnie couldn't determine that from the nature of the posts," said Blessing.

"DI Kemp was certain the same person carried out the two murders," said Alex. "I know we shouldn't assume it was a man, just by the cause of death, but surely everything points to a male assailant?"

"There was very little evidence recovered from either murder site," said Grace. "However, Tammie Kenyon was dragged one hundred yards from where the attack began. Whether she was dead when they dragged her to the next field remains a mystery."

"Either way, it's hard to imagine a teenage girl being able to do that," said Lydia.

"Can you add the social media aspect to the flip chart, please, Grace," said Gus.

He'd listened intently to how the team sifted through the mud, searching for the golden nugget that might break the case.

"Right," he said. "I suggested to DS Mercer that we'd try a different approach this time. So for the rest of this afternoon, we'll try a relaxed, informal approach. I want to encourage you to come up with thoughts that might seem daft. Don't be shy. Some will fall by the wayside. Others will spark more ideas. Maybe we'll find a way to make sense of the chaos we see before us at present."

"That was called brainstorming in the old days, guv," said Neil.

"As you know so much about it, Neil. You can write down everything that's said. So, turn the flip chart to a fresh sheet and prepare to be busy."

"Should we profile our killer, guv?" asked Lydia.

"You've studied the subject, Lydia. So go ahead, make my day," said Gus.

"We've got photos of the various crime scenes and the victims," she said. "Is there anything we can glean from close-ups of the wounds or other marks on the body?"

"The evidence from the neck injuries suggests the attacker wore gloves," said Neil. "All year round? That's odd."

"We know where the bodies were found, guv," said Blessing, "and where the attempt on Nicole Wyvern was made. Do we know who lives nearby?"

"Keep the murder files handy," said Alex. "We've got loads of background on the victims. Was there something we missed in their lifestyle, perhaps? A common denominator that different sets of detectives didn't grasp as significant."

"We know the attacks took place early in the morning," said Grace, "How long do we think each attack lasted? The killer was well-prepared, which was evident in Tammi Kenyon's case."

"The attacker is likely to have a family, too," said Blessing. "Whoever it was, they had to be able to leave home early without it raising a red flag."

"Weather conditions were different in all three cases, guv," said Alex. "Are we looking for someone who goes out in all kinds of weather for their job? A person who delivers milk, the post, or newspapers. Someone who works on the land."

"Neither murder suggests the attacker took advantage of a chance opportunity," said Grace. "Instead, they used cunning to lure the girls to the scene of the attack. So, how did they stop the victim from running away? Especially Imogen, who was a natural athlete."

"Forensics didn't find evidence of the victims struggling or attempting to escape," said Lydia. "They had to know the attacker well enough to let them get close in the first instance."

"When the attack came, it was swift and decisive," said Grace. "I believe it unlikely either attack lasted more than a few minutes."

"Which indicates a person with considerable strength and no hesitation in taking a life," said Alex.

"Local knowledge played a part in all three attacks, guv," said Lydia. "They were familiar with the fields they used, which links with your comment at the outset."

"So, do we believe our victims knew their attacker?" asked Gus.

"Yes," the whole team replied at once.

"If you have time this evening, think about the things Neil's listed, " said Gus. "We'll go again in the morning once we have the maps of our target area on the wall."

"It's good to be back, guv," said Neil. "Despite everything, we're still in business."

"Thank you, Neil," said Gus. "There's another thirty minutes before we finish. I'm sure I don't need to tell you how to fill it."

The team prepared for their digital contributions to the new case in the Freeman Files. Gus did the same, and everyone walked to the lift at five o'clock.

"I could be fifteen minutes late in the morning, guv, because of the roadworks on London Road," said Blessing.

"We'll cope," said Gus. "One item nobody mentioned was the scent the forensic pathologist thought she caught at the murder site in Leigh Road in January 2015."

"I think we all discounted it, guv," said Neil. "First, by her admission, it might have come from someone else in the tent. Second, those who have had the misfortune to attend a dead body try not to smell any more than the absolute minimum. I couldn't distinguish one scent from another after the first thirty seconds. Third, the pathologist couldn't confirm the scent she noticed around Imogen's body was the same one she smelt eighteen months earlier."

"All valid points," said Gus. "But we don't discount anything until we can rule it out."

The lift doors opened, and soon they were standing outside by their cars.

"It's always the same, isn't it, guv," said Lydia. "One day back, it's as if you haven't had a holiday at all."

"Some of us haven't," groaned Neil.

Gus followed the others as they drove from the car park, and Alex and Lydia were soon heading for Chippenham. Neil disappeared into the distance while Gus trailed behind the Smart car and the Micra until Grace and Blessing went their separate ways home. Suzie was waiting to greet him when he edged the Focus through the gateway at the bungalow in Urchfont.

"I thought I heard your car in the lane, darling," she said.

"I imagine you heard the news about Luke Sherman," sighed Gus.

"That *did* come as a shock," said Suzie. "What made it worse was nobody had heard a whisper until today. I've never known a hot potato to avoid being passed from pillar to post by the end of the day. The evening cleaners are generally the last to hear."

"Kenneth ordered me to drop the subject," said Gus. "Perhaps we should sweep the bungalow for bugs if you want to continue this conversation."

"You'll let me know when you want to chat, Gus," said Suzie. "I can take a hint. But, first, let's eat, then you can tell me what else happened today."

After they'd eaten, Gus told Suzie what Alex, Lydia and the others had done while he was home. Suzie was interested to learn Grace had reached out to her family but was disappointed to hear there was little prospect of bridges being mended.

"Families are so important, aren't they?" she said.

"Geoff was pleased to hear Grace refer to Devizes as home," said Gus.

"Mum and Dad will make her feel welcome," said Suzie. "A surrogate family isn't the same, but it's better than nothing. Did you get handed another case today?"

Gus gave her the bare bones of the Kenyon and Henderson murders. Suzie was interested in the attempted assault on Nicole Wyvern.

"Why would the killer draw attention to themselves? I don't understand that. They had committed two carefully planned murders without leaving evidence. If Julie Kemp were dealing with a serial killer, they would have been laying the foundations for their next target. They'd be checking their routines, calculating where and when they could strike with the minimum risk and the maximum chance of success —not jumping on a girl walking home from a sleepover seven days after killing Imogen Henderson. I don't believe Nicole's attacker knew she was a detective's daughter. That was a red herring. Sally Wyvern overreacted, which skewed the investigation's focus for her husband."

"The attempted assault certainly confused matters," said Gus. "The lack of motive for the murders had been the sticking point. Tammie and Imogen were fifteen and seventeen. One was flirtatious, the other reserved. They both attended the same school. DI Kemp and her team tried to find the motive among the students, teachers, and ancillary staff, without luck. What had those two girls done to deserve such a fate? Julie Kemp found nothing."

"What's your first move?" asked Suzie.

"After we've taken a closer look at the maps to see where every event took place, I want to call the owners to ask if I can take a walk in the countryside."

"I have every faith that you'll suss it out, Gus," said Suzie. "Would you like a hot chocolate to help you have a good night's sleep?"

"Wonderful," said Gus.

Tuesday, 23 October 2018

GUS WAS the first to leave the driveway in the morning. He wanted to read through the ideas on the flip chart once more before Blessing arrived with the maps. Suzie followed him along the lane, eager to pass, but passing spots were at a premium until they hit the main road into Devizes. Her Golf whizzed past before they reached the Fox & Hounds.

Gus returned Suzie's wave and was soon at the brow of Caen Hill and descending into the valley. Fifteen minutes later, he pulled up beneath the Crime Review Team office and parked next to Lydia's red Mini.

When he exited the lift, she was eager to tell him her news.

"We saw Tom Spencer in Chippenham last night, drowning his sorrows."

"I'll have a quiet word with DS Mercer. Tom will have a harder time trying to move on than the rest of you. Perhaps he needs an assignment that keeps him so occupied he doesn't have time to breathe. A spell on the south coast replacing Rick Chalmers could do the trick."

Gus could tell Lydia and Alex were shocked by his blunt response. He'd surprised himself, but Luke was his own man and would have to live with his choice.

The lift returned to the ground floor, and Neil arrived with Grace a minute later.

"I was just running through the ideas we came up with yesterday afternoon," Gus explained. "Neil, can you find out who the local landowners are, whether they have tenant farmers, and who operates in the fields we're concentrating on?"

"On it, guv," said Neil.

Blessing reached the office at a quarter past nine struggling with three cardboard tubes.

"Give the poor girl a hand, someone," said Gus.

Neil and Alex each grabbed a tube and extracted the maps Divya had produced. Blessing pinned the street map to the wallboard next to her desk. Gus and the team walked to study each map in turn.

Lydia checked the crime scene photos from Imogen Henderson's murder.

"I can see further proof of the meticulous planning that went into each murder," she said. "With Tammie, they had the cover of darkness, trees and hedges close to the site where the body was hidden to allow them to slip away unnoticed. Despite it being in broad daylight, the risk of killing Imogen where they did was a fraction of what it would have been on the other side of the field. The killer understood that and realised their quickest escape route was from that left-hand corner, should someone passing by have sensed something was wrong."

"Local knowledge coming into play again," said Alex.

"I've got the name of that farmer, guv," said Neil. "Rob Bean is his name. He deals in livestock rather than vegetables."

"He must have had a call from the police to drive over to unlock the gate," said Grace. "I wonder why they didn't record his details in the murder file?"

"Where does he live, Neil?" asked Gus. "Perhaps you could mark it on our map."

"Little Ashley, guv," said Neil. "One and a half miles west of the murder site."

"How old is Farmer Bean?" asked Lydia.

"Sixty-six," said Neil. "Married to Laura, sixty-one. They have a son, Sam, who's twenty-three. He doesn't appear to live at the farmhouse."

"Did the son attend St Laurence?" asked Alex.

"No record of that, guv," said Neil. "We could ask those two teachers on our list if they remember him."

"I can start trawling through social media, guv," said Blessing.

"It feels low-priority for the moment," said Gus. "Let's

call Rob Bean, ask for permission to visit the field, and then arrange to meet him and his wife."

"Anyone else you'd like contacted, guv?" asked Alex.

"Kemp, Quinn, Wyvern, and Anderson to kick off," said Gus. "I'm eager for us to speak with Shobna Patel to pursue this elusive aroma, even though it could be a red herring. Sorry, that slipped out."

"Would you like me to meet with the victims' parents, Gus?" asked Grace.

"I think the same pairing should speak with both sets, guv," said Lydia.

"I agree, Lydia," said Gus. "Why don't you work with Grace on this occasion?"

"No problem, guv," said Lydia.

"Who's going to Leigh Road and Woolley Street with you, guv?" asked Neil.

"That will be Alex," said Gus. "I'd like you and Blessing to hunt down Mrs Patel."

"On it, guv," said Neil.

"Blessing, can you continue digging into Sammy Bean until we've arranged a meeting schedule?" asked Gus.

"Got it, guv," said Blessing.

"While Alex is making phone calls, why don't we get the drinks, Lydia?" said Gus.

After the usual battle of wills with the Gaggia, Gus and Lydia returned with a tray of coffee and a single tea for Grace.

Gus sat enjoying his black coffee, watching the clock.

"We've got the all-clear, guv," said Alex. "We'll have to clamber over the gate as Rob Bean's too busy to drive over to open up. But he's happy for us to poke around wherever we wish. I've arranged for us to go straight to the farmhouse as soon as we finish. We can talk to him and his wife there."

"Pass the phone numbers to Neil, Alex," said Gus. We'll get going, and Neil can phone Polebarn Road and Bourne Hill. Face-to-face meetings in Trowbridge, Neil. A phone call with DI Quinn will suffice."

"What about Bonnie Anderson, guv?" asked Neil.

"You need to check whether she's still at Polebarn Road, Neil," said Gus. "Concentrate on getting hold of Shobna Patel ahead of Ms Anderson."

Five minutes later, Gus and Alex were heading for the ground floor.

"What state do you reckon this field will be in, guv?" asked Alex. "We came to work in Lydia's Mini. Unfortunately, I don't have any wellington boots."

"Nor do I, Alex," said Gus, "but I've got several pairs of overshoes I transferred from my old Focus. I'm more worried about the livestock Neil mentioned. There weren't cows, or pigs, in that field three years ago. I hope Farmer Bean hasn't moved into the alpaca, or llama, business."

"Diversification is rife in farming these days, guv," said Alex as they reached the car park.

"We'll take my car," said Gus.

"My first trip in the new wheels, guv," said Alex. "Very swish."

"Functional and economical, Alex," said Gus.

They arrived by the five-barred metal gate on Leigh Road within fifteen minutes. Gus searched the field for signs of life while Alex donned a chic pair of blue overshoes.

"Three horses on the far right-hand side," said Gus. "Looks like the field is rented out these days."

"They look healthy," said Alex. "Not that I'm an expert."

Gus had kitted himself out with his overshoes and was preparing to scale the gate.

"Do you need a helping hand, guv?" asked Alex.

"Don't you dare," said Gus. "Keep an eye on the horses. If they start running, shout."

Alex soon joined Gus on the other side of the gate, and they set off towards the furthest corner of the field, where Tammie Kenyon's body was found.

"Those horses must be females, guv," said Alex. "They've ignored us."

When Gus compared what he remembered from the crime scene photos with the scene that greeted them, it was apparent little had changed in three-and-a-half years. The trees were taller, and the bushes and brambles were even more overgrown. Yet, it was still a god-forsaken place to die.

"Let's move to where they discovered the second shoe," said Gus.

"I don't think the terrain has altered much in decades, guv," said Alex. "You'd need to be fairly strong to drag a teenage girl a hundred yards across this rough ground."

Gus stopped and looked back to the clump of trees.

"Just over a minute at a gentle pace. How long would it have taken? Three minutes?"

"The killer wouldn't have wanted to hang around. We can't be certain this was where Tammie died," said Alex. "It could just have been where she lost her second shoe. If I time our walk to the gateway, we'll know how much time elapsed from when Tammie was intercepted."

"No wonder DI Kemp and her team had trouble pinning anything down," said Gus. "The killer didn't *have* to be lying in wait on Leigh Road. They could have already been inside the field tending to the horses if they were being kept here then. Even if they weren't, what would Tammie have done if a voice she recognised called out for help or wanted a chat? The killer knew she'd walk past at that time on a Thursday morning."

"It was getting lighter with every minute, I suppose," said Alex. "If Tammie climbed the gate and ran towards where she heard the voice, she could have reached the spot in one minute, at a push."

"Then the killer struck without warning," said Gus. "Three minutes later, Tammie breathed her last. Three more minutes to drag the body into the next field. Add another minute to get the body into position to pitch it forward into the brambles. Remember, the autopsy report indicated Tammie was dragged backwards into the next field."

"We have a timeline for the murder that fits, but we still can't swear it happened that way, guv," said Alex. "What else can we glean from what we've seen here?"

"I'm standing by the gateway, and those horses are fully visible. What can you see of the hedge where the second shoe was found?"

"Only the top half, guv," said Alex. "As for where the killer dumped Tammie's body. I can see the trees but nothing of the hedge or the bushes and brambles beyond. The contour of the land gave the killer cover when they moved the body. So even if it had been light, nobody could have seen what was happening."

"Which means the killer didn't have to rush as much as we thought," said Gus.

"I wonder whether Neil's discovered who farms the field where Imogen's body was found yet?" asked Alex.

"Call him," said Gus. "We can drive to Little Ashley now for a quick word with Mr and Mrs Bean."

While Alex tried Neil's office phone, Gus drove to the crossroads where Karla Bates had seen Tammie crossing the road. He turned left, passed the Leigh Park Country House Hotel entrance, and followed the B3105 until it joined the A363. As he neared the left turn towards the Bean's farm, he spotted a familiar name.

"Great Cumberwell," he said. "That's interesting."

"We could tell from the maps that all three incidents were fairly close together, guv," said Alex. "It could mean something, but...."

"It could just as easily be another dead end," said Gus. "Did you get hold of Neil?"

"He's taken Blessing to Polebarn Road, guv," said Alex.

"Ask Amazing Grace to chase that information," said Gus. "Once we've finished here, I want to check where Nicole Wyvern was attacked and visit the field near Woolley Manor."

"Got it, guv,"

Gus soon drew up beside a battered Land Rover in the farmyard. Several other vehicles in an open barn had seen better days.

"Not a hive of activity, is it?" said Alex.

"Rob Bean should be thinking of retirement at his age," said Gus. "But farmers are stubborn beggars and won't admit defeat. No doubt he hoped the son would take over from him in his dotage, but if young Sam's not living at home, perhaps he realised the writing was on the wall."

As Gus and Alex crossed the yard, a grey-haired woman appeared from the side of the farmhouse.

"Come into the kitchen," she said. "Rob's inside, having a mug of tea."

Gus and Alex had to duck their heads to enter the side door. Rob Bean sat beside an ancient AGA cooker surrounded by wooden cupboards that looked like they'd been there for a hundred years. He nursed a large mug in gnarled hands, and Gus struggled to believe there was a mere four-year difference in their ages. Laura Bean hovered beside Alex. She, too, looked older than her years.

"Have you seen what you wanted to see?" asked Rob. "Get them a drink, Laura."

"Tea or coffee?" she asked.

"Coffee, please," said Alex. "White, one sugar. Mr Freeman will have a black coffee. I'm Detective Sergeant Hardy."

"How long have you had horses in that field, Mr Bean?" asked Gus.

"Five years or so," he replied. "Not the same ones you saw today, but it's a steady income."

"How many people do you have working for you?" asked Gus.

Laura Bean placed two mugs of coffee on the large wooden table in the centre of the room.

"Not as many as we once did," she said.

"Can you hear the birds?" asked Rob Bean.

"We understood you had livestock," said Alex.

"We've raised a wide variety of free-range poultry, including turkeys, geese, chickens, and ducks, since I was a teenager," said Rob Bean. "Most of the dozen people who work here are involved in maintaining our tradition of dry-plucking and hanging. All the birds live in small flocks, so we guarantee they receive the care and attention they need. If you tried, you couldn't be further from the mass production of supermarket poultry. We've sold directly from the farm to local residents, local farm shops, plus restaurants and hotels in the Bath area for years."

"You don't seem very busy at present," said Alex.

"The demand isn't as great as it was, and competition is fierce," said Rob.

"The younger generation prefers fast food or has decided to ditch meat altogether," said Laura. "There's no future in farming these days."

"Didn't your son want to inherit the business?" asked Gus. "So many farmers diversify, don't they? Perhaps he could have forged a new future for the farm."

"Sam went away," said Laura.

"We haven't spoken to Sam since he turned sixteen," said Rob.

Chapter Twelve

"THE ONLY TIME Rob Bean got animated was when he told us about his business," said Gus. "Forty years of hard graft, all for nothing. Sam Bean turned his back on his family and went away."

"Sad, isn't it, guv?" said Alex. "Let's drive to the end of this lane, find somewhere to park, and then we can cross over to follow the pathway from Great Cumberwell Nicole took."

Ten minutes later, they returned to the Focus.

"The crime scene photos helped us find the right line of oak trees," said Alex.

"I couldn't see anything that didn't gel with Nicole's statement," said Gus. "Her attacker had plenty of hiding places to choose from. He would have been on her before she had a chance to run. She was lucky."

"What did you make of her comment about the high-pitched voice?" asked Alex.

"Not every bloke has a deep voice, Alex," said Gus. "I was more interested in the glove. When I spoke to Suzie about it, she didn't think the person who attacked Nicole knew her father was a detective. As Suzie pointed out, there was zero planning for the attack, which didn't fit the profile. However, while we stood on the pathway, I could hear sounds from the Cumberwell golf course carried by the wind. DS Wyvern heard his daughter say when her attacker held her face-down on the grass verge, they wore a glove."

"Golfers wear a glove for added grip," said Alex. "A right-handed golfer wears a glove on their left hand. Nicole was pinned by a gloved left hand. So, you think it was a random attack by a golfer in the trees searching for a lost ball?"

"I reckon that's more likely than the option DS Wyvern persuaded his boss to follow."

"How would we find that person now?" asked Alex.

"We're after the killer, Alex," said Gus. "I suggest a phone call to Divya at the Hub might help the computer whizzes locate our man. If he's tried it once, I bet he's tried again since."

"I'll call her when we get back to the office."

They headed back to the A363 and collected the car. No sooner than they'd reached the junction with the B3105, Alex's phone rang. He listened and then ended the call.

"That was Grace, guv. She's leaving the office now with Lydia to speak to Mr and Mrs Kenyon. A Bristol developer bought the field on Woolley Street. He has dozens of hoops to jump through to get final planning permission. We might upset the locals who have objected to any threat to green space, but if we're quick, we should escape unscathed."

"Did Grace know who sold the field to the developer?" asked Gus.

"It was farmed by a chap called Cedric Norton, guv. He died in 2017, and his daughter disposed of everything except the farmhouse. That's about half a mile away, straight ahead. His daughter had the farmhouse converted into flats and rents them out."

"We're almost there," said Gus. "What's life without a little risk? Keep an eye out for angry residents who think we're here to see how many houses we can squeeze into the field."

NEIL AND BLESSING had arrived at Trowbridge Police station on Polebarn Road. After signing in, they were led to Julie Kemp's office. Neil made the introductions.

"Do you know why these murders are being reviewed?" asked Julie.

"Mr Freeman has had some success with cold cases, ma'am," said Blessing.

"The Chief Constable thought a fresh pair of eyes might help, ma'am," said Neil.

"We couldn't find a single person without an alibi," said Julie. "Every lead we followed went nowhere. I can't see how you can do any better."

"Why didn't you concentrate on the fields where the murders occurred, ma'am?" asked Neil.

"Forensics covered every blade of grass, DS Davis. They found nothing."

"I think Neil meant, who owned them, who worked there, and whether they were connected," said Blessing.

"Rob Bean owned the field on Leigh Road," said Julie. "He rented it to people with ponies and horses. Poultry is his stock-in-trade. Rob told me he rarely had people working in that field. He didn't have anyone there on the day in question."

"What about the field on Woolley Street?" asked Neil.

"Old Cedric's place?" said Julie. "That had been fallow ground for two or three years before Imogen's murder. Cedric was already almost ninety. His daughter stirred up trouble as soon as Cedric died by selling off his land and vehicles. Then she ploughed the money into refurbishing the farmhouse to provide luxury flats for people who couldn't afford the property prices in Bath."

"So, there was no connection you could see?" asked Neil.

"Laura Bean was Cedric Norton's daughter," said Julie. "That's the only thing the fields had in common. The father and his only daughter didn't get on. I don't think Cedric spoke to her after she married Rob. He had expected Laura to stay at the farm and look after him in his old age. The rumours started as soon as he died. Many locals thought Cedric would have left his money to charity, but the only will that came to light was years old, and Laura inherited the lot."

"Have you had further thoughts about the attempted assault on Nicole Wyvern?" asked Blessing.

"I never accepted that the killer was involved in the third assault," said Julie. "Tony Wyvern was adamant, though, especially because Nicole swore her attacker was wearing a glove when they grabbed her by the neck. But, alas, we didn't get a confirmed sighting of anyone close to Great Cumberwell or the golf course on the morning of the attack."

"Is DS Wyvern available, ma'am?" asked Neil.

"Two doors down the corridor on the right, DS Davis," said Julie Kemp. "Is that all you wanted to ask?"

"It might be a daft question, ma'am," said Blessing. "Would it be worthwhile conducting a house-to-house enquiry within walking distance of where the attacks took place? Both murders happened early in the morning. Surely, the killer must have lived nearby?"

"They had to leave home and get to the field without anyone seeing them," said Neil. "Then, return home afterwards."

"Maybe a family member has kept a secret for three years," said Blessing. "Or a passer-by saw someone but never connected them to the murders."

"Someone they were used to seeing in those fields," said Neil.

"The gap between neighbouring properties in the countryside can be significant," said Julie. "If the killer lived at home with a wife or mother, someone may have kept quiet for the past three years. But, if they lived alone and knew their way around, they could slip into any field unnoticed. That's what worries Tony and me the most. Because we never caught him, we dread hearing there's been another murder."

Neil and Blessing left Julie Kemp and went to question Tony Wyvern.

MEANWHILE, in Northleigh, Grace and Lydia sat outside Phillip and Debbie Kenyon's house.

"We'll bring back terrible memories, ma'am," said Lydia.

"Enough time has passed for both sets of parents to begin to live with their child's death," said Grace. "That's all they can hope for."

"Who said time was a great healer?" asked Lydia.

"An idiot," said Grace. "Come on. We can't avoid hurting them all over again. Losing a child must be the worst thing ever."

They left Lydia's red Mini and walked to the front door. Lydia rang the bell, and Phillip Kenyon answered before the sound of the bell died.

"Please, come in," he said. "Debbie won't be long. Her boss wasn't happy about her taking time off work."

Grace and Lydia followed Phillip Kenyon inside. While Grace explained who they were and why they were taking another look at their daughter's murder, Lydia looked around the living room. She recognised the photo of Tammie in her school uniform, aged thirteen, on a sideboard. It was the only one in the murder file from when she was alive.

Lydia heard a car pull up on the drive. Debbie Kenyon rushed into the room.

"Sorry, I'm late," she said. "What's this about? Have you found him?"

"Sit down, luv," said Phillip. "Just answer their questions, and we can get back to work."

"You haven't found Tammie's killer, then?" said Debbie. "You're useless."

Grace ignored the comment and turned to Phillip Kenyon.

"One comment the detectives recorded in the original investigation was from you, Mr Kenyon," she said. "You wondered whether you knew your daughter at all. What did you mean by that?"

"He was never here," said Debbie. "I made sure Tammie had clean clothes, never had time off school unless it was serious, and attended meetings with her teachers. We lived hand-to-mouth, but what can you do? I worked overtime whenever possible to scrape together money for little extras like that breakfast session."

"Is it fair to say Tammie spent plenty of time alone?" asked Lydia.

"After she was twelve or thirteen, she spent most evenings in her room," said Phillip. "She didn't want to sit down here watching TV with us any longer. So instead, Tammie did her homework, listened to music, and kept in touch with her friends on her phone."

"At fourteen, Tammie started going out two or three evenings a week," said Debbie. "Hanging around the town centre with friends from school, like Naomi Fletcher, and then there were the boyfriends, like Alfie Jones. Tammie was a typical teenager. She became secretive, did what she liked, and we grew further apart. We thought she'd grow out of it once she reached eighteen."

"Were you aware Tammie was sexually active?" asked Grace.

"I suspected," said Debbie.

"You didn't say anything to me," said Phillip.

"You were struggling to keep a roof over our heads," said Debbie. "Neither of us had the time to sit down for a heart-to-heart with Tammie. I kept my fingers crossed that boys like Alfie used protection. If Tammie had asked if she could go on the pill, it would have caused ructions. You would have hit the roof if you knew your little princess was growing up too fast."

Grace glanced at Lydia. The original investigation hadn't mentioned this level of conflict in the home.

"Did Tammie know Imogen Henderson?" asked Grace.

"Not as far as I know," said Debbie.

Phillip Kenyon shrugged his shoulders.

"Three years ago, you couldn't think of anyone that might have wanted to harm Tammie," said Grace. "Was there a person in the town that attracted attention?

Someone children and teenagers might make fun of or call names."

"What, like a tramp, one of the druggies, or meths drinkers?" asked Phillip. "Several roam the streets and the parks during the day. Some sleep rough at night. I can't remember hearing Tammie, or Naomi, mentioning being bothered by any of that crowd."

"Me neither," said Debbie. "Barbie was the only name I remember those two laughing about. I wouldn't know whether it was a girl from school or somebody they bumped into in town."

"Does Naomi still live in Bradford?" asked Lydia.

"Her parents divorced," said Debbie. "Naomi and her mother moved to Ireland within weeks of the police staging the reconstruction of Tammie's last walk to school. After that, we never kept in touch. A friend at work heard that Naomi's mother married again last year. No idea whether they're in Northern Ireland or the Republic."

Grace decided they weren't likely to learn anything useful by keeping Phillip and Debbie from getting back to work. She had already caught both of them checking their watches. Grace thanked the couple for their cooperation and left.

"Blimey," said Lydia.

"Tammie lived under the same roof, but she must have felt unloved," said Grace.

"She looked for love elsewhere," said Lydia.

"Surely we won't find the same situation in Springfield Avenue?" said Grace.

Lydia drove them into town; they arrived outside Steve and Elaine Henderson's house five minutes later.

"Zack will be at school," said Lydia. "I wonder if Rebel is still here?"

Grace rang the bell. The rapid-fire barking that followed told them all they needed to know.

Elaine Henderson answered the door.

"Police?" she asked.

"Detective Inspector Packenham," said Grace. "My colleague is Lydia Logan Barre."

"Stephen is securing Rebel, our dog. He's very excitable. Please come into the lounge."

Elaine sat, shoulders back, by the fireplace, knees together, hands in her lap. Grace and Lydia sat on a two-seater sofa under the window.

Steve Henderson joined them seconds later.

"Rebel has been out of sorts since Immie died," he explained. "He keeps expecting her to walk through the door. How can we help you?"

"We only have a couple of questions," said Grace. "Imogen wasn't the gregarious type, according to her teachers. She was single-minded and set her sights on getting the best grades possible in her exams. She didn't have a running partner. Is it fair to say Imogen spent a fair bit of time alone?"

"From the age of fourteen, Imogen spent most evenings in her room," said Elaine. "I was happy she didn't waste time watching TV like many others."

"Immie did her homework and read, listening to white noise through her headphones," said Steve. "We didn't disturb her or interfere."

"You denied her access to the internet and from owning a smartphone," said Lydia.

"That was in her best interest," said Elaine.

"Was she obliged to attend church with the family every Sunday?" asked Grace.

"Religion is important to us," said Elaine.

"Immie never complained, nor has Zack," said Steve.

"How did Imogen keep in touch with friends?" asked Grace.

"She mixed with those she wished to at school," replied Elaine.

"Did Imogen know Tammie Kenyon?" asked Grace.

"I hardly think so," said Elaine.

"You couldn't think of anyone that might have wanted to harm Imogen at the time," said Grace. "Can you recall anyone that attracted attention? Someone children and teenagers made fun of or called names."

"Imogen wasn't that sort of girl," snapped Elaine. "We raised her to be aware of her surroundings and sympathetic to the burden others carry. So it would be totally out of character for Imogen to pass a derogatory remark about another person. I sometimes despair at the way you people work. Why aren't you looking for her killer, not trying to say she brought it on herself by offending a down-and-out by calling them names?"

"What will Zack do tonight when he gets home from school?" asked Lydia.

"He'll take Rebel for a walk," said Steve. "Then, we'll eat together."

"Zack will have homework," said Elaine. "He'll go to his room to finish that, and then it will be time for bed. Why?"

"I was adopted," said Lydia. "But my parents always found time for me, even if it was only a cuddle, to tell me they loved me. When I was leaving to go to university, my mother asked me why I hadn't asked them to stop once I'd grown up. I told her even if it was only for a few seconds, it strengthened me. Whenever life at school got hard with the bullies and the racists, I knew I was loved. Nothing they could say or do broke my parents' shield around me."

"You can't come here accusing us of not loving our children," said Elaine.

"That's not what the young lady meant, Elaine," said Steve. "We assumed Immie was fine because she never complained. She never kicked back at the restrictions placed on her or told us she would prefer not to attend church. Perhaps we should have asked."

"Children have to have boundaries," said Elaine. "Look at the mess so many teenagers make of their lives."

"I meant we should have asked if Immie knew how much we loved her," said Steve.

NEIL AND BLESSING had left Polebarn Road and were en route to Winsley, a village two miles west of Bradford-on-Avon. When Neil rang her earlier, Shobna Patel told him she was visiting her sister and that it would be easier to talk to the police there. Mrs Patel lived on the far side of Bristol, near Almondsbury, with her husband, Bishan.

"DS Wyvern didn't approve of how we handled the case, Neil," said Blessing.

"That was an awkward fifteen minutes, I grant you, Blessing," said Neil. "No matter how hard I tried to convince him it wasn't a witch hunt, he thought we were trying to trip him up, get him to admit he'd not looked into every possibility."

"Well, they didn't do a house-to-house within walking distance of the attacks," said Blessing. "Nor did they pursue the social media angle as much as I would have wished."

"Ran out of time, I expect," said Neil.

"What about DI Quinn?" asked Blessing.

"I'll call him from the office later," said Neil. "Then we can update our files before we go home. Let's hope Gus and

Grace uncover more useful leads for us to follow tomorrow."

When a diminutive middle-aged lady answered the door in Winsley, Neil wasn't sure whether it was Shobna Patel or her sister.

"Wiltshire Police," he said, showing her his warrant card. "We'd like to speak with Mrs Patel."

"I'm Nitya Chowdury. Shobna is my twin sister. She's in the kitchen. Go straight through."

Neil and Blessing entered the kitchen.

"Something smells good," said Neil.

"Nothing to do with me," said Shobna. "My sister inherited our mother's culinary skills. I burn toast. How can I help you, DS Davis?"

"We've studied the crime scene photos of the wounds that Tammie and Imogen suffered," said Neil. "Did anything seem odd about them to you?"

"The bruising on Imogen's neck differed slightly on one side compared to the other," said Shobna. "That could have been because the left hand was the killer's dominant hand."

"What else could cause it?" asked Blessing.

"Perhaps the gloves the killer wore served different purposes in their occupation," said Shobna. "You would need to discover which profession might be involved."

"Did you check the crime scene photos taken of Tammie's neck wounds?" asked Neil.

"Of course, DS Davis, but the first body was exposed to the elements for far longer, and any detail that might have shown similar bruising had been degraded to such an extent, I'd be guessing.

"I've just searched online for industrial gloves," said Blessing. "What about a leather glove with a reinforced index finger, used by people engaged in construction or forestry."

"I'd need to see the glove in question, but it sounds promising. That could explain the slight differences I recorded on the left and right side of Imogen's neck."

"Could the leather glove account for the scent you recorded?" asked Neil.

"No, I could distinguish the smell of real leather from fake or cheap quality,"

"Hang on," said Neil. "Which side of the neck was it where you first caught the scent?"

"I leaned towards Tammie's body to look closer at the side of the neck closest to me. Then I walked around to do the same on the opposite side. The scent wasn't present on that side."

"So, if the leather glove was on the killer's left hand, that was the item that caused the more prominent bruising?"

"Correct," said Shobna.

"If the scent you caught wasn't from the leather itself, what else could it have been?" asked Neil.

"Perhaps the killer applied a shielding lotion," said Blessing. "If they wore a heavy glove for several hours, they were bound to sweat."

"Do you know many construction workers or tree surgeons with soft hands, Blessing?" asked Neil. "I can't see a rough, tough lumberjack moisturising, can you?"

"The killer could have had a skin complaint, DS Davis," said Shobna. "Your colleague may have a point."

"Would you recognise the scent after all this time?" asked Blessing.

"The unusual scent I smelt at the scene of the second murder was different from the one I remembered from eighteen months earlier. That confused me. But, if you identified a suspect and recovered gloves and a bottle of shielding lotion…."

"We might not need to identify the scent," said Neil. "People don't stick to the same brand of glove or lotion throughout their lives. Manufacturers change fragrances on a whim. We could show the killer had the tools needed to commit the murders. Then, your autopsy results would match the items we found."

"Did the police ever resolve the issue of motive?" asked Shobna.

"They didn't," said Neil. "We're working on it."

"Was there anything else?" asked Shobna.

"I think we've got what we came for," said Neil.

Shobna and Nitya stood on the doorstep as Neil reversed the car off the driveway.

"Like peas in a pod," said Blessing.

"What made you think of the lotion, Blessing?" asked Neil.

"My mother used gardening gloves when I visited her during the holiday. She's trying to match the garden Jacky Ferris showed her at the farm. There's a long way to go yet, but as soon as we returned indoors, my mother removed her gloves, washed her hands, and applied a hand lotion to keep them soft."

"Back to the office," said Neil. "A quick phone call to Salisbury, then we'll update our files."

When they reached the Church Street car park, Neil realised they were the last to return.

"We'd better get our skates on, Blessing," he said.

Gus and the others were hard at work updating the Freeman files when Neil and Blessing exited the lift.

"Welcome back," said Gus. "Have you seen everyone?"

"We didn't speak to Bonnie Anderson, guv," said Blessing.

"A call to DI Quinn was next on my list, guv," said Neil.

"Hold your horses, Neil," said Gus. "Why don't we take time out to recap everything we've learned today? We've only been back ten minutes ourselves."

Alex took the others through their visits to the two murder sites. He told them that horses had been in the field on Leigh Road when Tammie was killed, and her killer may never have set foot outside the field that morning. Rob Bean's father-in-law had owned the field on Woolley Street.

"So there was a connection between the two murder sites," said Lydia.

"Rob and Laura Bean had a son, Sam, who left home at sixteen, and it appears they lost touch," said Gus.

"How long ago did he walk out, guv?" asked Neil.

Gus tried to remember whether that had been mentioned.

"Not sure, but it could have been seven or eight years ago. We can check."

Alex had already called Divya once he and Gus reached the office. He told the others the attack on Nicole Wyvern was far more likely to have been a random attack by a golfer. Time would tell if he could be identified.

"Right, Grace, what do you have to add to the mix?" asked Gus.

"We believe Tammie and Imogen had far more in common than we thought," said Grace. "Why Julie Kemp and Alan Quinn didn't suss the friction in the Kenyon house is beyond me. We haven't spoken to the Family Liaison Officer, Bonnie Anderson, yet, but she must have noticed something."

"We got the impression Debbie and Phillip did nothing

but work, sleep, and argue," said Lydia. "They're still at it, three years after Tammie died. No wonder the poor girl turned to those lads for affection. There was precious little of it at home.

"Steve and Elaine Henderson had strict rules that Imogen was obliged to follow. She chose to shut herself away from most people at school, and at home, she was ignored. Both parents assumed she must be happy with the situation because she never complained. We believe the reality was that Imogen felt just as isolated and alone as Tammie did."

"We know their killer stalked them for a time, " Gus said. "Did they become targets because they were lonely and in desperate need of affection?"

"The attacker thought he could have sex with the girls because they were unloved," said Alex. "They resisted, and he strangled them."

"That could be the motive we're searching for, Gus," said Grace.

"I wonder whether the killer was suffering from the same feelings of being alone and unloved, guv?" said Blessing.

"That's a possibility too, Blessing," said Gus. "What did you two learn on your travels?"

Neil described the conversations with Julie Kemp and Tony Wyvern.

"Nothing much there then," said Gus.

Neil told them what had happened in Winsley when they spoke to Shobna Patel.

"Great work, you two," said Gus. "Now we're getting somewhere."

"What next, Gus?" asked Grace.

"We update our files for the rest of the day," said Gus.

"Scrap the phone call to Alan Quinn, Neil, and forget about Bonnie Anderson for now. First thing tomorrow, I want to speak to the two teachers Imogen had in her phone contacts. David Sayers and Rosemary Oram."

"On it, guv," said Alex.

"Can I get the rest of the team busy with anything while you're away, Gus?" asked Grace.

"Get cracking on Blessing's idea," said Gus. "A house-to-house on properties closest to the two murder sites. Be prepared to think outside the box."

Everyone found it hard to concentrate on their reports as they tried to fathom what Gus had meant. Finally, the team left the office at five o'clock and made their separate ways home.

Later that evening, Gus set out the rationale behind his thinking when he and Suzie relaxed with a drink after dinner.

"It's plausible," she said. "What type of a farmer was Cedric Norton? Do you know?"

"Apart from the field his daughter sold to a developer, all I could see was trees between me and where Alex reckoned the farmhouse stood."

"Dad's looked into planting trees," said Suzie. "They prevent soil erosion and protect crops and livestock against extreme weather conditions. Dad could get a grant for creating and managing woodland."

"Another way to diversify, I suppose," said Gus. "Cedric Norton was ahead of his time."

"Offsetting his carbon emissions before anyone had heard of them," said Suzie.

"Exactly," said Gus. "Trees don't look after themselves, though, do they? Someone has to inspect them and carry out remedial work. There were trees on two sides of the field on Leigh Road. I wonder who was responsible?"

"A tree surgeon would be the logical thought," said Suzie. "They could carry the right gloves and have permission to access the land. However, nobody ever spotted a vehicle, with or without signage, near either murder site."

"Also, the tree surgeon we met while investigating the case in Wilton stressed there were specific times of the year when jobs were carried out. For example, a bitterly cold day in January and a warm Sunday morning in May might not be considered peak season."

Epilogue

Wednesday, 24 October 2018

GUS AND SUZIE left the bungalow together at twenty-five past eight.

"A journey into the unknown lies ahead," he said as they reached their cars.

"I've told you which words to use and which to avoid," said Suzie. "Thank your lucky stars I've attended the seminars."

Gus drove out of Devizes and headed for the Church Street car park to collect a colleague.

Lydia had been Suzie's choice, and Gus couldn't argue.

While Grace looked after the rest of his flock, Gus and Lydia headed for St Laurence and an appointment with a Head of Year and a retired Religious Education teacher.

When they were seated in David Sayer's office, Gus decided to jump in with both big feet.

"Have you had any issues at your school with gender dysphoria?" asked Gus.

"Many teenagers question their gender, whether they feel female, male, non-binary or other terms used on the gender spectrum," said Sayers. "Although most people do not question their gender, their gender identity is more complex for some young people."

"I see," said Gus.

Lydia wasn't convinced he did, but she knew better than to interrupt when it was clear Gus had come here to check he was searching for the right piece of the jigsaw.

"For example," Rosemary Oram elaborated. "A child may struggle if their interests and social life don't fit society's expectations of the gender they were assigned at birth. That may affect how they think about their body. Puberty can be challenging and stressful for young people. Especially for those who feel distressed about their gender."

GRACE SET out her plans for the house-to-house near Woolley Grange and Leigh Park Country House Hotel.

"Neil, we'll take your car," she said. "You and Blessing work well together, so you will be one team, and Alex and I will be the other."

"Does that mean we're doing a lot of walking, ma'am?" asked Neil.

"Gus told us to think outside the box," said Grace. "Alex has been to Leigh Road and the Little Ashley farm. How far is it by road?"

"A mile and a half," said Alex.

"What about across the fields?" asked Grace.

"Half that," said Alex.

"We'll eliminate that side of the B3109 first," said Grace. "Then we'll drive to Woolley Street and tackle the centre section between the two roads. Finally, we'll move to the field where Imogen died and search between Woolley Street and the farmhouse that belonged to Cedric Norton. That covers the most likely area that our killer came from."

"How far do we search on either side of the fields, ma'am?" asked Alex.

"I've copied the detailed map of the area, so each of us can quickly identify the houses within easy walking distance of the fields in question. That should be sufficient. The killer lived locally and could arrive and disappear unseen."

"As soon as we hit a built-up area, we turn around," said Neil. "I get it."

"Some of these properties could be vacant, ma'am," said Alex. "It's the middle of the working week."

"The countryside is littered with second homes, too, ma'am," said Neil. "Owners only visit for the weekend after a tiring week in London."

Grace handed each of the team a copy of the map.

"If you check, you'll see I'm one step ahead of you," said Grace. "Properties marked with a cross have residents who don't fit the profile of our killer. The ones we're concentrating on had at least one male member of the family over fifteen living there at the end of 2014. We've established that the killer wasn't younger than fifteen. The upper limit, however, is undetermined."

"That cuts down the workload, ma'am," said Neil. "So, we'll knock on the doors of old-age pensioners. Firstly, they're more likely to be in, and secondly, they don't miss much. If DI Kemp had carried out a house-to-house, she might have heard a whisper of suspicious activity from a little old lady next door."

"We live in hope, Neil," said Grace. "Let's get to Brad-ford-on-Avon."

IN DAVID SAYER'S OFFICE, Gus was eager to move the conversation forward.

"Gender identity and sexual orientation are separate things," he said. "How would any distress be seen in the child's behaviour?"

"They may feel unhappy, lonely, or isolated from other teenagers," said Rosemary Oram.

"There could be social pressure from friends or family to behave a certain way," said David Sayer. "They may face bullying and harassment for being different."

"Something that's bound to affect their self-esteem and performance," said Lydia.

"You've explained gender dysphoria," said Gus. "What I'd like to know now is whether you could remember a student who found life difficult because of the gender assigned to them at birth?"

MEANWHILE, in Bradford-on-Avon, Neil parked his car in a lay-by on Leigh Park Road, which ran alongside the left edge of the field where Tammie Kenyon died.

"The map only shows a handful of properties backing onto the field, ma'am," he said. "But, apart from the ones you've discounted, there are dozens within walking distance of the murder site on the other side."

"Nobody came forward with information despite the media coverage," said Blessing.

"The message boards beside the road didn't produce anything," said Alex. "This could be a long slog with no reward."

"It can't be helped," said Grace. "Come on, Alex, let's start knocking on doors."

Progress was slow. The team learned people working for

Rob Bean could sometimes be seen in the field beyond the trees, but those occasions had become much less frequent over the years. Because of the lay of the land, the further the team walked along Leigh Park Road, the fewer residents there were who could see the far corner of the field where the horses were kept.

"Not a single suspect, ma'am," said Alex as they joined Neil and Blessing to return to the car.

"Let's move to Woolley Street next," sighed Grace. "I'm not giving up yet."

"Perhaps we should try Grange View first," said Alex. "Then, there's Woolley Grange itself. The eyewitness, Karla Bates, lives near there."

"The more I look at this central area, the less it feels right, ma'am," said Neil. "There's only one field between the busy corner where the Grange stands and the cul-de-sac that Alex mentioned."

"I wouldn't fancy my chances of getting from A to B without someone seeing me," said Alex. "Too many prying eyes on either side."

"We could come back," said Grace. "I didn't record many young to middle-aged males living in those properties. Let's switch our attention to the field where Imogen died. We'll head for the tree line, split up, and work our way to the farmhouse on the far side."

"There aren't any houses marked on the map," said Blessing.

"Not until that developer gets planning permission," said Neil.

"We're thinking outside the box, Neil," said Alex.

"Exactly," said Grace.

"Got it," said Neil.

Neil and Blessing made their way through the trees on

the left side while Grace and Alex headed towards the right. Grace's phone rang when she thought they must be a quarter of a mile from the farmhouse. It was Neil Davis.

"You'd better come and see this, ma'am,"

Grace and Alex turned left and threaded their way through the trees. In a small clearing stood a wooden hut, no more than ten feet by eight feet. Neil and Blessing came out to join them.

"No signs of life inside, ma'am," said Neil. "Someone has lived here in the past, though. There's a store for tools to the left of the door; saws, loppers, even an old scythe. They had a single bed, an armchair, a makeshift kitchen, and several Tilley lamps."

"A rough sleeper, perhaps?" asked Grace.

"We found gloves inside too, Grace," said Blessing, "and a bottle that could have contained hand lotion."

"We're getting closer," said Grace. "I can feel it."

"I DON'T RECALL a student like that," said David Sayers. "Not in my time at the school."

"What about before you came here?" asked Gus, looking at Rosemary Oram.

"There was a boy, who came to see me before his final exams, telling me he woke up every day like he was trapped in prison," she said.

"Go on," said Gus.

"That would have been seven or eight years ago now," said Rosemary. "Being intersex is a naturally occurring variation in humans. It isn't a medical problem that demands surgery. It describes a group of congenital conditions in which the reproductive organs, genitals, or other sexual anatomy don't develop in a traditional way."

"So, this person was raised as a boy," said Gus. "When he reached puberty, things got worse."

"The overriding feeling he should have been a girl was strengthened when he didn't develop in the same way as the other boys in his year. He told me he'd become a laughing stock. I asked why he hadn't come to us for help. Why hadn't he spoken to his parents about how he felt?"

IN THE CLEARING in the forest, the four team members stood outside the hut.

"What do we do now?" asked Neil.

"I think we'll find the answer at the farmhouse," said Grace.

"Cedric Norton's place," said Blessing.

"A quarter of a mile dead ahead," said Alex.

When they reached the forest's edge, an imposing farmhouse came into view.

"Someone's spent loads of money refurbishing this place," said Alex. "I reckon the monthly rental for a flat here would make my eyes water."

As they entered the courtyard in front of the building, a young woman emerged from a ground-floor apartment and walked to a sports car.

"Excuse me," called Grace. "Wiltshire Police. Could we have a word?"

"I IMAGINE this student's parents were unsympathetic," said Gus.

"There was very little the school could do at that stage," said Rosemary. "He'd sat his last exam and should have returned for final assembly. But instead, we never saw him again after he left my office. When his parents were asked, they said he went away."

"I presume we're talking about Sam Bean," said Gus.

Rosemary Oram nodded.

"It's clear Sam's story made an impression on you," said Lydia. "Why didn't you mention his name to the police when they were investigating the murders?"

"Sam's parents told us he'd left home," said Rosemary. "Tammie and Imogen wouldn't have known Sam, would they?"

"Social media can be a cesspit, but it is a tremendous resource," said Gus. "The original investigation uncovered dozens of examples of students using inappropriate language online when referring to students and teachers. For example, one name police thought was a nickname appeared on several accounts, but they couldn't attribute it to anyone at the school or in the town."

"You believe that person was Sam Bean?" asked David Sayers. "So, he returned to Bradford-on-Avon?"

"I don't believe he ever left," said Gus. "If my team thinks outside the box as I suggested, we might soon learn where he's been hiding."

"I'M due in Bath for a meeting," said the young woman. "What was it you wanted?"

"I'm Detective Inspector Packenham," said Grace. "Have you lived here long?"

"I moved in as soon as the flat was ready. It's my happy place. I owe it all to my grandfather. He was my rock."

"I can see why. It's a beautiful spot. And you are….?"

"Samantha Norton, most people call me Sammy."

"We've just visited the hut in the woods, Sammy," said

Grace. "Do you know what happened to the person who lived there?"

"They went away," said Sammy. "Barbie lived in the old woodman's hut after leaving home at sixteen because his parents treated him as subhuman."

"Barbie was the nickname Bonnie Anderson couldn't match to another person online," said Alex.

"I'd like you to call the people you were going to meet in Bath, Sammy," said Grace. "Sorry, but we need to speak with you further."

Neil ran back to collect the car while Grace called London Road.

Geoff Mercer contacted the custody suite on the outskirts of town to tell them to expect a new visitor, and when Neil returned, he had an extra passenger to ferry back to town.

GRACE CALLED Gus as they approached the custody suite to tell him the news.

"Well done," said Gus. "I sense we have some way to go before finalising the report on this case, but we have most of the pieces now. Sam's targets were girls whose parents ignored them. He felt they were kindred spirits. Tammie was sexually experienced and probably laughed at him. As for Immie, I can see her being sympathetic, given her upbringing. But, again, based on what we know, I fear she was unwilling to even talk to him when he approached her that morning."

"We'll see you in the custody suite, Gus," said Grace.

"You didn't ask about Barbie, Grace," said Alex.

"A slang term for a she-male that's now considered inappropriate," said Grace. "Yes, I've heard the term."

AFTER MANY HOURS OF QUESTIONING, Grace and Gus learned that Samantha Norton had transitioned in 2017. Her defence was that it wasn't her that killed Tammie and Imogen. Instead, Sam Bean was responsible, and after he went away, there were no further killings. However, Sam didn't stop it. Samantha stopped it.

"How do we handle that?" asked Grace as they stepped outside the building and took a break.

"We collect the evidence from the woodman's hut and build a case," said Gus. "Then, the CPS will decide whether they think a jury will refuse to believe a killer can claim their life started afresh after they transitioned."

Quick to Anger: Chapter One

Saturday, 27 October 2018

"Do you have any regrets?" asked Suzie.

"That's a tough question, darling," Gus said. "I've hardly had time to wake up. Do you mean about asking if you'd like to have lunch with me one Sunday afternoon in April?"

"That wasn't what I meant, and you know it," she replied as she poured his first cup of coffee. "Well, do you?"

"Not for a minute," said Gus.

"I was thinking of something more recent," said Suzie.

"The trip to Burnham-on-Sea?" asked Gus.

"It probably caused more problems than it solved," said Suzie.

"You can't win them all," said Gus. "A bit like the case we've just tackled."

"But you found the killer of those two young girls in a matter of days," said Suzie. "Surely that's a win? Or it should be when it gets to court."

"Nobody wins in a case like that," said Gus. "Why wasn't Sam Bean diagnosed earlier? Were Rob and Laura Bean aware of their son's trauma and ignored it? Could Rosemary Oram have done more once Sam bared his soul before leaving school? How is she feeling now?"

"I'd forgotten Immie Henderson was her goddaughter," said Suzie. "Rosemary had known Immie's mother, Elaine, since childhood. But nevertheless, that conversation between Rosemary and Sam was confidential. If Rosemary had breathed a word, it would have had ramifications in every school in the land."

"Yet, if Julie Kemp had learned there was an ex-student with gender issues, mightn't it have led her and Alan Quinn to alter their approach?" asked Gus. "A few hours checking Sam Bean's whereabouts to confirm an alibi rather than ploughing on with the tried and trusted methods."

"It's what we do, Gus," said Suzie. "We play the percentages."

"There were too many instances where police and public weren't working together as a cohesive unit," said Gus. "Nobody came forward with information despite extensive media coverage of both murders. Those message boards beside the roads didn't produce a single positive response. What does that tell you? Kemp and Quinn ignored the murder site itself in both Tammie Kenyon and Immie Henderson's murders. It proved to be key, as I suspected."

"Why, though?" asked Suzie. "What made you so certain that was where you would find the answer?"

"Because nothing else they had gone through with a fine-toothed comb had turned up a possible suspect. Therefore, the killer had to have a connection to somewhere they didn't place under the microscope."

"What do you have planned for the weekend?" asked Suzie.

"I'm free this morning for whatever you're building up to ask. I need to visit the allotment this afternoon, and then tonight, I think a trip to the Lamb is in order. Tomorrow will be a day of rest, as it should be. I've done enough running around this week."

"Mum wants a hand moving a few bits and pieces from my brother's bedroom, ready for Grace's arrival next weekend. Then, if we leave in half an hour to do the weekly shopping, we can drop by the farm on our way home. I don't think it will take that long, but Dad muttered something about fence repairs last night. So Mum reckoned that means she won't see him before sunset."

"No problem," said Gus. "I'll be showered and dressed in fifteen minutes. Then, if you get your skates on, we'll be in Worton before eleven."

Monday, 29 October 2018

"Rise and shine, Gus," said Suzie.

Gus opened one eye and tried to focus on the clock on the bedside table.

"How can it be seven-thirty already?" he groaned.

"Your turn to get breakfast," said Suzie. "I'm off for a shower."

Gus eased himself out of bed gently. When Jackie Ferris said a few bits and pieces needed moving, she hadn't explained how heavy they were. No wonder John made himself scarce. After an hour of struggling with heavy furniture items, two hours on the allotment hadn't done Gus's back any favours. He was feeling all of his sixty-two years on Saturday evening.

Sunday was every bit the quiet day he and Suzie had planned. Gus pottered around the bungalow, trying to keep moving. They dined at home and spent the evening listening to Greg Allman and Carlos Santana. After a few glasses of Malbec, Gus was mellow and relaxed when he went to bed.

Suzie emerged from the bathroom to find a bowl of fruit and fibre ready and waiting.

"That looks good," she said. "What did you have?"

"One slice of toast with honey," said Gus. "My new regime, starting today."

He finished his cup of coffee and headed to the shower.

Thirty minutes later, he and Suzie stood outside the bungalow.

"Usual time tonight?" asked Suzie.

"I sincerely hope so," said Gus.

Suzie edged through the gateway into the lane, followed by Gus in the Focus. A leisurely drive through the lanes followed until they reached the main road into Devizes. Suzie turned off for London Road while Gus carried on towards Caen Hill.

As he parked behind the Old Police Station building, he wondered what lay in store in the days ahead. Despite leaving Urchfont at twenty-past eight, he was still last to arrive. The others were upstairs, awaiting his arrival. Gus gave a deep sigh and called the lift.

"Morning, guv," said Neil.

Lydia, Alex, and Blessing all looked up from their computer screens.

"Grace is fetching coffees for everyone, guv," said Neil. "We knew you wouldn't be long."

"I'll give her a hand," said Gus. "I hate to interrupt people when they're working."

"We're putting the finishing touches to the Burnham

reports, guv," said Lydia. "You'll have everything you need for your meeting with the Chief Constable before your coffee gets cold."

If I get the call, thought Gus. I'm not sure if he's still speaking to me.

"Very considerate, Lydia," he said. "I hope you did as I suggested?"

"Yes, guv," said Alex. "We took every opportunity to remind him that you pointed out that all roads led to Burnham-on-Sea in the original reports on the Fennell and Roker case."

"Right. That might tame the storm," said Gus. "What about last week's enterprise?"

Grace was already on her way back from the restroom.

"Morning, Gus," she said. "I'm handling those reports. I'll pass you the files in an hour, and you can check I haven't missed anything. If the boss doesn't want you at London Road until lunchtime, you should be able to take two sets of completed reports with you."

"Amazing, Grace," said Gus.

She gave him an old-fashioned look as she handed him his cup of black coffee.

"The pause was for a comma," he said.

"I'll believe you. Thousands wouldn't."

Gus finally found time to reach his desk. No sooner had he sat down when his phone rang.

"Saved by the bell, guv," said Alex with a grin.

"Freeman speaking," said Gus.

"Morning, Gus. Kenneth is expecting you at a quarter to twelve."

"That's very precise, Vera," said Gus. "Tell him I accept the challenge."

"You know what he's like, Gus," said Vera. "He has

meetings scheduled throughout the day. But, somehow, he always manages to find time for you and Geoff Mercer."

"It keeps him grounded," said Gus. "We provide a generous dose of common sense to counter the rubbish he has to endure from his peers and superiors."

"I hope this phone isn't tapped," said Vera. "That's dangerous talk these days."

"They can cancel who they like," said Gus. "Just as long as Geoff and I can get our bacon baps and chicken wraps."

"See you later, Gus," chuckled Vera. "Don't worry, your lunch has been ordered, and Kassie spent yesterday baking."

"Don't tell me Number Eight has been given the elbow," said Gus.

"Not by Kassie," said Vera. "Noah caught a stray elbow in the face not long before the end of Saturday's match. He was having his nose straightened in Swindon yesterday."

"Ouch," said Gus. "It puts my bad back into perspective."

"Old age creeping on," said Vera. "You need to slow down."

"That's quite enough from you, Ms Butler," said Gus. "Blame Jackie Ferris for not persuading her two strapping sons to take their bedroom furniture with them when they flew the nest."

"I heard Amazing Grace was moving to Worton Farm," said Vera.

"You don't need to wonder what lay behind the switch. Monty is still in Grace's good books," said Gus. "He wasn't charging her over the odds or looking for sexual favours. Instead, Grace simply felt isolated on the edge of Salisbury Plain with no friends nearby."

"Grace won't have any shortage of conversation with Jackie and Blessing under the same roof," said Vera.

"I fully expect John Ferris to find urgent tasks as far from the farmhouse as possible," said Gus.

"He'll never change," said Vera. "Anyway, I must get on. Bye for now."

Gus sat drinking his coffee. There was nothing to do but wait for the promised reports.

"I've finished, guv," said Neil. "Shall I start the big clear-up?"

"We didn't have the street maps and murder scene photos on the walls for long, did we, Neil?" said Gus. He glanced at Neil's folder and finished his drink.

"Come on. We may as well do it ourselves while the others are playing catch-up."

The residue from the Kenyon and Henderson files didn't take long to remove. When Gus returned to his desk, Neil pulled up a chair. He had news.

"I escaped for an hour on Saturday night, guv," he said quietly, "and went into town for a drink. I was in the Cavalier on Eastleigh Road."

"I remember it well, Neil," said Gus. "Although, I haven't been back since we were there with your Dad."

"I avoided it for months," said Neil. "But several of my mates still use the place, so recently, I started meeting them there for a pint before we walked into the town centre."

"Is this another Amelia Cranston story?" asked Gus.

"Heavens, no, guv," said Neil. "I haven't seen her for ages. Thank goodness. Rick Chalmers was slumped in a corner. I reckon he'd been drinking since lunchtime. Rick wasn't making much sense but wasn't a happy bunny."

"I'm still waiting to hear where they're sending him next," said Gus. "DS Mercer thought the south coast operations were too expensive concerning the number of people they intercepted. So I don't think Rick will return to the Jurassic Coast anytime soon."

"Avon & Somerset won't be keen on taking one of ours on an undercover gig again," said Neil. "Not after what happened with Luke."

"Water under the bridge, Neil," said Gus. "So, what could Rick tell you?"

"He's off to Gablecross, guv. Jake Latimer got his promotion through. I rang and confirmed it with Jake yesterday. He's moving to Winchester to join Anna Cromwell's team."

"You need to get a move on, Neil," said Gus. "Jake's a good detective, but you're every bit as capable. Don't fall into the same rut as your Dad and get left behind."

"Got it, guv," said Neil.

"Why would Rick be unhappy with a move to Swindon?" asked Gus.

"I think he was hoping to join the Crime Review Team, guv," said Neil.

"I suggested that to DS Mercer, but he reminded me the Chief Constable wanted Amazing Grace to stay with us until the end of the year. I can understand the thinking. Kenneth Truelove will retire sometime next year, and if the CRT were to carry on, it would be more palatable for the powers that be if there's a DI in situ ready to assume command when they award me the DCM."

"Don't Come Monday, guv," said Neil. "Yes, I remember."

"That's why you need to look after Number One, Neil. If they pull the plug, I want you to be on the next rung of the ladder or ready to take the leap."

"Forewarned and all that," said Neil. "We don't want to

see you go, guv. Why would they dismantle a winning team? It's not as if we have many of those; wherever you look across the country."

"It's all politics, Neil," said Gus. "I steer clear of it as much as possible."

Grace and Blessing were collecting empties on their way to the restroom. As she passed Gus's desk, she picked up his cup and nodded to his monitor.

"You'll find everything you need in your inbox, Gus," she said.

"Thanks, Grace," said Gus. "I'll read, mark, and inwardly digest before leaving for London Road."

Neil returned to his desk and started reading Grace's report. Things were on the up; she hadn't taken credit for the positives from Wednesday's trip to Bradford-on-Avon. According to Grace, old-fashioned, solid teamwork had brought results.

Neil was interested in the interview sessions Gus and Grace held at the custody suite on Thursday and Friday with the killer of the two teenage girls. He didn't profess to understand Samantha Norton's condition and wouldn't want to be on the jury when the case reached the Crown Court in Swindon. Still, Grace had provided a suggested checklist for colleagues to consider when facing similar problems. Say what you like about her; Grace was a sensitive soul at times, no matter how hard she tried to hide it.

Gus couldn't find fault with Grace's report either. Armed with a hard copy of the relevant files, he was soon ready to leave the office. Only a slow-moving bin lorry in Seend could prevent him from reaching his destination in time. But, if memory served, that was a regular Tuesday stumbling block, so he should be fine.

"I'll see you this afternoon," he said as he walked to the

lift. "Try to make good use of the time. Just because we're between cases, it doesn't mean you can sit and chat. Give your CV's a spring-clean, and check which blanks you can fill to smooth the path for your next promotion."

When the lift doors closed behind him, everyone started speaking at once.

Downstairs, Gus smiled as he left the lift, started the Focus, and eased into traffic on Church Street. That put the cat among the pigeons. He hoped he had a few more cases in him, but you never could tell. As Neil had said, being forewarned was always wise.

At London Road, he parked as close to the main building as possible, strode up the steps to the front door, and signed in. Gus glanced at the clock as he climbed the stairs to the mezzanine. He had three minutes to kill. Where were Vera and Kassie?

Gus could hear Kassie's voice in the distance. She must be doing the refreshment round with her trolley and was currently behind a closed door. Kassie's voice wasn't troubled by such trifles.

"Well done, you made it in time," said Vera, who suddenly appeared at his shoulder. "Geoff's still in his office. Kenneth's alone if you want a head start."

"No, I'll wait for Geoff," said Gus. "I can hide behind him when the bullets start flying."

"Get on with you. Kenneth's a pussycat," said Vera.

Geoff Mercer appeared at the end of his dark corridor. He spotted Gus and waited while he crossed the admin area to join him.

"All set?" asked Geoff.

"As ready as I'll ever be," said Gus. "When were you going to tell me about Rick Chalmers?"

"That appointment isn't general knowledge yet," said

Geoff. "I would have told you as soon as it was appropriate. You're developing a better intelligence network than the legend that was Terry Davis. How on earth did you hear about Rick?"

"Neil saw him on Saturday night," said Gus. "Rick had had a few, so loose lips. Then, yesterday, Neil rang his mate Jake Latimer at Gablecross for confirmation."

"Did Jake tell him his partner, Janina, is pregnant?" asked Geoff. "By the look on your face, he didn't. Good to know I've got some secrets left. Not that her condition had anything to do with Jake getting the promotion. Anna Cromwell headhunted him. She was adamant Jake was the right man for the job. Of course, we would have liked to keep him here in Wiltshire, but when the opportunities arise for our people to move up the ladder, you can't blame them for grabbing their chance."

"A moving target is harder to hit," said Gus. "I should have remembered that. I stayed at Bourne Hill for far too long. Anyway, time to join the boss and let battle commence."

Geoff tapped on the door and waited for gruff permission to enter.

"Good morning, Sir," said Gus. "I trust you had a good weekend?"

Kenneth Truelove turned away from the window overlooking the overflow car park and returned to his desk.

"I had a lot on my mind, Freeman. No thanks to you. My Sunday church visit seems to come around far quicker than it used to when I was younger."

"Confirmation you're getting on in years, Sir," said Geoff. "It happens to all of us."

"Look on the bright side, Sir," said Gus. "Surely you have less to confess now that time flies past so quickly?"

Kenneth sighed.

"We had a brief get-together following your efforts on the Fennell and Roker murders," he said. "As usual, you created as many problems as you solved. Because you were conducting interviews at the custody suite on Thursday and Friday last week, I didn't get the chance to pass on the good news. As you know, Sam Webber and Ian Hood were collected from the Black Horse in Chippenham about an hour after you and DI Packenham arrested Becky Hood. While you were on holiday, the CPS took their sweet time studying the evidence and finally agreed to pursue the charges we indicated. Why it took them so long, heaven knows. Hood and Webber will face charges of bringing drugs into the country, distributing them across a significant part of Wiltshire, plus dealing direct to a discreet clientele within a five-mile radius of their home town. Becky Hood's solicitor indicated his client was willing to provide information on the gang's network in return for a lighter sentence. The CPS probably had enough evidence to proceed without a deal, but belt and braces won the day."

"What did they charge her with in the end?" asked Gus.

"Becky Hood didn't intend anyone to come to harm when she set that fire," said Geoff. "However, she had to accept the lesser charge of reckless endangerment."

"The loss of life cemented the charge as Category One," said Kenneth. "There's a change to the law in the pipeline, and by the time Becky Hood gets to court, she could be looking at a minimum of a four-year sentence. If she gets a hard-line judge, that term could double."

"Perhaps Helen's sister knew more about the gang's business than it appeared when we spoke to her," said Gus. "If so, the added benefits her evidence might bring could help her cause."

"Her husband and Sam Webber will be lucky to escape a life sentence," said Kenneth.

"I won't be shedding any tears," said Gus.

"I hesitate to ask what's in the folders you're holding on your lap, Freeman," said Kenneth.

"The larger of the two contains the secondary element of the Fennell and Roker murders, Sir," said Gus. "You were aware of the headlines before our holiday. However, we didn't have all the information to hand until we returned. My team has included updates from DI Jill Crooks and DS Kurt Burgess. There was a downside to letting the case run away from us, but the overall results speak for themselves. Several unsavoury criminals have been arrested and will be charged."

"Several others have disappeared, fate unknown," said Kenneth.

"I would ask you to refer to my earlier comment regarding Hook and Webber, Sir," said Gus. "The other file contains everything we thought relevant from our trip to Bradford-on-Avon."

"Do you have any doubts about who killed Tammie Kenyon and Imogen Henderson?" asked Kenneth.

"None whatsoever, Sir," said Gus. "Sam Bean was responsible."

"Tricky business," said Kenneth. "That defence has been used before. Did you know?"

"Not in the UK, Sir," said Geoff Mercer.

"I fear it will stir up a hornet's nest when the press gets hold of it," said Kenneth.

"When you read DI Packenham's report, I think you'll agree we've gone as far as we can," said Gus. "It's down to the doctors, shrinks and CPS now."

"You never close a case with a clean finish and a neat bow, Freeman," said Kenneth.

"I can offer something that might cheer you up, Sir," said Geoff. "A detective from Polebarn Road phoned me just before I left the office. They caught an amorous golfer at Cumberwell. He was up to his old tricks again early on Sunday morning. While Sam Bean planned his attacks precisely, the golfer's attacks were random. He tried his luck when he spotted a lone female by the edge of the woods. Little did he know she was a rugby-playing police constable named Jenny Collins. She pinned him to the ground and called it in. Blessing worked with her brother, George, a few weeks ago. It was DC Collins who rang me with the news. The culprit admitted five other offences, one of which was Tony Wyvern's daughter, Nicole, back in May 2016."

"We try our best," said Gus. "Despite Tony Wyvern's daughter being attacked close to where the murders occurred, it was clear to me the events were unconnected."

Grab your copy…
vinci-books.com/quicktoanger